MW01148223

WRONGFUL CONVICTIONS

Thank you to the people that helped me
with the things I am not very good at:

Shawna and Dolly Poncelet, Monica Tappe, Brianna Hurlburt, Jana Alberg, Chastity Peterson, Zina Evje, Theresa Renecker, Jenny Tuck, Janet Poncelet, Abby Flottemesch Robinson, Evy Schneider, Leslie Blakeburn, Troy Russell, Brian Dewitt, Ted Snyder, Dorothy Barnes, Brodey Kroupenske, Aaron Zierden, Beth Ott, Debbie Peterson, Jaime Mulder, Adam Gack, Dominic Chiapusio, Phil Demulling, Jeff Haugen, Elizabeth Pangerl, Kate Arens, Tina Mitts, Ryan Ladd, Debbie Tuck, Niklas Liedtke

Prologue

1999

The Crown Victoria roared down the gravel road, shattering the tranquility of the warm sunny June morning. A dust cloud woke from its slumber to furiously chase after the rusted beast. The wheels of the titanic auto ripped across the washboards left by the recent grading of the backwoods thoroughfare. The Vic really couldn't be distinguished from any number of cars that traveled this road; a modestly kept former logging trail that connected the main highway to the heart of the Leech Lake Reservation. The car was obscene in its size and shabby appearance; its price more than made up for its dilapidated exterior. The interior of the car was in no better shape, with the exception of the stereo system added by its teenage owner. This was the one modification necessary to allow its owner to forget that the quarter panel of the vehicle had been completely eaten through by rust, and the doors on either side were not far behind. The cancer on this vehicle was terminal; its owner however was not yet ready to give the automobile its last rights. Despite the shortcomings of it aesthetics, the 305 cubic inch V8 roared with the same ferocity it had the day it rolled off the assembly line in Detroit ten years earlier, and it was for that reason that the beast still had not been put to pasture.

The road traveled by the behemoth was particularly well maintained as far as gravel roads in Cass County were concerned. With the exception of these few washboards common to all gravel roads, overall this road was unusually smooth and exceptionally wide. It was not the main road to Old Agency but cut several miles off the paved highway that came out of Walker past the casino. This road was closed in the winter, as funds were not available to keep it plowed and most residents of the reservation used the "Onigum Road" instead, a direct route from Onigum to Walker across frozen Leech Lake.

The occupants of the vehicle sat in an unusually muddled silence for teenage boys. Their gazes focused on the trees that blew past the windows. There were four of them, the oldest no more than seventeen. This trip was atypical of most trips taken by kids this age. The stereo normally blaring loud abusive rap music was silent; there was no playful banter about the boys. No conversations about the Minnesota Twins season, or talk of the local girls, instead they sat in resolute silence their minds singularly focused on the task at hand.

The driver was the oldest of the boys, with long black hair pulled back into a ponytail and the thin mustache of a boy in the midst of puberty. The passenger was a particularly ugly kid with gnarled red hair and crooked teeth; he wore a dark sweatshirt with the hood pulled over his matted mass of hair despite the seasonably warm temperatures. Two more kids sat in the back, a baby faced boy who resembled the driver as brothers resembled each other. The other was the youngest in the group. A twelve gauge shotgun in his lap, however, suggested he should be taken the most seriously. He wore a Pittsburgh Pirates baseball cap backwards and twisted to the left, and sported a Native Mob tattoo on his left arm: a representation of his affiliation with the Vice Lords. The young man wore each with pride.

As the vehicle approached its destination, the driver took one last hit from the sherm, a combination of PCP and marijuana, and passed it to the Vic's other occupants. The ugly kid with the red hair was fondling a .32 caliber revolver in his sweatshirt pocket. He took the cigarette in his left and took a deep drag coughing a little as he inhaled. The boy in the back passenger seat finished the forty ounce bottle of malt liquor he was drinking before taking the cigarette and burning it almost down to his fingers. The killer behind the driver waved off the roach when it was offered. He wanted his head clear for this; he needed to prove his loyalty. He was on a mission.

The silence of the trip was broken only once, when the boy with the shotgun pulled the slide back to make sure that a shell was chambered. The driver's knuckles turned white around the steering wheel. Sweat beaded on his forehead, as the car approached a corner they saw their destiny in the clearing in front of them.

*   *   *

Harold sat on the rickety porch in front of a ramshackle trailer house. The white tin building was heaped in a pine clearing just off the gravel road. The yard was adorned with two decrepit vehicles; one was completely charred to cinders, the other, an old Pontiac, looked as though it hadn't been used in a thousand years. Prairie grass grew up through its floorboards, the sun faded paint was covered with a thick layer of dust. All of the tires were flat.

The trailer house itself was in marginally better shape, though the siding was filthy from the dust churned up by passing cars. Most of the windows were broken and the panes replaced with cardboard, save the one just to the right of the porch.

Harold had been out of prison for only a week. He had been a resident of the Oak Park Heights Correctional facility for the last five years. Every day that he had been out he had started with a cigarette on the porch. He enjoyed the feeling of the warm sun on his face while he smoked. He sat, his eyes fixed on the bend in the road and the sound of an approaching engine in the distance. He wore no shirt this morning. His chest decorated with a tattoo that read "Native Pride" over his heart and the symbols of the Red Nation gang were emblazoned on his right pectoral and both arms. Another tattoo on his chest, a six point star with a pitchfork protruding out of the top right, had been done in a jailhouse, rough but clear. Harold had been a member of the Native Disciples gang while he lived on the Red Lake reservation with his mother before going to prison, but prison had changed him. He loathed every second of the experience and vowed never to return. He no longer wanted to be part of the gang; being locked in a cage away from his home and family had changed him. Simply thinking about this caused him to look down at his chest with regret. He rubbed the tattoo and felt the resentment of five wasted years. His mother had died while he was in prison. His aunt had taken in his little brother, then she offered him a place to stay once he was released. He had taken her up on the offer in an attempt to escape the pitfalls awaiting him in Red Lake if he were to return. Harold had also landed a job working for the Chairman of the Leech Lake Tribe, Clifford Banks as his head of security. He felt he had a new lease on life.

Harold's brother was in the house looking out the one good window at him. Harold looked over his shoulders and waved, and the boy waved back. He had gone into prison an arrogant punk kid and came out a man who understood his responsibilities to his family. He knew that his brother was more important than any of the bullshit he had been involved in before he went away. He knew it was dangerous for a Red Laker to be in Leech Lake and even more dangerous that he was about to give up some information on one of the leaders of the Leech Lake Native Mob. It was the deal he had made with the devil, he was no snitch, but he had a job now. His job was security and he had to do what he had to do. While in prison, he had learned the name of a man who was the largest supplier of drugs on the reservation. The deal he made had gotten him this new job and his new boss had helped him get out of prison early. He doubted anyone knew he had been released early. He was sure that no one knew he was the snitch. Banks had his back. Banks was power. As the Crown Victoria rounded the corner and he got a clear view of it, he realized that nothing could have been farther from the truth.

1

Marcel Wright had been taught that boxing is a difficult sport. He learned that It took discipline, strength, speed. But most importantly it took heart. Heart, Marcel knew, wasn't something people were born with, it was something forged out of struggle. He had been a student of the sweet science and knew the all time greats had come from the world's toughest corners; Brooklyn, Tijuana, Manilla. He couldn't imagine a world champ coming from Beverly Hills or Dubai. His reasoning was simple: for people that are faced with a fight for survival everyday, simply surviving the ring is nothing. On the other hand, for people who have a safety net and no real fear of what tomorrow has to offer, it is impossible to find the motivation to dig deep enough into one's heart to stand toe to toe with another man - hurting, completely exhausted, and entirely alone - and go another round. He hadn't known that world, but held firm that this was more fact than a personal opinion. Marcel knew the only way to become truly great at the sport was when a man only had one true possession, dignity. The experts told him that It was the same reason most world champions didn't go out on top. Once they earned the pay days and the lifestyle of a champ, there was nothing left to fight for. Marcel defined it in simpler terms: they lost the fire. Marcel had seen a documentary on Mike Tyson. He had explained this proposition very eloquently. He said every time he fought he was afraid he was going to lose, he was afraid of being humiliated, he was afraid of everything. He said while he was training, he was always afraid the guy he was going to fight was going to beat him. He dreamt about the guy beating him. That was early in Tyson's career and it is what got him to the top. By the time he fought Buster Douglas, he no longer had that fear. For guys like Mike Tyson and Marcel, losing meant going back to the streets. It meant a life not really worth living, and that was all the motivation Marcel needed.

Marcel snapped a double jab at the heavy bag, then followed with a left cross, right hook, left cross and quickly moved to his right, dancing around the bag. Sweat poured from his face. His sleeveless t-shirt was drenched and there were a thousand dots on the concrete floor beneath him where the perspiration was spraying. The warehouse gym he worked out in wasn't equipped with air conditioning and in the one hundred degree August heat the gym trapped the smell of sweat and dying air inside the building and all around him. The front door to the gym, a loading bay fifty years earlier, was open and several industrial sized fans made futile attempts to circulate the dense air through the gym. Though they moved air, they did little to move the mercury down from ninety two inside the gym. There was no saving grace on a day like this. The humidity in the air made it feel like a hundred and forty degrees. There was no escape. Minnesota had been experiencing a severe drought and the air simply refused to let go of all the water it had stored up since May. It was as if the air knew it had to rain but the clouds had forgotten, caught up in the magnificent warmth of the sun.

Marcel loved to work in the heat. Cutting weight was easier but the heat and humidity did so much more for his stamina. Just as cyclists went to Denver to train in the thin mountain air, a blanket of hot moist air could do wonders for a boxer. Though this heat was excessive, it didn't slow him down. Marcel simply bore down and pushed himself a little bit harder. Marcel had motivation.

Marcel was also determined and disciplined. He got into the fight game after being uprooted from Minnesota to go live with his grandfather in Longmont, Colorado. Marcel's grandfather Henry was a police officer who trained amateur fighters, many of whom were cops. Henry insisted on teaching his grandson self-reliance and the importance of hard work. Henry also strove to teach the importance of education, but Marcel preferred to focus on discipline. These had been lessons that Henry had failed to teach his own son, Marcel's father. It was a mistake he wouldn't make again.

Marcel took to the sport immediately. He was a natural. His grandfather had the opportunity to see him win his first Golden Gloves title when he was sixteen, two weeks before his grandfather died of a massive heart attack. Even though Marcel spent the next few months bouncing around various foster homes, he had acquired the values that his grandfather had tried to teach. Those values made the foster homes tolerable. Marcel studied at the gym when he wasn't working out and set his sights on bigger things.

Marcel's foster homes weren't the kind that showed up in a Channel Four expose, but they weren't the loving families that other kids in his class grew up in either. He didn't like spending his free time there and regularly escaped to the gym to do his geometry homework or just training before going to live with Jarvis. He was seventeen years old when the Olympic trials for the 2004 games in Athens rolled around. If you had asked any of the old boxing people around the area, he was the odds on favorite to make the team. In his first two fights, he looked like a lock to make the team. However, a broken hand in his third fight was the end of his Olympic dream as well as the first loss of his amateur career. He won a scholarship from USA Boxing to the University of Colorado Boulder and graduated with honors despite the disappointment, or perhaps because of it. He had considered another run for the 2008 games in Beijing, however around the same time he had been accepted to Law School at St. Stevens in St. Paul, Minnesota. He decided that he would turn pro and set his sights on a Middleweight title.

Jarvis Lane was a long time trainer, and a man who had been the face of amateur boxing in the Western US for forty years. He demonstrated the virtue of a Spartan lifestyle; he explained to Marcel how guys like Bernard Hopkins and Roy Jones never drank or smoked. He had taught Marcel to eat right and treat his body like a temple. The only TV Jarvis ever watched was Friday Night Fights on ESPN. His time, he had once told

Marcel, was much too valuable to spend watching other people's lives and fantasies. He would much rather live out his. Jarvis for the most part, had lived his fantasy. He had trained three different world champions, and he had traveled all over the world for fights. Furthermore, he had also fulfilled his life's ambition of owning his own business, a gym.

Jarvis had stayed in Colorado through Marcel's college days and it had been on his suggestions that prompted Marcel to return to Minnesota for law school.

Law school had been Marcel's grandfather's dream for him. His grandfather had wanted him to become a prosecutor for the US Attorney's office. In Henry Senior's years on the force he had dealt with many attorneys, and the ones that most impressed him had been the US attorneys. Those men and women had put a few dipshit defense attorneys in their place on more than one occasion. Henry had always been tickled by that. Marcel on the other hand, had never really been too keen on being a lawyer. Nothing about wearing a suit all day and sitting in a stuffy courtroom had ever appealed to him. His love was boxing, but Jarvis had convinced him that the more education a man has, the more doors that would be open to him. In the end, the offer of a scholarship at St. Stevens had closed the deal. St. Stevens wasn't necessarily Marcel's first choice, but as Jarvis often said, a man gets to chose his own path, he just doesn't get to choose where it leads.

Marcel was a little apprehensive about returning to Minnesota to say the least. It had been a long time and he desperately wanted to continue training with Jarvis. But Marcel's discipline and Jarvis's encouragement won the round, so he packed all the possessions he owned into a single backpack and got into Jarvis' van. He never looked back.

"We got abs." The gravel in Jarvis' voice followed the bell to signify the end of the round.

Abdominal work with Jarvis was twelve grueling minutes that began with crunches and came to a crescendo with the old man slamming a twelve pound medicine ball into Marcel's midsection every time he did a sit-up. The workout was intense, but effective. Marcel's torso was cut from steel and he was better than most fighters at absorbing punishment to the body. Marcel knew the problem with body shots were twofold. First, getting hit in the right spot is devastating. Marcel watched on pay per view as Oscar De La Hoya, who Marcel considered one of the greatest fighters of all time, was KO'd with a liver punch from Hopkins. Second, a punch to the liver leads to another problem. Fighters who go down from body shots have their heart questioned. That was exactly what happened with De La Hoya, though fans and experts all over boxing claimed he took a dive. In reality, it doesn't take much of a shot to that part of the body to leave the toughest champion all but paralyzed for several seconds, maybe even several minutes. Once others start questioning a fighter's heart, it is only a matter of time until the fighter begins to question himself. Jarvis had preached that once self doubt creeps in, and a fighter starts to question whether or not they can still go on, their career is over. Jarvis had told the story of Oliver McCall over and over. His promising career came to a crashing halt in his second fight with Lennox Lewis, when he gave up in the fifth round and began sobbing. Shortly thereafter his life began spiraling out of control and he ended up in prison. Marcel had no interest in being knocked down with a body shot or having anyone question his heart, so he endured the grueling workout thanking Jarvis when it was over.

When the final bell of the workout sounded, Marcel grabbed a seat on a bench ringside a cold towel draped over his head. He took a second dry towel and mopped as much sweat from his face as he could. The towel quickly became soaked and he tossed it into a bucket on the floor in the corner.

"Coming by for dinner?" Jarvis said as he sat down next to him. During camp, Jarvis always cooked for his fighters. He was a master nutritionist and had no intention of leaving such an important facet of training to one of his youngsters.

"I have class, first night, I brought a turkey sandwich," Marcel answered. He could hear exhaustion in his own voice.

"No cheese?" Jarvis inquired.

"No cheese."

2

J oanne Hart-Benson got hit with a blast of
sand that had been carried by a ferocious
wind gust across the parking lot. Although
the sun was hot, the wind gust signified a front
was moving in and a storm was just around the
corner. Everyone in Minneapolis and St. Paul
was praying for relief. This was the hottest summer on record. Today was the fourth day in a
row the mercury had touched triple digits and
the Twin Cities had seen nineties every day
since July twenty-fourth, more than a month. A
thunderhead was forming on the western hori-

zon and anyone who had spent any time in Minnesota knew that humidity like this was going to be followed by one hell of a tempest. St. Paul hadn't seen rain since early May; the typically lush green St. Stevens campus had browned up after the watering ban was put in place in early July along with the rest of the city. There had been watering bans in place throughout the Twin Cities, and the normally beautiful green of the metropolitan area had long since dried up and turned brown.

Joanne had been a professor at St. Stevens for eight years now. The first six had been a breeze, but the last two on the other hand had been more of a struggle. The trouble hadn't surprised her. The last two years of her life had been a struggle. A wave of disdain washed over her, and Joanne understood that she was beginning to hate the university.

Joanne didn't fully understand her state of mind. The school had been very good to her. The job certainly paid well. She was given a ton of leeway to set her own schedule and she had the respect of her colleagues. When Joanne paused for a moment and looked at the building, a realization came to her: it wasn't the university she hated, it was the students. Each new class that entered seemed to have an added degree of arrogance. Her mind played back her first year. She had seen a fire in their eyes, a passion for the law. As she stood in front of them, sharing in their discovery of the law, she saw idealists. They had an aura that suggested a healthy fear and a determination to change the world. That determination fueled her passion like spraying lighter fluid on a bonfire. Joanne herself was an idealist, unlike many of her own classmates. Her passion to change the world had not burned out when she got her first big check. Instead it raged, burning hotter and hotter with every case.

Joanne had graduated from the Cardozo School of Law in 1993 and she had been a member of the first Innocence Project, a non–profit legal clinic that focused its efforts on exonerating innocent people based on DNA evidence. After graduating law school, she went to work at the New York State Defenders office, and in her first year had oral arguments before the Supreme Court of the United States on a death penalty case. That case had been argued successfully. Her first win. The decision was not a landmark by any means, but it was the first in a series of victories against the death penalty that set her on a path that lead her to St. Stevens University. Along the way she met Frank Dekalb and the two of them founded the American Innocence Institute that was based at St. Stevens. It was at St. Stevens that she met Shannon McCarthy.

Shannon McCarthy was a legacy at St. Stevens. Her great-great-great-grandfather had been one of the first five men to enroll at the Saint Paul building on September 22nd, 1880.

She was a fifth generation student. There was a building on campus named after her grandfather. To say that Shannon came from money was an understatement. Shannon's family was money, at least in Minnesota. The fact that Shannon had taken her mother's maiden name in high school was not a sign of embarrassment about her family's wealth, but it was symbolic of her desire to blaze her own trail in life. Unlike many of her current classmates at St. Stevens, Shannon didn't live lavishly off her trust fund. She didn't spend late nights partying on Grand Avenue in St. Paul and only touched the trust when an emergency arose, or for a large purchase like the down payment on her house in Northeast Minneapolis.

Shannon was a modest woman who worked full time while going to law school. She had a certain amount of resentment for her classmates whose family connections assured them jobs after law school. Her resentment wasn't based in jealousy, for she certainly had her own connections, but rather contempt for her classmates' lack of self-reliance. Yes, she had connections, but she had no intention of using them.

It was Shannon's self-reliance that first caught Joanne's attention, a quality that Joanne felt was one of her own most endearing traits. Joanne had taken Shannon under her wing over the summer and had put her to work with the institute. The work was tedious but Shannon never complained, and Joanne's respect for her protégé grew. Joanne hadn't met Marcel Wright yet, but she had heard plenty about his brilliance from Shannon over the summer and was looking forward to meeting him this fall. She had gotten her class rosters a week earlier and both Shannon and Marcel had been on her roster for Wrongful Convictions. If Marcel was half the legal mind Shannon had made him out to be, his skill combined with Shannon's work ethic would make this a truly special class. Special was what she needed. The institute had suffered a series of high profile losses within the last couple of years, and Joanne had been dealing with her own personal issues as well. Some new blood would do everyone good.

3

Shannon wheeled into the parking lot at St. Stevens as Joanne Hart-Benson was walking across it. She pulled into a parking space between a black Toyota Corolla and a red Nissan 380zx and watched Joanne walk up to the law school. She observed the woman pause at the front and take a long look at the name above the door letting all entrants know that they were about to cross the threshold of the St. Stevens University School of Law. St. Stevens University carried with it an air of superiority, and it wasn't shy about letting everyone know it. Joanne's pause was odd. Everyone else passed in and out of the vestibule with little thought. Why would a woman who had been working at the school for eight years all of a sudden be captivated by the name above the door that had greeted her every day? Shannon had observed a lot of odd behavior in Joanne recently.

Shannon had class with Joanne this evening. It promised to be the most interesting class she would take at St. Stevens. 1L classes are the same for every student in every law school in the country. Everyone took Civil Procedure, Contracts, Torts, Criminal Law, Legal Writing, Property and Constitutional Law. Those classes were mostly foundational, and there is nothing particularly sexy about any of them. Constitutional Law one was interesting. Shannon, a self proclaimed history buff, had enjoyed the interplay between the social issues of the day and the Supreme Court's ruling on cases and how those cases shaped our present day. Contracts, on the other hand, was a brutal exercise in fortitude; the year long class didn't apply to her beyond 1L and provided little entertainment.

The second year of law school was designed for students to load up on the heavy subjects that most interest them: white collar crime, wills and trusts, consumer protection, the meat and potatoes of the law. 3L or the third year was where students coast home with clinics and practicums, Trial Practice, Lawyering Skills, the hands on applications that were vital to post-graduate employment. Wrongful Convictions was a course that fit somewhere in between, a year long course with a heavy emphasis on case law and writing during first semester. The second semester was a practicum with the Innocence Institute.

Like most other students, Shannon had enrolled in the class this year because rumors were rampant about the future of the American Innocence Institute at St. Stevens. One of the fascinating things about law school was the tendency for adults to revert back to high school students once they were accepted. Where college was a journey for young adults to find themselves, law school is a rumor mill filled with pettiness, backbiting and treachery. It was an ultra competitive forum for people that never had to compete on an equal playing field and didn't feel the need to start. From stolen materials in the library to all out false information campaigns, law school was really a finishing school for sharks. Circling the waters waiting for the smell of blood, attacking when the time was right. Joanne Hart-Benson was not above the rumors and the respect she once garnered at St. Stevens had started to wain. There were rumors about her drug use, cocaine primarily but more recently there was talk that she was suffering from a paralyzing addiction to Narcodone. Attorneys and drug use were not a new phenomenon. In fact a survey of lawyers in the Twin Cities would probably find most had some form of addiction: drugs, sex, booze, gambling, whatever. It was the nature of the business: long work hours, isolation, ego, money. But the most recent rumors where more damning, the type of allegations that brought censure and disbarment, ended careers, and sometimes lives.

Shannon was the type of person that would know better than to believe every law school rumor, however there were signs that no one could miss. Joanne had aged about ten years in the last eighteen months. She had been an attractive woman, hosting her own show on Cable TV. The show was a roundtable program with a pro-defense bias that generally humiliated a backwoods law enforcement officer or bumbling prosecutor every week. The show was canceled after poor ratings because most people that watched garbage like that were not looking for her liberal opinions. Moreover, everyone suspected that Joanne's looks going to hell weren't helping her plight. She had become more haggard; the combination of stress and drugs no doubt has that effect on a person. Shannon herself hadn't seen anything in person working alongside her, but in her experience functioning addicts could be very adept at hiding their plight. After Joanne entered the building, Shannon exited her car and made her way to the building herself.

4

Marcel parked his bike in the parking lot on the rear side of the law school, separated from Shannon and Joanne's parking lot by Thol Tennis Courts and the graduate buildings. Marcel always parked in that lot because there were designated spots for motorcycles that were always open. During the day it was the only way he could get a parking spot within eight blocks of the school. At night, however, parking was more abundant, but Marcel was a creature of habit. His route to the parking place was a rote act at this point.

Jarvis hated the thought of Marcel riding a motorcycle. Jarvis, as always, had a cautionary tale. This one was a fighter named Diego Corrales. Jarvis mentioned his name every time he saw the bike, so often Marcel now began to tune him out. Marcel was not a thrill seeker and figured it was the aggressive look of the Kawasaki ZX-6 that most scared Jarvis. Though Marcel knew it was capable of reaching a ridiculous top speed, he himself had never really tested it out. For Marcel it was more about the versatility that riding the bike gave him. Plus he thought it was sexy.

Marcel was excited about the upcoming class, which was more than he could say about any of the classes he took as a 1L. When he had sat down with his friend Shannon last spring to look at the course catalog and plan out what they were going to take, that had been the course that most intrigued him. He had seen Joanne Hart-Benson's show on TV at a friend's once. He didn't really care much for it, but the thought of having a celebrity professor was kind of cool. Not that Marcel cared much about celebrity, but he hoped she would bring some experiences to the classroom that were foreign to him. Marcel also liked the idea of the American Innocence Institute. He was very aware of what DNA was doing to shake up the criminal justice system, and he was shocked by how many innocent people had been convicted of crimes they didn't commit. The thought reminded him of his own childhood fear, that someday he would be sent to prison for something he didn't do. The idea of being locked away in prison was a horrifying thought to Marcel; he couldn't envision himself living as a caged animal, much less doing so because of something he hadn't done.

The notion of prison brought with it a tornado of emotions to Marcel's conscious. His own father had died in prison the victim of a petty dispute. The thoughts of his dad's death brought great sorrow, but it also brought great anger, thinking about the life his father had chose to live. Rather than raising his kids, he chose drugs and crime. The twenty-five year sentence he'd died serving had been his third stretch of hard time. He had pulled the first when he was eighteen, two years for stealing a car. His Dad, Henry Wright Jr., or Junior, had been released as a twenty year old felon without much hope for the future. It wasn't long before he was a repeat offender, this time earning a seven year sentence for possessing enough methamphetamine to supply the entire Midwest for six months. He was released at age twenty-eight, now hardened from an adult life behind bars. He had become adjusted to that life and had no fear of going back, but he had also gotten clean and wanted to try and do right or at least that is what Marcel had been told. Junior moved away from Colorado to escape the drug influences. That was when he met Marcel's mother. Junior and Caroline were together on and off for a few years, long enough to sire two sons. Junior had been clean most of the time, gotten work as an auto mechanic at a local shop and attempted to be a citizen.

Marcel always wondered if going to the reservation was the right choice for his father. On the one hand, his felony record didn't automatically exclude him from being part of society. People that lived hard lives understood hard choices. There were a lot of other ex-cons living in Northern Minnesota, especially on the reservation. No one judged his father on his past. The problem was there were plenty of other dirtbags around to pull his father down which was exactly what happened.

Looking back, his dad should have never had the gun. As a convicted felon, he lost the right to possess a firearm. The gun wasn't his only misdeed. An addict shouldn't have been in a bar, either. Unfortunately in Northern Minnesota, the forms of entertainment were extremely limited. Forget going to a ball game, a movie, a fancy restaurant if a man were without a driver's license his only real form of entertainment was the local VFW club. Besides hanging around outside the gas station, which closed at ten, it was the only thing in town.

At first, his father would only go out on Friday nights. Then it was Friday and Saturday, and pretty soon there weren't many nights when his dad wasn't at the bar. Take a shot of Jack Daniels, mix it with an ex-con and a dead end town, add ice, and you have a volatile cocktail. It began with him slapping Marcel's mother around, then he put her in the hospital a couple of times. Finally, when rumors started flying around the VFW that she was running around with Nip Johnson, Marcel's drunken dad had loaded his .357 with hollow points and put four of them into Nip. Two in the chest, one in the leg, and one in the face that closed the casket. Marcel's mom was only shot once. She had lingered in a coma for two weeks before eventually dying. Marcel hadn't been old enough to remember any of this. He was still an infant. His mother's mother had taken him and his brother in and raised them like her own sons. That was until she passed then he lived with his older brother Henry Wright the third.

Marcel shook off the memory, dabbing his eyes that had started to well up with tears. He knew he had to get it together. He gathered himself and walked up to the building, looking off to the western sky at the gathering clouds. He was a little irritated at himself for not checking the weather report in the morning; he had left fairly early for a run with a couple other amateur fighters at the gym, then had worked the front desk until his training session with Jarvis. It hadn't rained in months. He hadn't planned on that changing, so he had ridden his bike like every other day. He had a feeling he would be regretting this later.

The St. Stevens University Law School was connected to the Grad School by a third floor skywalk. At ground level they were separated by a sidewalk that connected the back parking lot to the front parking lot. Marcel and Shannon reached opposite ends of the sidewalk at the same time. Marcel saw Shannon's smile from one hundred yards away. Marcel was happy to be greeted with that big smile. Marcel considered her a friend; friends were a rare commodity at St. Stevens. At St. Stevens there were colleagues. It was much too cut throat an environment to have friends, and if one was naïve enough to think otherwise, they would have been eaten alive in 1L. Shannon was different. She didn't care about law review or being top of the class. Much like Marcel, she never planned to practice law. Shannon said she had her sights set on the business world. Marcel thought that Shannon was a very attractive woman; she had thick flowing black hair that complimented her dark eyes perfectly. She was small in stature but had a big personality. She was brimming with a positive energy that always invigorated Marcel. Without her dynamism Marcel doubted he would have survived the grind of civil procedure. Marcel was also intrigued by Shannon's element of class: she was proper, she dressed nicely, spoke right, didn't cuss, and had appeared to Marcel to have a high degree of ethics. Marcel and Shannon did not come from the same worlds. Marcel's world was harsh and cruel, Shannon's was prim and proper. Marcel liked having that respite. Marcel loved boxing, and though governed by the Marquis of Queensbury rules it had migrated from a sport of nobility to a sport that existed on the fringe. Shady characters abounded and a boxing gym wasn't the place for those offended easily. Marcel had always wondered how Shannon would react to his gym. He thought that most likely she would be appalled. He had wanted to invite her to his last fight, but had chickened out. He didn't want to risk alienating the one person he had a connection with at St. Stevens.

Marcel had been in Minnesota for about eighteen months. In those eighteen months his social life consisted of road work with younger fighters, hundreds of rounds of sparring and one date. That had been an abject disaster. The date had been Jarvis' idea, set up not long after Marcel had moved to Minnesota. The thing Marcel failed to consider when accepting a blind date through Jarvis was that Jarvis was from the hood. Being from the hood, his associates also came from the hood. Marcel wanted nothing more to do with the hood. The woman's name was Chandra, a stripper with a penchant for drugs and partying. Jarvis had no idea, at least about the drugs. Marcel had no doubt that Jarvis knew she was a stripper. Marcel knew plenty of girls who had danced their way through school, they were women with goals and a slightly broken moral compass. That didn't mean they were dope fiends with no future. Chandra was a dope fiend with no future. She had no self-esteem, and stripping was a way for her to get male attention at least that's how he assessed the situation. On the date she had gotten high during dinner, attempted to make fools out of both of them, and Marcel had decided to excuse himself from the situation for the bathroom. He paid for his meal and left her at the restaurant. He never talked to Jarvis about the incident, and Jarvis never asked.

"Ready for 2L?" Shannon had made her way down the walk to him and pulled him from his daydream.

"It has to be better than 1L right?" He smiled.

"But I am looking forward to this class." This was a half truth. He wasn't about to tell her about the memories of his family.

5

The room began to fill up as the clock drew nearer to seven. The class was titled Wrongful Convictions. Judging from the capacity of the room, there were a lot of other 2L's who had been intrigued by the class like Marcel was. Marcel had thought that the Innocence Institute would be a nice break from the monotony of the classroom. He certainly didn't care as much about building a resume as most of the other fifty students in the class had been. It was clear, regardless of motivation, that none of them wanted to be in a case law heavy lecture class for the next two and a half hours.

Marcel had started law school with no real inclination of the type of law he was most interested in. Criminal law was sexy and that was what his grandfather wanted, but he had plenty of experience with the criminal justice system and none of it had been pleasant. His grandfather had wanted him to be a U.S. Attorney and prosecution did have its appeal, at least compared with corporate lawyers who sat in offices and pushed paper all day. Personal injury attorneys made bank, and they were in court a lot. The problem was that he didn't like the idea of being an ambulance chaser. Marcel's legal future was clouded by dreams of a middleweight title belt, and nothing else really mattered to him right now.

Marcel and Shannon had conversations with each other about what their futures would hold. His grandfather's dream was the reality Marcel concocted for the sake of conversations. He had never shared his dream of being a world champion with anyone. This was a symptom of superstition where he felt that if he said it out loud the idea would vanish forever. Shannon's version of the future was almost incomprehensible to him. One of the biggest differences in their social class was their view of what things were achievable. Shannon's dream was to start her own consulting firm. She planned to start a business whose sole purpose was to teach other businesses how to run more efficiently. This concept was beyond the realm of Marcel's reality. He had no ability to conceive the nuts and bolts of how to get something like that started, nor could he envision the type of people that she would work for. It was one more example of the divergent worlds they came from.

Joanne entered the classroom at about four minutes before seven o'clock. Marcel had quickly learned that you could tell a lot about a professor based on their ability to make it to class on time. There was a small group of professors whose own arrogance prevented them from arriving to their class any earlier than the posted start time. It was especially hard for Marcel to respect anyone like that. He took pride in his own punctuality; his grandfather had ingrained in him the belief that there was no greater currency than reliability, and that one of the best ways to lay a foundation of reliability was to be punctual. Marcel didn't really consider four minutes early punctual, but given Joanne's status as a television personality and St. Stevens's celebrity professor, he had figured it would have been about ten after the hour before she came strolling in.

Joanne went to the front of the classroom, flipped on the projector, and began her introduction. There was a familiarity about her that Marcel acknowledged. He hadn't seen her on TV much, but anyone who has seen a TV personality in person knows that make up and lighting did amazing things for people. Here standing in front of the class, familiarity was the best word to describe Joanne's television personality. The Joanne that stood in front of the class tonight looked about twenty years older than the one he had seen a couple years ago on TV. The in-person Joanne had bags under her eyes. Those were the eyes of an addict, eyes Marcel knew well. Her lips were thinning and the lines in her face were deepening. Her skin was losing its elasticity prematurely, and anyone who knew drug people could see that Joanne Hart-Benson had a severe drug problem.

Kids that grew up like Marcel develop an ability to see the dark side of people much easier than kids who grew up in protected environments. Marcel had thought about this often and believed it was a survival instinct, an evolutionary quality that man's prehistoric ancestors surely possessed. A sixth sense for assessing the danger of foreign tribes. It was a sense that had been dying out in mankind as the world got smaller and life got more comfortable and safer. This was a sense now possessed only by those who grew up in a constant state of chaos and danger; certainly not by many in the room tonight. Marcel was very aware of one constant with drug addicts. They could be dangerous, especially when they held positions like the one Joanne held.

"Good evening, my name is Joanne Hart-Benson, this is my tenth year teaching Wrongful Convictions at St. Stevens." Her voice was crisp and captivating.

Marcel could instantly understand why she had been so successful as a litigator. Confidence flowed from this woman and Marcel was compelled by a force deep within himself to turn off his danger indicator and allow himself to be mesmerized by her voice.

"Before coming to St. Stevens I worked to establish the first Innocence Institute at Cardozo School of Law in New York. Since that time, two hundred seventy two people have been exonerated because of DNA evidence. Seventeen of those people were sitting on death row." Joanne was now in full stride.

"The average sentence served by those two hundred seventy two innocent people was thirteen years. Take yourself back thirteen years, what were you doing? Some of you were in Junior High, some of you may have even been in elementary school. For some of you that is more than half your lifetime."

Marcel gave a quick glance around the room. His colleagues were as captivated as he was.

"How does this happen? How can we prevent these things from happening in the future? What can be done about those innocent people currently incarcerated right now? Those are the questions we are going to explore this semester in Wrongful Convictions."

It was clear to everyone, Marcel included, that Joanne was in her element. It was of no consequence that this was an audience of future lawyers rather than a jury. A live audience was her canvas and the facts of the case were her oils. A live audience was different than a television audience. With a live audience, Joanne could build a relationship with the men and women in front of her. That wasn't the case with a television audience. She worked the inflection of her voice. Her tone and tempo were such that the people sitting in front of her not only believed what she was saying, they couldn't help but liking the woman as she said it. Marcel could feel her passion fill the entire room; it was like a gas that would overtake them all and eventually suffocate their good sense. He wondered how many jurors over the years had been won over simply by her style, evidence be damned. When class was over, everyone in the room would find in favor of Joanne on this night.

"On July 25th, 1984, nine-year-old Dawn Hamilton was kidnapped in Baltimore, Maryland. She was raped, her panties were flung into a tree and her neck was stepped on, strangling and killing her. Her body was left in some woods in a working class suburb of Rosedale. A grizzly murder, with the most innocent of victims." Joanne was really ramping up now.

"The narrative of a case always put the police

under the gun to find a suspect in a hurry. This case was no different. Luckily there were witnesses." She paused and surveyed the class to ensure she had everyone's attention. She was about to lay out her case.

"There were two boys who were near the woods before little Dawn was killed. They saw her with a man they described as about six foot five inches tall, white, with flaming red hair and a mustache." She started to move about the room, injecting more emotion.

"A man named Kirk Bloodsworth, a commercial fisherman from Cambridge, Maryland, had been working near the woods where the little girl's body was found at a furniture store. Bloodworth was only six foot tall and on the heavy side; he did have flaming red hair and a mustache, however." Marcel and the rest of the class hung on her every word.

"The police put together a composite sketch and a tip came in that a man working at a nearby furniture store matched the description. Police brought Bloodsworth in for questioning, where he steadfastly denied the charges. Nonetheless, his picture was used as part of a photo lineup. One of the witnesses said that Bloodsworth looked similar but had a different hair color." She paused so the jury could digest point number one.

"The other witness was not able to identify a photo in the lineup. This was the basis for an arrest warrant." Marcel could feel the reasonable doubt dancing around the room.

"Police were under a lot of pressure to solve the case and decided Bloodsworth was their guy. They brought him in and put him in a lineup. Again one of the witnesses was unable to identify anyone. The second picked out a police officer from the lineup. This, ladies and gentlemen, was not enough to cast doubt in the eyes of the police. No, the police had their man." Joanne's voice marching toward a crescendo.

"Police continued their pursuit of Bloodsworth; they questioned him relentlessly. They showed him pictures of the crime scene, including a picture of a bloody rock. When in a later questioning Bloodsworth made mention of the bloody rock, police took it as an admission of guilt. He was the easiest target: he had no alibi, he worked in the vicinity and had a vague resemblance to the initial identification."

"Despite their inability to identify the man in either a photo lineup or an actual lineup both witnesses, boys, testified at trial he was the man. Prosecutors failed to disclose that there were other possible suspects and no biological evidence was offered. He was convicted on circumstantial evidence and sentenced to death." She paused again. Marcel could tell she was waiting to bring it home.

"On the evidence we just discussed, Bloodsworth was sentenced to death." She let it sink in and then continued.

"He appealed his case, all the while sitting in isolation on death row."

Marcel couldn't help but think of his own father sitting in prison and how his life ended in one violent moment. Marcel thought about his father often, more often than he thought about his dead mother. This was a fact that burdened him with guilt. His mother had done nothing to deserve her fate while his father was a man filled with evil and consumed by violence. Yet he had no memories of her. He did, however, have memories of his father even though he only saw him behind the glass partition of a maximum security prisoners' visiting center.

Marcel realized he had drifted off and tuned back into Joanne's narrative.

"...a book named *Blooding*, anyone ever hear of it?" Joanne posed the question to Marcel and his classmates. Shannon and a few other's raised their hands.

"Tell us about it, Ms. McCarthy." Joanne passed the baton.

"Written by an ex police officer named Wambaugh, Jim Wambaugh maybe." Shannon furled her brow trying to recall the author's first name. Marcel admired that quality of hers, the never ending quest for precision.

"Anyway, it's all about how the British were using DNA to solve crimes, the book depicts the first uses of DNA for solving crime."

"Very good, Ms. McCarthy. Bloodsworth wrote his lawyer because the little girl's panties contained a semen stain. The FBI had originally found nothing of use on the panties and in most cases the evidence would have been destroyed in the eight years Bloodsworth sat in prison since it wasn't shown to be useful originally. Serendipitously in this case it wasn't. It had been sealed up and boxed away."

Marcel wondered how often the world breaks the right way for people like Kirk Bloodsworth. He knew how often it broke the right way for him. Marcel could not help but feel a kinship with Kirk Bloodsworth. His story was a caricature of Marcel's own greatest fears.

"...stress this, it is important for all of you to understand that the Innocence Institute is not a job. It isn't a civil litigation firm where you are serving a dual purpose, doing some good, but also making a windfall of cash. No ladies and gentlemen, the Innocence Institute is a passion." She paused to emphasize her next point.

"Bloodsworth's lawyer took ten thousand dollars out of his own pocket to pay for the testing."

Another pause and Marcel was back into the swirl of his own thoughts again. He was trying to imagine what it would be like to be able to go to a bank to withdraw $10,000 to put towards someone else. Neither Marcel, nor anyone he had ever known, had more than enough cash on hand to do anything more than buy groceries for the next few weeks. In these moments he felt isolated from his classmates, proof he was from a different world.

"...the arrogance of the prosecutors in the case was on display in 2000, in an interview with CNN. They continued to doubt Bloodsworth's innocence, coming up with nonsensical alternative theories." Joanne's disdain for government attorneys was on full display for the class. Marcel instantly felt a contempt for the woman in front of the class, as if she were disrespecting his grandfather.

The thing most of his classmates, like Shannon McCarthy, could never understand about guys like Marcel was that when people struggled to make ends meet, respect became the prevailing currency. In some places that currency was so valuable people would kill for it.

"...in 2004, Bloodsworth was completely vindicated and the DNA evidence was used to convict Kimberly Ruffner of the crime. Ruffner had been convicted of an unrelated crime a month after Bloodsworth's initial conviction and was serving forty-five years in a cell directly below his own. The irony of the criminal justice system is very, very real." Most of the crowd joined Joanne in a good chuckle. Marcel however, couldn't escape his own circumstances. First hand experience with trials and prison, a murdered mother and brother and a father who spent time in prison and finally met with a violent end himself. He shuddered.

6

J oanne felt good when the lecture had finished. Recently success was a more fleeting proposition than it had been when she was younger. Her audience tonight had been captivated. They had asked pertinent questions, and she knew that she had been dazzling. She felt like the star she had been in her thirties, charming the hell out of the juries and winning acquittal after acquittal. She had tried only one case in the last two years and had lost. That defeat was excruciating. It was after that adverse verdict that she had really amped up her drug usage.

She always had a taste for cocaine, but coke never dulled the pain - at least not like narco. But damned if narco wasn't the most addictive shit she had ever been around. Narcodone had all the benefits of oxi but for half the cost. With coke she could always take it or leave it, but not with narco. Narco was like the all seeing eye; a hostage taker that even the best trained negotiator couldn't deal with. The sort of captor that a woman like Joanne could fall in love with and she had certainly developed Stockholm Syndrome in this case.

At first she used drugs to quiet an unexplored pain; that fact was stipulated to by all parties. Eventually, the pain was silenced and was replaced by the siren's song of the medicine. For Joanne, simply getting out of bed was an act that now required medication. If she was really being challenged and was also being honest at the same time, she would admit that it was the narco more than her disdain for the last loss that prevented her from taking new cases. She always had the common sense to know that the quickest way to disbarment was being doped up during a trial. With coke it was no problem, but with narco she wasn't sure she could make it through a trial clean, so rather than risk it, she quit taking cases. It was easier than to quit taking the dope. Despite Joanne's addictive personality, she certainly wasn't addicted to the courtroom, not anymore. Out of law school, the court room had been her addiction, but that was before the television mess and before narco.

Joanne was now at a crossroads. She had an amazing opportunity in front of her. Earlier that day her protégé, Tavian Springs, had come to her office with a case that had the possibility to turn everything around. Tavian was just out of law school and had a good legal instinct, but unlike most young guns, knew that he wasn't ready for a case of this caliber yet. It was a death penalty case in Texas. The death penalty was right in Joanne's wheel house and this particular case had all the makings for a grand return to the big stage for her. The defendant in the case was Esteban Diaz. Diaz had been convicted of killing another teenager, the son of a Texas State Patrol officer, as part of a gang initiation in Brownsville, Texas. Diaz' public beating by police in the aftermath of his arrest had made headlines but had not spared him from a trip to death row in Texas. The case had initially sparked outrage because of the beating, but it continued to linger in the press because of his claim of innocence. Diaz had produced three separate alibi witnesses, two of whom were discredited by the prosecution. The third was killed in an altercation with police after a traffic stop in what appeared to most outside observers as nothing more than a government sanctioned hit. The officer who had pulled the trigger had disappeared under mysterious circumstances, the witness was buried, and Diaz was sentenced to die. Diaz had made contact with Tavian and Tavian had brought the case to Joanne.

Tavian had a hard time masking his excitement when he first approached her about the case. He had yet to handle a murder case, much less a capital case, and was anxious to get his feet wet. Joanne had not actually seen Tavian in court but he had developed a reputation of being diligent and ruthless. In the time she had known him, Tavian had made an impact on her. He was the hardest working young man that she had ever come across. He had a singular focus when he was tasked with a project. Joanne knew she could count on him to put in the legwork. Before even approaching her, he had already begun the investigative work; it was this vigor that had convinced her to get back into the game. However, the real draw to her was the proposition of getting back into the limelight and resurrecting her once prominent career. Tavian was well aware of her thirst to get back to center stage in the war against the death penalty, and she knew this was the real reason he had brought it to her. In all things, Tavian was loyal. Loyalty to Joanne was very important.

With the Diaz case in front of her, there were two big moves she needed to make. The first was to get her partner at the Innocence Institute, Frank Dekalb, on board. Dekalb's specialty was research and writing. With her courtroom savvy and Tavian's investigative skills, the three of them would be an unstoppable force. The second thing she had to do was kick the damned narco. That would be tougher than getting Frank on board. She had made the decision on her way in to St. Stevens that tonight would be the night to quit; she knew it would be a tougher fight than any she had ever faced in the courtroom. She was preparing for a sleepless night, likely the first of many. For a split second she considered stopping off at Applebee's for a scotch to help her with sleep, but she decided against it. Joanne wasn't sure that booze was the right way to kick a drug habit, and she didn't want to create a whole different set of problems for herself. The thought of being hungover and in opiate withdrawal was terrifying. She decided against Applebee's but did make a stop though. It was a stop she made regularly, and of late more frequently. In a parking lot outside of Ridgedale Center was a nondescript trash receptacle made of concrete and pebbles. The receptacle had a false bottom with a locking door on the base that thousands of people who drove by it every day and never noticed. Inside the door was a Louis Vuitton bag with twenty five thousand dollars that would need to be washed.

7

Clifford Banks sat in his office looking through a file that had recently been dropped on his desk. Clifford had been the Chairman of the Leech Lake Band of Ojibwe for almost fifteen years. Clifford had done a lot of really good things for the tribe since moving back to Cass Lake. His first task as general manager of the casinos was to help increase profits a hundred fold. This put people to work and allowed him to increase funding for tribal police, which in turn had lowered crime on the reservation. Crime stats weren't yet where he wanted them but they were going in the right direction. Clifford fancied himself a reformer. Everything he did was to benefit his people. Some of his actions may have been considered questionable by outsiders, but Clifford was of the mindset that the ends justified the means.

The rez had suffered under the watchful eye of the white man for a hundred and fifty years. In more recent times, with the population decimated by alcoholism, unemployment, crime and an overall sense of despair, the white man had given up and turned control back to the people. The problems of the rez were not about to fix themselves. The rez needed a reformer. They needed Clifford.

Clifford knew he was not the only visionary, but he felt he was the only one capable of giving back the Leech Lake band their proud heritage. Returning a people to an ancient splendor was no small task. Clifford saw it as a war, and in war there were casualties. Clifford was not concerned with the loss of innocence; innocence for the native peoples was lost when Columbus set foot on Hispaniola. Clifford was concerned with the prosperity of his people. He was willing to do whatever it took to accomplish that end.

Gangs had been one of the many plagues on the reservation. Clifford was looking at a file that contained information on several gang related murders from the recent past that had went mostly unsolved. The reservation gangs were not connected to the big city gangs, but rather copycats that were less organized but equally violent. The violence stemmed from control over the drug trade. From an outsider's perspective, drugs certainly could have been one of the areas where Clifford's morals could be called into question but to Clifford there was a big difference between him and the gang-bangers killing each other over weed and meth. Clifford had a hard and fast rule about selling within the borders of the Rez. Yes, Clifford had managed the Leech Lake Casinos and, yes, he was now Chairman of the Tribe, but Clifford's primary business was the manufacture of prescription drugs. When gangs started selling dope in Cass Lake and in Onigum and started killing each other over the profits, he worked tirelessly to stomp them out. In some cases he put them in his employ. In other cases he took the measures necessary to make sure they were out of business. It had taken some time, but he had brought peace to the reservation. It was the key factor to his popularity. Clifford, however, had no problem selling to the rednecks and tourists around Walker and made most of his money selling to housewives and to prisoners in penitentiaries across the country.

Clifford had claimed to have grown up on the White Earth Reservation, leaving for ten years to attend Harvard and earn an undergraduate and a PhD in economics. What Clifford had done upon graduating changed depending on who he was talking to. Some stories revolved around him traveling to Pine Ridge and working with the Bureau of Indian Affairs there. In other stories, he had returned to Mahnomen where he worked with some white bankers. The fables all revolved around how he had missed home, not really ever being able to put his finger on what it was that called him back. He would say the quality of life on the reservation didn't offer the things that are considered a good measure of quality of life: no pro sports teams, opera houses or symphonies, and no shopping malls. Clifford would laugh when he told people that the Cass Lake Panthers were his basketball champions and the loon's song was his opera. Tranquility and history were his quality of life. Another of Clifford's claims told of his family having been in northern Minnesota for generations, members of the Bear Clan. They had been here long before statehood, before the first Norwegian settlers had ever set foot in the land of sky tinted water. His family had helped run the Dakota out of the Shakopee Valley. He went on and on about his spiritual attachment, and how all the shopping and fast food in the world couldn't replace that.

Though Clifford told many stories about his Uncle Dennis, the founder of the American Indian Movement and the Alcatraz takeover when the students at San Francisco University had occupied the Island, none could be verified by people who were there. There weren't any of the old people who could recall a baby named Clifford being born anywhere in the family. To many this was of little consequence.

The real story of Clifford Banks, AKA Jesus Ramirez, was very different than the yarns he spun glad handing the locals. Though he did have indigenous heritage, his ancestors were not Ojibwe. In fact he had grown up in Mexico, escaping the brutality of the cartels by running con games until he saved up enough cash to buy his way across the border into New Mexico. In New Mexico, he became Clifford Ramirez, complete with all the right documents to land a good paying construction job. Not the day labor so many of his fellow countrymen sought, but a union job with high pay and good benefits. It was in that capacity that he discovered both politics and the plight of the American Indian. In 1983, he was part of a project to build a card club for the Cabazon and Morongo band of Cahuilla people. Not long after, the State of California tried getting its hands into the cookie jar and the U.S. Supreme Court told them not so fast. Thus tribal gaming was born. Ever the entrepreneur, Clifford saw an opportunity. After a little background research, he became Clifford Banks. He greased the right folks and got himself enrolled in the White Earth Band of Ojibwe, becoming a distant relative of the renowned civil rights activist Dennis Banks. Somewhere along the line his fake heritage and real life became blurred. He grew to love his adopted people. Maybe that was the nature of con men in general or maybe it was simply his nature, but Clifford Banks was the biggest believer in all of his scams.

Though Clifford was a con artist, he was not a violent man. However, violence had been a way of life in his family. He had survived the cartels in Mexico and maneuvered Southern California's gangland in the eighties. As a young man, he learned quickly that violence was politics by other means, but it was a tenuous relationship. He himself would never allow violence to be the end. If violence was the end, then power was illegitimate. Violence as an end was despotism and despots were not about making life better for their constituents. Service of the constituents is what created the real power.

Clifford had real power. Clifford served his people and made their lives better. Violence to Clifford was a tool, a hammer wielded to drive the nails into the frame of a new school or hospital. Violence was the conduit for his passion and his passion was the reservation. The people of the tribe could see his passion and that was why he had been elected chairman; it was why he would continue to serve and why he believed he would be the first Native American elected to Congress from Minnesota. It didn't matter to him at all that he wasn't really Native.

Clifford thumbed through the police reports

until he came to the one he was most interested in, that of Henry Wright. Between May and
August of that year there were eleven murders
on the reservation, ending with the murder of
Henry Wright. Of the eleven murders, Henry's
was the only one that had been solved. Ken
Northbird had been the sole conviction in the
crime. Retaliation was the motive. Henry had
been in front of his house when a hooded assailant walked up to him and shot him point blank
killing him.

Clifford knew the story well. There were in
fact two different stories of what had taken
place ten years ago on his reservation. One was
the real story. The other was the official story
that was told to the jury. According to court
records, Wright had been at a bar in Walker
and had been involved in a brawl with five or
six other men, one of whom was John Jackson. Henry had been thrown out of the bar
and hitched his way back to Onigum. There
he found a party, where a lot of alcohol was
being consumed. Two hours after the incident in
Walker, Jackson showed up at the party alone. It
wasn't long before he crossed paths with Wright,
who stabbed him twice. The second puncture
plunged into Jackson's liver, killing him almost
instantly. Wright took off with Tess Whitebird,
who drove him to her house. Shortly afterward Jackson's brother, Ken Northbird, arrived
on the scene just in time to see Jackson being

taken away in the ambulance with the word that he was already dead spreading throughout the party. Wright had kept a low profile for the next ten days. Most believed he had went to the Twin Cities for that time to try and round up enough money to get out of Minnesota and head to Denver in an attempt to avoid both the police but more importantly Northbird. The rumors were mostly correct. When his body was found he was carrying a thousand dollars cash and two bus tickets to Denver. Henry had returned to the Walker area, apparently to pick up his younger brother Marcel. His plan was to start all over in Denver. He never made it out of Walker. He was shot to death in front of his home by Northbird as his younger brother watched. Marcel Wright had identified Northbird, who was sentenced to life in prison.

The file he had been looking at had come from Jefferson Buckley, the special agent in charge on the case for the FBI. Buckley shared Clifford's vision for cleaning up the rez and was a man that knew sometimes some eggs needed to be broke in order to make omelets. Over the years Buckley and Banks had broken some eggs together, and they had enjoyed some pretty damn good omelets. When Buckley retired he handed the file to Clifford. Buckley hadn't been interested in anyone sniffing around the case and figured it was time to be put to bed. Two years later Buckley lost his battle to prostate cancer, which left only three other people, not including himself, that knew anything about the contents of that file. One of them was Clifford's top lieutenant, a man he trusted. The second was Ken Northbird, residing under Clifford's keen eyes in the Florence federal supermax in Colorado. It was the third that Clifford was most concerned with right now. Clifford had recently learned that the third had just resurfaced in the Twin Cities. Clifford knew it was in his people's best interest if he kept an eye on Marcel Wright. He knew exactly who he could count on for that job.

8

Marcel walked out of St. Stevens alone. Shannon had hung back to chat up Joanne after class, but Marcel knew that he was on borrowed time with the approaching thunderstorms. The walk to his bike was a short one, and as he walked he peeked back over his shoulder. He could see flashes splashing all over the sky to the west over the skyline of Minneapolis. The thunderclaps followed later telling him there was still time. On the western horizon he could see the torrents of rain. He hopped on the bike and fired it up. He was so caught up in the approaching squalls that he didn't notice Shannon slip into her SUV and pull out of the parking lot shortly after he did.

Once on Snelling, Marcel wound up the six hundred cc engine and quickly darted through the south bound traffic on the way to the interstate. From St. Stevens it would be a quick shot this time of night to the Cathedral Hill neighborhood where he lived. During rush hour, Shannon had no hope to keep up with the crotch rocket, but at this time of night she could easily maneuver the traffic following at a distance safe enough to keep him from noticing.

As Marcel entered Interstate 94, a few streaks of rain smeared across the shield of his helmet and he quickly twisted the throttle of the Japanese racing bike. The arrow on both the tachometer and speedometer shot to the right and he took off like he had been fired from a gun. Shannon was able to see him from a distance. She entered the interstate and stomped the gas pedal hard towards the floor. Her BMW traveled in the same direction as Marcel, but she was barely able to keep the gap between them close enough to maintain visual. She was just close enough for her to see his exit on West 7th Street. Marcel slowed once off the interstate to a more reasonable speed for the considerably more congested main thoroughfare through downtown St. Paul. Marcel turned right at the Cathedral and made his way around to his apartment on Summit

Ave, a couple blocks from the historic church. Shannon was able to close the gap considerably at this point, so much so that she had to pull back a little to prevent him from seeing her once he parked abruptly in front of the old Victorian that had been divided up into apartments sometime during the 1980's. Shannon wheeled into the parking lot of the Cathedral and watched.

9

M arcel couldn't stop thinking about Shannon. They had spent a lot of time together in Libraries during 1L and though they never had conversations about their past, Marcel was able to piece together some of her background. Shannon was the daughter of a prominent philanthropist. Her father was a snowbird, spending summers in Minnesota and winters in Florida. Shannon had went to high school in Florida but considered Minnesota home. After high school, she attended the University of Florida where she majored in Art History and Criminology. The two majors didn't really have many overlapping classes and it had taken her a full five years of study to complete the two programs but she did so in grand fashion, graduating magna cum laude and earning the opportunity to speak at her graduation. After graduation, she really didn't know what to do with herself, so she went to work with her father's foundation as a supervisor on missionary projects in Africa for a year and a half. She was a restless soul and grew tired of remaining in any one place for too long and quit the foundation. After leaving Africa, she spent six months and thousands of dollars of her father's money exploring Europe. She returned to the States shortly after 9/11, based on a warning given to her father by the state department that she was to be the target of a kidnapping. When she returned to the states, her father talked her into going to graduate school. Since he was footing the bill, she acquiesced to his demands.

Though she never said it outright, Marcel got the impression that Shannon was a loner. She never seemed to have a problem meeting people, but she didn't seem to have any friends. Marcel believed that most people were intimidated by her perfection. She had shared a story with Marcel about how lonely overseeing the St. Theresa school project in Africa was. There were a few locals and some older men that supervised the construction but most of the missionaries were women and she found they were none too friendly to her. Marcel wondered if her assessment was accurate or if there was something else.

Marcel couldn't help but wonder about her past relationships. He knew that she had traveled with a couple guys in Europe but it hadn't been anything serious, more relationships of convenience. He himself wasn't experienced at all when it came to dating and women. He tried to convince himself that his lack of social life was due to his focus on becoming champion but in reality he was scared.

It was Marcel's impression that depression had set in when she had returned to the states and recognized the depths of her loneliness. That had been two years ago. He wouldn't have guessed it. She didn't carry any of that pain with her. He knew depression. He knew what it looked like. He had been around it his whole life. Shannon was comfortable and relaxed with him. She was also completely present in their conversation. He almost felt she approached their evening the way she approached the assignments in class with an all encompassing focus.

Marcel was an expert at reading people's underlying emotion; it was a skill most abused kids learn like a survival instinct. Marcel was starting to believe that his entire sense of self was a complex combination of survival instincts. Tonight, however, he hadn't been focused on survival.

Marcel was a man who was confident to the point of self-destruction. He was different from the others at St. Stevens, from the tattoos to how he dressed and spoke. He rode a fast motorcycle and he was a pro fighter. Marcel lived on life's jagged edges, and he could tell that Shannon was a woman who desperately wanted to live there as well. A majority of the decisions she made in life were the result of this quest for danger. Marcel understood this well. That trait, that relentless pursuit for adventure, was what created criminals and heroes and they both possessed it. Sitting at the table, Marcel knew they shared a common bond. Each had needed adrenaline to make themselves feel normal. There were people in the world who chased that dragon with drugs. The people like he and Shannon chased it in more natural ways.

10

M arcel unlocked the door to his unit and was unimpressed with the warm stale air that greeted him. Though the apartment was on the first floor, there was no air conditioning and given the current run of sweltering temperatures there was never time for the place to cool down. Marcel walked in and instantly pulled off his shirt, tossed it into a hamper in the corner, and walked to his bedroom in the back of the apartment. He sat on the edge of his bed contemplating the evening and examining the depths of his own emotion.

Marcel thought about his friend Shannon. He wondered how it was that people from two completely different worlds could have enough in common that they could be friends. Shannon was knowledgeable about a number of different things, and that made conversation easy. What made it interesting were their various differences.

Marcel also thought about Bloodsworth and how so much of his life had been taken from him. Locked away in conditions that Marcel couldn't fathom all for the sake of expediency. The thought made him shudder. His mind was brought back to his own family. Memories of seeing his own father behind glass.

A new thought made its way in. The thought of the man who killed his brother sitting in his own cell. Marcel had never entertained this thought before. The events were compartmentalized in his brain, due in large part to his understanding of the world as a boy. His father's prison sentence and his brother's killers trial were two separate and distinct events because that is how he had seen them. But tonight, somehow the barrier in his brain had been unlocked and now he came to comprehend how the two were related.

Marcel wondered what Shannon would think of his family tree. Their upbringings were so different. Did Shannon have any comprehension of living with poverty? He knew of course she had no idea what it was to be poor, but did she have any idea what life surrounded by poverty was like? Shannon had traveled the world; had she seen the by-products of a life lived on the razor's edge of survival? Did she know the drug culture, had she been around addicts? Had she known the violence of the drug trade? Marcel knew that rich people were not immune from addiction. In fact he felt that they were even more susceptible to its throws, however he rarely saw them suffer from the collateral damage that the market created. Had Shannon ever been shot at? Or, better yet, had she ever visited someone close to her in prison? He doubted it. Even if she had, he knew the experience would be very different. The maximum security facilities he had been to were very different than the federal minimum security camps white collar criminals were sent to.

The irony of his own life struck him and made him chuckle out loud in the stuffy room where he sat all by himself. Marcel had competed in the Olympic trials and was a professional athlete. *A professional athlete*! He shook his head. When people thought of professional athletes they pictured Lebron James on a Banana Boat. They never pictured the minor league baseball player making fifteen hundred dollars a month or the pro golfer struggling to keep his tour card. They certainly didn't think about the nameless boxers in gyms all across the country making five hundred bucks on undercards beating the hell out of each other with no hope of every making it to the bright lights of Las Vegas. At least Marcel had that potential. But, here he was, in a small apartment with no air conditioning, no food in the fridge and barely enough in his bank account to meet the bills each month.

Marcel looked out the large bay windows in his bedroom. The rain continued along with the spectacular lighting show. A flash lit up his apartment, followed instantaneously by an explosion of thunder that flickered the power out in the entire building. The place he lived was the bottom floor of an 1890's era Victorian mansion. The building itself was large. Perched at the end of Summit Avenue on Cathedral hill, it had an amazing view overlooking downtown St. Paul. Jarvis had hooked him up with the landlord and he had gotten an incredible deal for it. It was really the only way he could afford such a nice place. The apartment was not without its flaws; it had no central air conditioning and most of the rooms were unbearably hot except for his bedroom, which had a small window unit that kept the temperature in the high seventies. This allowed him to at least sleep at night even though the west window faced the fiery late afternoon sun which seared through the glass and got trapped inside. This in turn increased the temperature to a point where even the heartiest organisms struggled for life. Even after the sun dropped below the horizon, it remained unbearable even with the windows open and fans circulating the air.

Marcel yanked himself back to reality, got up from the bed and put on a pair of basketball shorts. He remained shirtless as he sat on his very comfortable armchair, an addition found at a thrift store not far from his apartment.

The power flickered again. Marcel could tell that the wind was picking up outside. This flicker wasn't a result of a lighting strike; this one was a result of a branch hitting a power line somewhere in the neighborhood. He prayed that the power wouldn't go out tonight. Even with the storm, the temperature outside was still in the high eighties and incredibly humid. He decided to round up some candles as a precaution. He had a couple in a drawer in the kitchen. He pulled them out, and then he carried them over to the coffee table in front of his thrift store armchair. The action of looking for the candles combined with the sauna like climate of his apartment lead to a glistening sweat beginning to cover his upper body. He went to the pantry outside the bathroom and took out a bath towel and wiped his forehead and chest, then went back to the thrift store armchair and sat back down. He wiped his chest again and looked down as he did so. He traced the lines of a tattoo over his heart; the memorial he had dedicated to his brother all those years ago. He never talked about his brother's murder, not with his grandfather, not with Jarvis, not with anyone. He had thought by moving away to live with his grandparents in Colorado that he could escape all of the things that had happened to him, and he had for the most part. The tattoo was done as a reminder of a time he no longer wanted to be in and the family he once had.

Life hadn't always been tough for Marcel. The time with his grandfather had been good, however short it was. Marcel's grandparents lived between Boulder and Denver in a very nice farmhouse. Apart from being a police officer, his grandfather also raised horses. He had always wished his brother could have shared that portion of his life with him. That was just one of the many things that Marcel had wished he could have done with his brother. Another was baseball. If Marcel had just one wish, it would have been for the opportunity to play baseball with his brother. Baseball back then had been fun. He had enjoyed the company of the other kids. Marcel knew his brother would have enjoyed that part of baseball as well. One of the best parts of living on the ranch was that he had friends then; he was even invited to Teddy Cramblit's birthday party at the Boulder Reservoir. It was the best birthday party he had ever been to. Marcel had always wanted a birthday party, but had never had one. A funny thought entered his head: maybe next year he would throw himself a birthday party, invite Shannon and Jarvis, have a Dairy Queen cake and party hats. He laughed to himself at this prospect.

Marcel hadn't been a star on his Legion base-ball team, but he played. For Marcel it wasn't about how he performed, it was about the game itself. Baseball was timeless; people hated the Yankees in the Great Depression as much as they hated them today. He always enjoyed watch-ing baseball. He remembered Kirby Puckett and Kent Hrbeck in the World Series and of course game seven. He had been to a couple of Rockies games out in Colorado, but the thing he enjoyed most was listening to the games on the radio. That was the timeless nature of the game: no matter how technology changed, baseball was best enjoyed in its most basic form. Even bet-ter was baseball in September. There was some-thing magical about baseball in September, es-pecially if your team was in contention. The Twins had been in contention most years in the 2000's. This year was no different. Joe Mauer and the rest of the Twins were making a run at catching the Detroit Tigers who currently lead the division. Marcel reached for the stereo and flipped on the game. It was already in the fifth in-ning, the Twins were up one nothing on Kansas City. Delmon Young had parked a solo shot into the left field seats in the second inning and Liri-ano had given up only two hits thus far. Bert Bly-leven and Dick Bremer's calls were that of two old friends showing up to talk with him about the game.

Marcel looked over his other tattoos. Symbols of a past that he had tried to mostly forget. The tattoos made him think again of Shannon. One of the things that he was most appreciative of was that she avoided the topic of family. Discussing family for most people was in the realm of safe chit chat. It didn't cross the danger zones of politics or religion, subjects that most people steer clear of. Marcel wasn't like that. Neither was Shannon. Telling people about his mother and brother being murdered, or his father's incarceration, were not topics he ever wanted to discuss with new acquaintances. He would much rather talk about Christianity, Judaism, Islam, whatever anyone was interested in talking about. He could discuss points of the Republican party or the Democratic party. He really didn't have a position. What he did have were books. He was well read, in large part because it allowed him to talk about subjects other than himself or his violent family tree. He had no doubt that eventually the subject of family would come up with Shannon, but he hoped against hope that the subject wouldn't come up in class. That was the realization that he had been struggling to come to all evening. It was that level of exposure that he wasn't sure he could handle. It was funny to him. He could stand toe to toe in the ring, knowing that he could be physically humiliated in front of thousands of people on any given fight night with absolutely no fear, but he was petrified of speaking about his family in front of fifty classmates. He considered Shannon for a moment. Exactly how much of his past would he be willing to share with her?

Justin Morneau's Double down the line drove in Denard Span from third and Alexi Casilla from first. He refocused on the game and everything else, fear included, dissolved. Burt and Dick were recapping the at bat. As far as Marcel was concerned, Burt Blylevn was the best announcer in sports. He communicated a genuine passion for the game that was impossible not to catch if you were a fan. It was part of what he loved about listening to the games on the radio. Marcel sat on the thrift store armchair immersed in this moment, smiling, for now everything in his world seemed right again. A stark contrast to the fear that gripped him only moments before. There was a certain cosmic balance that he felt right now. A balance that didn't exist when he got the tattoo on his abdomen. He traced the tattoo with his finger, a feeling of regret washing away the temporary contentment of the baseball game. That tattoo was different than the one on his chest. That tattoo was a permanent reminder of things in his life he had been running from for so long. The tattoo took his mind to the girl he had known long before Shannon.

Marcel pictured her clearly in his mind's eye as he got up and walked to his bedroom. It was separated from the living area by a set of French doors that matched the crown molding in the rest of the house perfectly. Marcel kept the glass spotless. Cleanliness was yet another of Marcel's great virtues; there wasn't so much as a paperclip out of place in his apartment. A cool blast hit him as he walked through the doors. It was refreshing. He shuffled across the hardwood floors, a deep red oak, to the large bay window and looked over the city which continued to be illuminated by the persistent bolts of lightning that gave no sign of letting up. St. Paul was quiet; its normal hustle and bustle drowned by the continued downpour. The wind was fierce and there were some hailstones starting to fall. For a moment, Marcel thought he could hear a civil defense siren going off somewhere in the distance. Shortly thereafter the baseball game was interrupted by the emergency broadcast system. A tornado warning was in effect for Anoka and Sherburne county. Several funnel clouds had been spotted by trained spotters near the cities of Ramsey, Elk River, Zimmerman and St. Francis. Just then there was a blinding flash and an explosion that shook the old house to its foundation. For a moment Marcel thought it was going to collapse. That lightning bolt knocked the power out for good. The radio was silenced as was the humming of the air conditioner. It didn't take long for the heat to start seeping in through the cracks in the ancient insulation in the walls. Marcel doubted he would sleep much tonight.

11

A cross town on Lake Minnetonka, Joanne knew that she wasn't going to sleep either but for an entirely different reason. She normally took 200 mg of narco before bed. She hadn't done so tonight. She felt the withdrawal deep in her joints; it was as if she could feel every individual vertebrae in her back aching. Her knees were on fire, and the pain pulsated in her fingers. She tried to tell herself the pain wasn't real, that it was simply a side effect of her addiction. It didn't help.

The power had went out in her ten thousand

square foot prison a few hours earlier, but the back up generator had kicked in and kept the lights and the air conditioning in her master suite running. Non-essentials had been shut down, the hot tub and pool, lights in her library, the theater in the basement. It was like being in solitary confinement.

She had won the house in the divorce. She had never wanted it. What she cared most about was winning. The monstrosity was a continued reminder of her lowlife husband, who had fucked every woman whom he came across. A good number of them in this house. In fact it was in the kitchen where his philandering had finally been discovered. Her husband, Richard Benson, was an accomplished plastic surgeon. The woman, who had been taking it from behind in Joanne's kitchen, was a nineteen year old college student who worked in his Bloomington office. At the time she wished she had a gun. One of those little dillingers, or derringers, whatever those miniature single shot bastards were that sexy widows always had tucked in their bags in the detective movies. She, however, didn't have one. Even if she did, she wouldn't have known how to use it and probably would have ended up shooting herself in the foot. But oh, how she wished she could have put a bullet right between his eyes at that moment. She couldn't say that it had come as a huge shock to her. Before she was the third Mrs. Benson, she was the previ-

ous other woman. He had been fifteen years her
elder and married the first time she had gone
down on him in a parking garage downtown. She
had just moved to Minneapolis from out east and
was working as a waitress at Manny's steakhouse
where they met. He drove a Mercedes convert-
ible, bought her lavish gifts, and had not treated
her like a waitress he was hitting on in a bar. This
made him different than so many other scumbag
married men that had come through the restaurant on a nightly basis, or so she had thought.
Richard had a penchant for younger women. By
the time she turned thirty she was too old for
him. That's when the sex ended. It was also when
her career was taking off so she never really addressed it. She was on the road a lot, not that she
could have fixed it anyway, but when she came
back into town he was always there to pick her
up, take her out to dinner and play the role of the
loving husband. With the exception of the sex.
He had played that role until the last night of
their marriage when she walked in on them.
That night he hadn't been at the airport to pick
her up, so she had taken a cab back. She had been
foolish, fearing something had happened to him.
A heart attack perhaps. Though he worked out
religiously, the rest of his lifestyle was condu-
cive to any number of heart problems, from his
high cholesterol diet to the smoking, booze, and
drugs. Richard loved the drugs. He was the son of
a bitch who had introduced her to cocaine while

she was still working at Manny's. She would have never been able to afford it on her own, but with Richard there was a ready supply on hand all the time. In hindsight, there had been all kinds of warning signs about Richard. The least of which was her being the other woman at one point, and that made her hate herself even more. This house was just one big damned reminder of her failures, and damn, how she wished she had a gun that night.

So there she sat with aching joints, unable to sleep, and unable to escape the reality that in her relationship with Richard she had been a rube. He had run a scam on her and left her a middle aged addict with a career on the brink of ruin, and a gigantic house that had a tax liability higher each year than the salary she had once made as a waitress downtown all those years ago. She thought again about the mini pistol and if she had it right now, she just might well swallow a bullet. Suicide wasn't really an option, though. If she really wanted to say good-bye, there was enough pills in the house to do so. It was more an alternate ending like on the special features section of a DVD. An end to the story that was once written, but no one really liked once it was filmed. Suicide was admitting defeat and throwing in the towel. That wasn't how Joanne operated. Joanne, for all her flaws and misgivings, was a fighter. She had once been a "Champion of the World" and she was determined to get her belt back. If she was able to get back on top, then she could walk away with her legacy intact. If she bowed out now, she would be best noted as an also-ran. A one hit wonder. A fluke who let reality catch up with and destroy her. That wasn't going to happen. Tavian had got her back in the ring. A win would put her on track for another title fight.

Joanne had once heard the saying, "Every journey begins with a first step". At the time she thought it was corny. Now that she was in the midst of withdrawal she decided that her own first step was to lay on her bed, wallowing in pain and withdrawal. Soaking in the sorrow of her current predicament and accepting it because she couldn't change it. Her journey would lead her back into the spotlight and success she once relished. She put her head in her pillow and wept until the sun came up.

12

Texas Department of Criminal Justice inmate number 999569 sat in his cell in his Polunsky State Penitentiary where Texas' execution chamber was housed. The fifty-four acre unit was located near downtown Huntsville one hundred and sixty miles southeast of Dallas down Interstate sixty-five. It was Texas' oldest penitentiary and has been inmate number 999569's home for the better part of ten years. Today he sat on his bunk and looked for a long moment at the package he had just received, a manila envelope with a post mark from St. Paul, Minnesota. He had been waiting a long time for this package: all of his adult life. The State of Texas had accused him of shooting and killing a gang member with a twelve gauge shotgun. He was convicted by a jury of his peers solely on the testimony of a jailhouse snitch who got a nice deal in exchange for his testimony. There was also circumstantial evidence, evidence that could have applied to any number of the boys in El Paso with Mexican heritage.

Before he was inmate 999569 he had been Esteban Diaz, a sixteen-year-old honor student with a bright future. A member of the student council and the centerfielder for his high school's baseball team that had made the state tournament just two weeks before the murder he was convicted of took place. His youth was gone. He was a hardened man now, but the judges words still shook his soul.

"For the offense of murder in the first degree for the benefit of a gang, count one of the indictment, I sentence you to execution by lethal injection." When he heard those words bounce off the walls of that cold courtroom, the air was forced out of his lungs, then the blood rushed to his head and his body went numb. His head swirled and all he could remember hearing were the shrieks and cries coming from his mother whose collapse was prevented by his grandmother and aunt. The pain that this affair had caused his mother hurt the worst. His mother always believed in his potential and believed in him. She had moved to Texas from Mexico when she was sixteen all by herself. She had been pregnant with him, and she wanted so badly for him to have an opportunity for a future. A future that evaporated when those words came out of the judge's mouth.

He knew that watching him being led away in handcuffs had killed her, though she didn't physically die until three years later. His aunt had sent him a letter explaining how his mother had taken too many pills two weeks after he had heard that his appeal had been denied. The stress of it all had been too much for her and she snapped. He wept when he read the letter. It was the last time he cried. This place had taken his innocence and his passion. It had made him hard.

He had proclaimed his innocence every step of the way; he had never been involved in gangs. Gangs had taken the lives of so many people around him, and he saw no future in any of his peers that had given themselves over to the pull the gangs had in the neighborhood. He had avoided gangs at every turn. The cruel irony of the whole situation was that gangs had ruined his future even without his involvement.

The envelope he held in front of him contained his salvation. He had heard about the American Innocence Institute from a fellow inmate who had tried to get them involved in his case. The only problem was that guy was guilty. They refused to take his case. Estaban on the other hand, was innocent. They were his last hope. His mandatory appeals had been used up. If they couldn't do anything for him, he would be dead in less than three months.

Estaban didn't waste a lot of time savoring the outside of the letter. He paused briefly to realize and discard the fear that his request to review his case would be denied. He exorcised it and replaced it with hope. The move tired him greatly, and he felt like it was the last little bit of hope he could muster forever. Something inside him told him he deserved it, that he deserved to have hope for all that was taken from him. He was right to have hope because inside this envelope would be the answer to his prayers.

13

Joanne sat on the sofa in her suite at the Austin Hyatt. Her team was there too, an eclectic mish-mash of lawyers and law students, all dressed in sweatshirts and jogging pants. Many of the team were catching quick cat naps since no one had slept much in the last forty-eight hours. They had been pouring over witness statements, reading through notes of prosecutors, investigators, defense attorneys and anyone else who had any involvement in the case of Texas v. Estaban Diaz. This was how it began. The team always descended upon the locale of a case to thoroughly investigate before even deciding to meet with a petitioner. The number of prisoners in this country who claimed innocence was staggering. Living on the word of a convict alone would lead an outsider to believe the United States of America was in the business of prosecuting primarily innocent people. Most prisoners were flat out full of shit. Some, however, were in denial; they were unable to admit or realize that their actions in fact made them guilty of a crime. In most of those cases, the convictions were a result of accomplice liability. Joanne and her team were not about to meet with an accomplice. The Innocence Institute was not about to do anything that would cast her group in an unfavorable light. The only clients they would meet with were the ones who could make a showing of actual innocence. It was important that they fought the good fight.

Joanne had no idea what time it was; she didn't really know what day it was. She had been clean for almost a week. Most of that time she had been sick, suffering the physical symptoms of narcodone withdrawal. The drug had symptoms so severe that they were akin to heroin withdrawal, and as such, doctors never recommended quitting cold turkey. But that was Joanne's style. She had gotten everywhere she was on her own and was damn sure going to get there this time too.

Tavian came into the sitting room of the large suite. He had been sleeping in the bedroom for the last two hours. He had led the charge out into the community to meet with witnesses and got into the thick of things.

"Wow, Joanne. You look like hell. When is the last time you slept?" There was genuine concern in his voice and Joanne could only imagine what he saw. She had often wondered if he knew she was a dope fiend. She thought she hid it pretty well, but she doubted she could hide it from someone who was so close to her.

"No time to sleep," She lied. Joanne couldn't have slept if she wanted to. The ache in her joints was damn near unbearable, but he didn't need to know any of that. What was the saying from the spy movies? Need to know.

"What day is it?" She stood up from the sofa, pain shooting from her lower back directly into her brain. She wanted to cry but couldn't.

"Monday." Tavian walked to the counter and poured two cups of coffee.

Joanne looked down at her watch. It was only a little after six AM. Her flight was leaving in a couple hours. She had to be back in St Paul by seven for class.

"Any word from Frank?" the young man asked as he poured sugar into each cup and stirred.

Tavian was a twenty-five year old prodigy who had joined the team from Georgetown Law. He was a brilliant legal mind and not hard on the eyes. There was more than one occasion where Joanne had caught herself fantasizing about him. His six foot two inch frame was perfectly chiseled, and his smile could set a room on fire. She assumed there weren't many of his juries that didn't include women. But at the end of the day she was a professional and a relationship, even a tryst, was out of the question.

"No, the execution is scheduled for six PM, I don't imagine that we are going to hear from him until much closer to that time," she responded, taking the cup of sugar from him.

Frank Dekalb was one of Joanne's partners, and they had founded the American Innocence Institute years ago, long before she met narco. Back then she had been been a rising star, fueled by cocaine and ambition. Frank was a square who looked the part of an attorney all the way down to his red bowtie and white pressed shirt. He was currently the lead attorney in the case of Ali Sharif, a man accused of killing a cop in Georgia. It was a death penalty case, though not associated with the Innocence Institute. Frank was now dealing with the governor of Georgia, seeking a commutation of the sentence. Though Sharif was guilty as sin and had taken full responsibility for the murder, his remorse and conversion to Islam while on death row awaiting his appeals gave Dekalb the hope that the governor might be willing to commute his sentence. The new governor of Georgia was a wild-card, a moderate Republican who had voiced some concerns over the death penalty. Dekalb knew that he was a Christian and his faith had a big role in shaping his feelings about the death penalty. The case gave them all hope that they might be able to spare a life. While the Innocence Institute would never touch a case like Sharif's, Joanne, Frank, Tavian and the rest of the folks in this room all detested the death penalty. Many times they would work together outside the Institute on garden variety death penalty cases. They all ran in the same circles.

"What is your gut telling you on this one, boss?" Tavian asked thoughtfully. He took a seat at the kitchenette table where they had sat the night before until four AM discussing the contradictions in several witness statements.

"The thing I have learned in all these years are that politics are a delicate matter, Governor O'Connor is a rising star in the political world. If he has any designs on the White House, we can forget it. He is too moderate to win the Republican nomination, and he would need to bolster his conservative image. This case would give him that opportunity. If the White House isn't on his radar, then we have a shot. Frank knows that he has some personal moral objections to the death penalty, and that is where hope lies." Her answer wasn't very definitive, however they all knew that was the nature of the game. A craps table provided more guarantees than the political world. However if she were to wager, and she had discussed the case at length with Frank who shared her position, they both bet this would be a winner. Frank didn't think O'Connor had designs on the White House, and he believed that at the end of the day, shutting down death row in Georgia would be a legacy O'Connor's would be happy with.

There was another factor turning in their favor: Frank and Governor O'Connor had been undergrads together at Georgia Tech. Both had been political science majors. Frank went on to law school while O'Connor became a grad assistant at Tech and eventually a full professor at Emory. He was elected to State Senate in 1988 and became Governor in 1999, He was the first Republican elected in the state of Georgia since 1872. The two men had kept in touch through it all. That was a morsel that Joanne and Frank had kept to themselves.

"Roll the dice, huh?' Tavian responded

"If you want guarantees, this is the wrong line of work. If you can't handle disappointment, run away now." That was definitely Joanne's strong suit. She handled disappointment like a champ. Her failure to shoot her ex-husband was proof positive of that, but she had also handled the disappointment of losing her television show like a professional as well. That was if numbing herself with narco and dropping out of society for three weeks was considered professional. In her experience it certainly was the way her colleagues handled it.

"So let me ask you, Tavian, what is your feeling on this one? Is Estabahn Diaz an innocent man?" She asked shifting the subject back to their task at hand.

"You know I don't operate on feelings." He flashed that charming smile "I operate on evidence and facts we can prove, and until I get out and interview the principal's of this case, I have no opinion." The dispassionate, almost robotic way that he approached every case was so sexy to her. Her heart twittered just a little listening to him talk.

Their conversation was ended, as was the sleep of everyone else in the suite when Joanne's cell phone rang, an old school rotary phone ring in a digital song.

"Hart." Joanne's answer was curt. The caller ID let her know it was Frank but she would have answered the same had it been Ruth Bader Ginsburg on the phone. Joanne looked at a digital alarm clock on a night stand in the room. It was an hour later in Georgia, but she thought it was still a little early for him to know anything. She glanced around the room, several young disheveled faces watching her conversation intently. Red eyes and wild hair looking for hope.

"Joanne." The voice was strong and confident through the earpiece.

"Yeah Frank, where are we at?" The quality

that endeared Frank to Joanne, the reason they were partners, was his ability to dispense with pleasantries. Small talk in Joanne's mind, was nothing more than high priced bullshit. When they communicated with each other, words were not wasted.

"I had breakfast with O'Connor this morning." The confident voice was a dam on the verge of collapse, barely holding back a flood of emotion. Joanne could hear it and knew that Sharif was going to die at six PM tonight.

"O'Connor declined." He said.

"He is planning on putting his hat into the presidential race isn't he?" She converted her disappointment to indignation.

"Yeah, he was pretty frank with me. He laid it out, and it was exactly what we discussed. He knew he had to move right in the next twelve months and this was on opportunity to do it. He is holding a press conference at Five Thirty tonight." Joanne could hear contempt in her partner's voice now. For a poli-sci major, Frank never really enjoyed the realm of politics. He had been unable or unwilling to play the game at the public defender's office. Others with half the legal acumen had moved on to judgeships, but not Frank. Ultimately that was how Joanne found him, and she was happy she did. He was a brilliant legal mind, a tremendous researcher, and the best tactician in the Innocence Institute. It was Frank who put together the game plans for a majority of the cases taken on by the Innocence Project nationwide.

"What's the story on Diaz?" Frank was true to form. Frank would never dwell on defeat and he had already moved on from Sharif. As much as the loss hurt Frank, Sharif was a dead man now, and lawyers feeling sorry for themselves weren't going to change that.

"Well, it is too early to make a definitive statement on this one." Joanne wanted to tell him that it looked good on its face but there was a growing audience and she didn't want to taint their objectivity with her opinion. Though she didn't have much influence on court television, she did have some in this room.

The eyes around her were drenched with despair and pity. Some of it for her, some of it for Sharif, but most of it for themselves. They were a collective group of young lawyers and law students who were not accustomed to losing. Joanne thought they better get used to it in a big damn hurry. She remembered crying after her first execution. Her mentor, Vivian Monroe, had pulled her aside and ripped her a new asshole. She laid it out in the cold hard matter of fact way that most lawyers dealt with the gruesome details of the crimes they prosecuted and defended. "Defendants are not our friends and family," she had said. "They are people who had their chance at life and fucked it up. Our job isn't to cry for them; our job is to make sure that the government follows the letter of the law to the T. Our job is to ensure innocent people don't get convicted, and our job is to end a barbaric practice. Nowhere is there room for pity or regret. We do everything within our power to protect the rights of the accused, but at the end of the day there are people out there that do horrible things. And there are enough people out there who believe that killing them is the appropriate punishment." Those had been hard words for her to hear, but she remembered them always. The saying Vivian had used the most, that resonated with Joanne and she adopted as her own mantra, was that at the end of the day, win, lose or draw she would go home, they would go to prison. She thought it applied now as well as any other.

"Well most of you probably heard but Ali Sharif will be executed at six pm tonight. There will be no stay." She saw tears start to well up.

"For those of you that are new to this, keep this in mind: we go forward. We don't dwell on any one case, and that is what Sharif is, a case. Remember this always: at the end of the day, we go home, they go to prison." She focused on a girl who couldn't have been more than twenty-two years old. The girl had looked as if she was about to give her a damn hug before she started talking. Now a river of tears cascaded down her perfect cheek. She had a look of horror on her face. Joanne's predatory instinct kicked in. She had learned from the best after all. The great Dr.

Deviant. Joanne couldn't help but see her own naïve self in the woman. She saw the self that had trusted her pussy connoisseur of an ex-husband standing there in front of her, weeping like the weakling she had once been. She had been naive to the con of men, yes, and she had been naive when it came to the tough cases as well. That was, of course, before Monroe had dressed her down in front of a crowd not all that dissimilar from this one and she knew what she was going to do. She didn't really want to do it, but it was necessary.

"What in the fuck are you crying about?" She directed the question at the crying woman, fully expecting an answer.

Her assault left the girl in shock. As Joanne watched, she saw something else wash over her. It was the same look she saw in the medical assistant's eyes the night her ex-husband had not picked her up from the airport. She saw embarrassment. A rage grew in Joanne's belly. No longer was she interested in helping this young woman. At that moment she hated this woman as much as she hated her husband and the chippy he was giving it to in her kitchen. She hated all of the people who had short changed her all of her life. For a moment Joanne thought of the pistol. If only she had the pistol. She would have shot the bastard that had turned her into the animal she was now. She would have shot him first in the balls, then in the face. She would have destroyed her tormentors. Instead she was left here to un-load with her tongue on this young woman. A woman who she saw so much of herself in. She did this because now she was the predator.

"Well? I am waiting for an answer. Because if you are standing in my five hundred dollar a night suite crying your eyes out, I believe I have the right to know why. I mean, because if Sharif was your uncle, or your boyfriend, then that is something that should have been disclosed to us immediately. However, if he isn't your squeeze, and in fact he is not someone who you have ever even met before, well, then you are crying for no apparent reason here in front of everyone." She could feel Tavian looking at her, but she didn't take the lasers off the woman.

"You see, if you are going to cry over every case you lose you aren't going to make it very long. You are much better off giving up defense work and getting a job as a prosecutor. Or better yet, give up law altogether. Go be a flight attend-ant, jet off to some sunny location where every-one is happy because quite frankly hun, most of the people you are going to work for are going to end up in prison. And some of the people we work for are going to die. Shit! We didn't even work for Sharif; he was Frank's client. So the way I see it, you have two choices. Shut the fuck up, or get the fuck out." The young woman was now bawling.

When Joanne finished, the young woman

picked up her bag from the end of the sofa and left. It reminded Joanne of her uncle's dog. When Joanne was a kid, the dog pissed on the floor one night. Her uncle beat the dog within an inch of its life. When the beating was over, the dog walked away much the way this tart did. Joanne took pleasure in it. She hoped she would never see the woman again, not because she didn't want to deal with the emotion of the aftermath of a brow beating like this, but simply because she hated this woman and wanted the woman to know it.

"Tavian, make sure that bitch never comes back."

Tavian simply looked back at her, knowing that he wouldn't have to worry about it.

14

C had Hunt could tell that Tavian couldn't quite believe what he was seeing. Tavian and the others had always thought of Joane as a cold fish and a bit of a hard ass, but neither Chad nor Tavian could imagine her doing what she had just done. He wondered what this girl had done to draw her ire.

Chad was a paralegal who had been with Joanne for most of her years with the Innocence Institute. He had been there as part of the team in the glory days when wins were commonplace. Those days were now long gone, but he stayed on anyway.

Chad knew it wasn't Sharif. He knew she wasn't lying about not giving a shit about Sharif. She didn't give a shit about any of the defendants she worked with, but there had to be more to the story. Some of the lawyers in the room assumed it was her way of staying sane. Chad, on the other hand, thought just the opposite: that she was on the brink of insanity. He had been with her for a while and she had never been the type that had ever forced her world view on anyone else.

Chad thought that for the past two days she didn't seem like herself. Or at least the self she had evolved into over the years. She had been irritable and looked like hell. In the past couple of years she had morphed from being a very attractive woman to a woman who now appeared to be aging as fast as the clock ticked. Chad had discussed the possibility of drug use with Tavian the night before at dinner, and the two men had come to the conclusion that she had a fairly severe drug habit though neither of them had first hand knowledge. Joanne had exhibited mood swings, increasingly slurred speech, and declining appearance. They both also saw another warning sign: she hadn't handled a case in several years. Not handling a case, above all else, lead them to this conclusion. Chad knew that if she were using drugs regularly, she risked disbarment if she handled any cases. Chad looked at Tavian and knew that there was more than one person in the room that wondered if her tongue lashing was part and parcel to withdrawal.

Chad was surprised when she had taken the lead on this case. He figured Tavian had brought it to her, thinking she would offer her help, but allow him to be the first chair. That hadn't happened. Chad knew that Tavian had been hiding his disappointment, but he hoped Tavian would be monitoring the situation very closely.

Chad knew emotion was a dangerous commodity when defending people sentenced to death. The crimes were always violent; the stories were always sad. He couldn't remember ever working on a death penalty case where the victim was a child molester, and the defendant was a nun. Sure, there were good people who did bad things, and there were bad people who got killed, but never the twain did meet. Ali Sharif had kidnapped two young women who were both police officers. He had taken them to a barn in the middle of shit ass Georgia, where he tortured and raped them for two weeks before eventually killing them. When the cops closed in on him, he tried shooting his way out. He killed a young officer in the process. These were three women who had families whose lives had been destroyed by this low life. Chad personally didn't give a shit about Sharif's conversion to Islam or his remorse. More importantly, he knew Joanne didn't give a shit either. The emotion on display, berating the young woman, was almost as dangerous as the young woman's tears. The thing that Chad knew, and that Joanne and everyone else in the room did too, was that every team needed the passion of youth. Joanne needed the passion that the young woman brought to the table because there would come a time when things fell apart. When the case was at its worst, that passion would be all they had. Chad was too old to have much passion left. Joanne's was misguided, and Tavian made rocks look firey. He feared that if Joanne chased away all the young idealists, they wouldn't be able to survive a case like Diaz. Although Sharif was a piece of shit, Diaz was a kid doing the best he could to raise himself out of a bleak situation. Diaz was innocent. Losing the Diaz case would really mean something. Losing the Diaz case would be something they would all cry about.

15

Marcel's training camp started the day Joanne had flown to Texas. Training camp meant his time was limited for things outside of boxing and school. He hadn't spoken with or even thought about Shannon since they had class together almost two weeks ago. Now, on his way to class, he thought about seeing her again. He wondered what she did outside of school. Despite being the closest thing to a friend he had on campus, he didn't really know her at all.

Marcel had considered asking Shannon out

on a couple different occasions, but stopped himself. There was something about those type of encounters that changed people. What was it about the whole process of dating that could change how two people approached each other? Marcel wondered if he was dealing with fear right now or if he was simply being a realist. Was Shannon really someone who he would share some sort of fairytale romance with, they marry, have a family, and live happily ever after? If that wasn't the case, then in all likelihood his one friend in law school would transform into the one person that he was bound to have a series of awkward encounters with. No, he wasn't afraid. In Marcel's world there were no fairytale endings.

The complexity of his feelings for Shannon wasn't the only internal storm he was dealing with. This week, each student in class would get their first big assignment. Normally school assignments didn't have any bearing on him, but this wasn't a normal assignment. It also didn't help that his entire body was aching from the intensity of the workouts he had been put through twice a day, for two hours every day. It had slowed him down mentally as well as physically, and he was having a hell of a time processing everything right now.

When he opened the door to the room, he saw that he would not be the first one to arrive for class that evening. The room was in the lower level of the school. It wasn't a very large room, compared to the large lecture halls on the main floor. The room seated at maximum forty-five people and the class had pushed the limits of that capacity. Unlike a traditional classroom, there were not individual desks in the room. This was different than the other rooms in the lower level. Instead the room had two rows of long tables in the shape of a large U. The back row was elevated above the front row.

Shannon was already in a seat in the center of the U in the back row, reading over some papers in front of her. Upon hearing the door open, she looked up from her papers and their glances met. A smile lit up her face and at that moment he once again considered asking her out. He took the short walk to where Shannon was sitting.

"Hey," He said taking a seat next to her. "Early start?"

"I didn't get the reading done this week," she responded focusing back on her papers.

"Really?" Marcel was surprised. Their friend-ship formed because both had a studious nature, both were focused and driven. Marcel approached everything in life like this and he assumed it is how Shannon approached her life too.

"Been a crazy week." She didn't offer any more and Marcel didn't press. He knew she needed to get the reading done, not so much for class but for her own sense of determination.

Marcel opened his bag and took out the reading packet they had been assigned for class. He didn't get a chance to start it before the door to the class opened and Joanne came in. She was early, which surprised him, but that wasn't what grabbed his attention. It was her physical appearance.

Joanne looked like hell. She had gotten off the plane two hours ago. On a normal flight she would have been in a cool, comfortable place: sleeping in a blissful narco-laced cold comfort blanket. On this trip, however, she was tormented by pain. She was also still pissed off at the conversation she had with Tavian after she set the little tramp straight in the hotel. The plane had also arrived late so she didn't have a chance to go back to her penitentiary on Lake Minnetonka. Instead she met with a reporter from the Star Tribune who was running a piece on Sharif. It was the typical boiler plate bullshit she passed off to reporters when a case like Sharif's came down and they lost. Explaining a loss was something she had always hated. It felt like reporters assigned the blame to her when a client was executed as opposed to assigning blame to the asshole who raped and murdered police officers.

It was difficult for her to keep her patience with this particular prick this afternoon. In the last few hours she had concluded that sobriety and patience could not coexist. Nonetheless, she had willed herself through the interview with every ounce of politeness she could muster.

As she made her way to St. Stevens, she thought about stopping by the Old 88, a bar on the South Side, where she knew she could get some blow at any time day or night. A little bump before class, she thought, would set her up nice. It would give her a little balance and help her push through the sleep deprivation that was starting to overcome her.

"Holy Hannah," Shannon whispered in shock. "Must have been a rough week." She continued, forgetting about the reading in front of her.

Marcel and Shannon were not the only ones in the room that noticed. Several of their classmates exchanged bewildered glances with them, and they all shared a smirk at her expense.

"Please forgive me. I just got back from Austin. the A-I-I is down their working on a case right now, and it has been a crazy forty-eight hours. Added to which my partner Frank Dekalb's client, Ali Sharif, was executed at 6PM tonight down in Georgia," Joanne spoke, sensing the concern of her students. No mention of dope though.

"Did you work on the Sharif case?" an older woman near the top of the U on the right hand side asked

"No, Sharif wasn't an A-I-I client, he was one of Frank's. Sharif wasn't innocent by any means, he was guilty as hell. He admitted his crimes and made peace with them." Joanne's voice sounded like she looked.

Joanne peered out through bloodshot eyes, over the class, and up at a clock on the back wall.

"Well, let's get started. Class is going to be cut short tonight, however I am going to be passing around a sign-up sheet with time slots for individual interviews. Before next week I want to meet with everyone individually to go over the assignment so you will have to plan accordingly." Her voice didn't have the same pizzazz it had a week ago. "I am asking everyone to partner up on this assignment. Are you all familiar enough with each other to pick your own partners?" she asked awkwardly.

The class agreed they could find partners on their own. This gave Marcel an opportunity to team up with Shannon, which meant they would get a chance to spend some time together outside of school. Maybe this could be the way around his fairy tale conundrum. Jarvis would probably be pissed, but Marcel didn't care. They were officially in training camp and Jarvis would have pitched an absolute shit fit about him working alongside a woman that he was attracted to. Jarvis was from the old school and would have told him to pick some fella to partner up with, or at least the ugliest girl in class.

"Want to get going on this tonight?" Shannon asked Marcel.

"Tomorrow, a.m? I have plans tonight," he answered, opening up his bag and stashing the reading packet back into its folder.

"Oh, okay." She sounded disappointed.

"I have to work," He explained quickly not wanting her to get the wrong idea.

"Oh, where do you work?" Shannon asked and packed up her own papers.

"At the 'House of Pain' gym. I am working with a group of kids tonight, putting them through a workout."

"House of Pain?" Shannon gave a curious glance.

"Boxing gym in Northeast."

"You teach kids boxing?"

"Yeah, Jarvis, my trainer, has a program for low income kids; I help."

Marcel was humble about his work with the kids. He loved doing it but didn't feel it was necessary to share with the whole world. Shannon had him backed into a bit of a corner, though.

"Wow, that's really cool, I guess there is a lot about you I don't know, a lot of different layers. So you're a fighter too? I mean you said you had a trainer." She shot him an approving smile.

"Nah, I mean, yes I am a fighter but what you see is what you get. Not much for surprises with me. We will spend a lot more time together and you will see. I mean on this project." He felt like an idiot.

"Yeah, I think we will. I guess I will see you

tomorrow." Shannon got up and walked out of the room.

16

Marcel left the school and headed for the parking lot where he had left his motorcycle. Tonight was the first time that he wished he didn't have to go to the gym. He loved the gym, and the work he did there. He also liked the people he met. To him, the gym was his home; his apartment was just a place he slept. Working with the kids was an especially fun time. He saw so much of himself in the boys he worked with. None of them had shit. Most had messed up family lives. For them the gym was a sanctuary; the one place where they knew they could get some food and be safe. But tonight he wanted to be working with Shannon. That made him feel a little selfish.

Jarvis couched it as teaching the kids to eat healthy, but Marcel knew that the reason he did it was because this might be the only healthy meal the kids would get all week. Jarvis would fire up the grill in the pit, and would go to work grilling chicken or fish. The pit was an adjacent lot that he owned that housed a sand pit and some other archaic workout devices, such as a tractor tire, that he used for cross training. Jarvis would always have some kind of greens as well. This group of kids never had to be told to eat their vegetables. Marcel always thought it funny how kids always appreciate things they don't have, even vegetables. All of this of course, was paid for out of Jarvis' own pocket.

Jarvis did his best to get parents involved, and they were always welcome to come in and eat. There were a couple from time to time, mostly single moms. There was also a dad who was there every week. Marcel thought he was a good dude; he was doing the best he could to raise his two sons on his own. The man reminded Marcel of his grandfather.

A couple of the kids were already at the gym when Marcel arrived. Other than them, the place was deserted. One of the boys, Isaiah Green, was the one whose dad came every week with him. His older brother Isaac wasn't in the gym today.

"Marcel, what's good?" Marcus Green, the brothers' dad extended a hand.

115

"Where's Isaac?" Marcel took the man's hand and they embraced.

"Man, you know that time of year, Football tryouts." Marcus' smile was ear to ear

"Tryouts huh, what position is he trying out for?" Marcel went to his locker and tucked his school bag away and pulled out his workout bag.

"Fullback and linebacker. Me personally I'd like to see him on the defensive side, given licks rather than takin em, but you know kids man, touchdown's what everyone cares about." The man's gregarious personality spilled out in the words.

More kids started to come through the door. A couple with adults, including to Marcel's surprise a woman he faintly recognized. She was with Deshawn Thunder, a ball of energy from Little Earth, who came and worked his tail off every week. Every other night he had been dropped off by his grandmother.

She looked at him with familiar eyes and started making his way over to him.

"Marcel?" Her voice was soft and a little bit raspy. Marcel thought it sounded sexy which, not unexpectedly, fit the rest of her.

"Yea," he responded, looking long and hard at her, trying to get past the feeling of recognition to remembrance.

"You don't remember me. Don't worry it was a long time ago, I guess. You were just a boy." The woman spoke with a thick Native accent.

Marcel dove deeper into the depths of his memory and started rifling through old files. There were places inside his head he hadn't traveled in almost fifteen years. He dwelled on her face for a second more and finally the name appeared.

"Tess?" he asked, remembering more names from the old days rather than actual faces. The thought of rhubarb jelly filled his head. Tess had looked after him when he was younger and he recalled how much he had hated the rhubarb jelly she would occasionally use to make him peanut butter and jelly sandwiches. He didn't get them everyday, he had no idea what he had gotten for a snack on any other day. On the days he had gotten the rhubarb jelly though those sandwiches had been hidden under her sofa. He wondered if she had ever found them. In hindsight it had to be a hell of a mess under that couch when it was finally moved.

"Yes, oh my gosh, how long has it been?" She stepped forward and gave him a big hug. Jarvis materialized from his office and shot him a disapproving glare.

"Ten years." The words sounded vast coming out of his mouth.

"Oh my goodness, you were just a little kid."

She looked at him; looked through him. Sizing him up. Measuring the amount he had changed in ten years. She was older than he was, and it was likely she had changed a lot less than he had. He simply remembered that she was beautiful. He was quite surprised she had recognized him after all this time. He likely didn't bear much resemblance to his fourteen year old self.

"Yeah, and look at you." He nodded at her.

Tess, now in her thirties, was stunning. Marcel thought he would describe her as beautiful, despite the signs of a hard life. She had long black hair that matched her very large black eyes. She had olive skin, darker than most Native American girls. It was her claim that she was pure blood; no white people in any of her lineage. She was thin and fit, and he could tell that she had started to take better care of herself now that she was older.

"Me, I haven't changed much, but you are all grown up, I mean look at you," Tess spoke gently touching one of his shoulders.

"Yeah, well I guess everyone does. Someday Deshawn will grow up too." He thumbed behind him to the boy who came in with her.

"So I hear you're a fighter?" Her eyes lit up ever so little, this struck Marcel as a little odd. He wondered how long she knew he was here, and more importantly how she knew.

"Yeah, keeps me out of trouble, I guess." Marcel was sorry he'd said it as soon as he had.

"Trouble huh, you..." He knew what she was asking without her having to say a word. It was the exact reason he felt remorse for his prior statement.

"Like I said this keeps me out of trouble," He interrupted before she said anything more.

"I doubt it." She shot him a skeptical look and her tone was serious.

"I got a whole new life moving to Colorado." It was Marcel's turn to look through her.

"I take it you don't talk with anyone from the rez anymore." He knew from her tone that she certainly didn't.

"If anyone, it would have been you, I guess." His words were sincere. Tess had been his brother's girlfriend at the time when he was murdered. Marcel really liked her. She would play with him, give him attention. She was a sort of surrogate mother for him, though no more than a kid herself. That's how it went though. None of the crew he grew up with had much for families, so they took care of each other. It was no wonder why things went to hell so quickly.

"Yeah, I graduated, got the hell out and never looked back. Now I am helping my Auntie take care of Deshawn. My cousin works out of town a lot and can't always do it, and Auntie is getting older and can't keep up with him. She's almost eighty now, and you know Deshawn, he can't sit still."

Marcel sensed regret in her voice. It didn't surprise him. There was some great and terrible magnetism about the rez that kept pulling people back. Maybe it was that sense of home, or maybe it was the sense of being a foreigner everywhere else. Whatever it was Marcel had seen it many times, including with his own father.

"What about your mom?"

"She passed away eight years ago, cancer."

"I am sorry." Marcel really didn't know what to say. For the first time since returning to Minnesota, he realized that a lot of things had changed in ten years.

Marcel had spent years dreading his return to Minnesota and crossing paths with his old life. Now that it had happened, his initial apprehension melted. He longed to catch up, but Jarvis was starting to get the guys going, and he knew he needed to get to work.

"Look Tess, it's great seeing you again. I would really like to continue our conversation. I gotta get to work, but what are you doing after this?"

"I gotta get Deshawn home then I gotta get to work. I am on the overnight shift at the hospital. I would like to get in touch with you though, why don't you give me your number." She pulled out her cell phone and opened the address book.

17

J oanne had promised herself she would stay
sober, but by noon on Tuesday it fell apart.
She hadn't slept in three days, and she felt
like her body was dying. She had a flight back to
Austin at 3:00PM. where there was a shit ton of
work to do. She needed the sleep to be sharp. She
found a bottle of narco she had stashed in her
kitchen with the spices. There were two 100mg
tablets left in the bottle. This would be perfect,
not too much, just enough to allow her to sleep
on the plane. She popped them in her mouth and
washed them down with the last swig of sweet
tea she had left. Taking the pills meant she had
to get to the airport in a big damn hurry now because if the drugs kicked in and she got stopped

by a cop, she would be fucked. And not like the tramp in her kitchen either.

She grabbed the keys to her BMW off the granite countertop, and hopped into the car. On the way to the airport, she got a call from Tavian. He informed her that the bawling bitch had not returned. The tart had spoken with one of the other interns on the team and shared her plan to resign her position. The tart was a 3L at the Cecil C. Humphrey School of Law in Memphis, and she planned to return there and complete her course work.

Joanne didn't give a shit.

He also updated her on the witness interviews; things were looking good. His remaining two alibi witnesses hadn't waivered on their testimony at all. After all this time, their story was the same as it was in the moments after the crime. Another of the interns had also gotten a lead on some possible new evidence that they were tracking down, evidence that could blow the whole case open. They had contacted the prosecutor and he was on board tracking down the lead. It was time to meet Diaz.

Tavian had switched her ticket into Houston. He also had an intern waiting with a car to drive her the hour and forty five minutes up to Livingston. He figured it would give her more of a chance to sleep. Tavian and Joanne had discussed her inability to sleep, and she had assured him she would try on the plane.

She did just that. Shortly after taking her seat, she was out. When the plane landed, she had to be woken up by the passenger next to her. It felt glorious. Joanne's first thought was thankfulness that Tavian had lined up a driver. She was still pretty tuned up, and she was definitely in no shape to drive. She wondered how 200mgs could have messed her up so bad. She hoped she could catch her wits by the time she got to death row. She got into the car with the intern and Chad and again passed out in the passenger seat for the duration of the drive. It took close to two hours. It wasn't enough for the drugs to wear off.

The car pulled into the grounds at about 7:00PM. The unit was on lockdown, and the guards did a complete search of the car: trunk, glove box, center console, their private bags, everything. Joanne was apprehensive at first, hoping to hell she hadn't accidentally left any dope in her suitcase. She knew she hadn't. Years of practice in covering up her addiction had taught her better than to try and take dope on a plane, much less to a prison, but the initial fear still scratched her interior a little.

She, and Chad checked in the intern waited outside. They were required to remove their shoes and socks, which were then searched for contraband. There was no line, as visiting hours were closed. Joanne knew the warden personally and had called in a favor to get in despite the late hour. There were two corrections officers waiting to pat them down; a female officer to pat down Joanne, and a male to pat down Chad. The search was pretty thorough. She wished she had more dates that had went this well. After the search, they went through the metal detector. She remembered the first time she had come to a place like this and had worn a bra with an underwire. She had ended up going through the detector with tits in hand because the bra kept setting the dumb thing off. From that point on, she kept the girls packed in a sports bra when she went to prison. The experience of going through a metal detector at a prison topless had been just a little too humiliating for her.

After the state-sanctioned molestation, they were lead into the visiting room by the corrections officers. The visiting room at Polunsky could best be described as a concrete box only slightly bigger than a public restroom stall. The inmates were separated from visitors by a thick sheet of plexiglass. No physical contact was allowed. There was enough space for two visitors at a time. Each visitor had a black phone that he or she could communicate with the inmate through; a direct line to the other side of the glass. Communication with other inmates was strictly prohibited. On the inmate side of the glass there was only one phone, and a steel cage was locked behind the inmate. It was an ominous place for visitors. It was reality for those condemned to die in Texas.

As they were being lead to the visitors' room, she could feel the guard eyes picking her apart. She was high as a kite and knew it. She was certain their well-trained eyes could see it as well. She spoke as little as possible so as not to give herself away with any slurred speech.

She had told Chad that she wasn't feeling well and asked him to handle the intake questions. She had given him the paperwork and he had accepted she wondered if he could tell that she was high.

Diaz shuffled in shortly after they were seated. His legs and arms were shackled. He was dressed in a white prison jumpsuit, with the letters DR on the back in black block letters. Joanne's initial impression was that this was a young man who did not belong on death row. He was well groomed, no tattoos or scars. When he spoke there was a certain thoughtfulness about him that impressed her, and she was immediately glad they took the case.

"Who are you?" His voice was soft and meek. She felt he never would have survived the general population.

"I am Chad Hunt from the Innocence Institute, this is Joanne Hart-Benson, head of the Innocence Institute," Chad spoke through the phone.

The inmate on the other side sized them both up and waited for them to continue speaking.

"How are you, Esteban?" Joanne slurred. She could tell he wasn't quite sure how to start, and it was up to her to keep this thing from turning into a shit show even though she wanted to talk as little as possible. It was of utmost importance for an attorney to develop a rapport with a client, especially in a case like this where candor was a necessity.

"I sit in a six by ten cement box twenty-two hours a day with no contact with another living soul. On weekends I sit there all day. All I can hear is the prison ruckus. It's maddening. I get a few minutes for showers, at least there I am alone, I don't gotta worry about taking it in the culo from some honky bubba. Other than that I live in hell on earth. How the fuck do you think I am?" His tone wasn't harsh, but certainly frank.

"Can I get you anything?" Visitors were allowed to bring twenty dollars in change into the prison to buy food for inmates in a vending machine.

"I'm good bro," Diaz had a thick Spanish accent but spoke English fluently. Though he had been raised by an illegal alien he himself was a citizen.

"So, Ms. Benson, are you going to take my case?" He directed the question at Joanne, paying no mind to Chad.

"Well, Mr Diaz, first there are some questions that we have to ask you." Chad tried to get the attention back to him.

"Who are you again?" Diaz turned his face to Chad. It wasn't a malicious question.

"I mean, 'cause I sent Ms. Benson and Mr. Springs a letter, and I know that you're not Mr. Springs." He was curious and a little untrusting.

"Chad Hunt, Mr Diaz, I am a paralegal with the Innocence Institute." Chad was reeling just a little.

"Misster Dias, Chad is my personal assistant on thiiissss caasse." She could hear the words slurring and knew that she needed to keep her mouth shut.

Diaz' face turned back to her.

"So, let's have the questions, Ms. Benson."

"Well first we have to ask this, it is of utmost importance that you shoot us straight." Chad was regaining his footing. Joanne jumping in had steadied him.

"Shoot." Diaz was still looking at Joanne.

"Did you kill Javier Ortiz?" Chad asked bluntly.

"No." Diaz looked Joanne directly in the eye as he answered, as if trying to read her.

"Were you in the car when he was killed?" Chad continued

"No."

Joanne's eyes were locked with Diaz' as if by some magnetic force. She was afraid he was going to see that she was high, but she was also afraid that if she turned away from his gaze that it would be a dead giveaway so she held eye contact.

"Do you know who killed Ortiz?"

"No."

Diaz' one word answers made Joanne even more nervous. She felt like he was doing it on purpose in an attempt to get her to talk. She suddenly realized the drugs were wearing off and paranoia was setting in.

"What were you doing the night that Ortiz was killed?" Chad had moved into full trial mode now and was hitting his stride.

"We had a baseball game that night, game started at five fifteen. It was hotter than hell. I remember that. The game was at Franklin, across town. It went into extras. Man, they had this pitcher that brought heat man, but It was three to four and I drove in the winning run in the tenth with a smash to the left center wall. That was my best game ever; my last game ever." Joanne could hear a melancholy in his voice that hadn't been there before. She guessed she would probably feel much the same way if her life had been snatched away from her in her prime. The simplicity of youth simply disappearing forever, never to be returned. All within a year this young man had gone from playing baseball in high school to being locked in this hell.

"Me, Chico Rodriguez, Donny Nichols, and Miguel Nunez, Miguel is the one who was murdered. All of us played on the team. Chico was a pitcher, Donny at First, Miguel was behind the dish and I was in center. We were so excited about the game that we decided to go out and celebrate. Game didn't get over until after eight, but before eight-thirty. We then went over to Chico's house, showered up, got ready and went to Juarez."

Diaz lived in El Paso and it wasn't uncommon for kids to go down to Mexico for booze. A special curfew was put in place in the city specifically targeting the young people who would head down to Mexico, use the international bridges to come back, and then raise hell in the neighborhoods.

"Did you have any interactions with border patrol?"

This question was the key. The new evidence that Tavian had come across earlier that day had to do with a retired customs agent who claims he was coerced by local law enforcement to keep his mouth shut about an encounter.

"Yeah man, all along we said that there was a border patrol officer who gave us shit on the way back. Some old white bastard, but none of us could really describe him, and didn't remember exactly what he said. We were all pretty fucked up. We never got his name neither. I told the cops, my attorney, everyone."

There had been no mention of the border patrol in any of the notes that the group had. As far as they could tell, no statement had ever been taken. They doubted the prosecutor had even known about the border patrol officer.

The story Tavian had heard earlier that day was that the local cops had found out the border patrol officer was allowing a Mexican national free access to and from the US for an occasional knob slobbing. The problem wasn't so much a Mexican tourist coming and going as it was the contraband he brought with him, including cocaine and ephedrine used for producing methamphetamine. It also just so happened that the border patrol agent had a wife, five kids and three grandkids. Homosexual trysts were not something his family expected of him, and the fear of exposure was too great to spare an innocent man from the needle. The cops had wanted this "spic" put away for killing a brother's son. However, in the last year his wife had had a stroke and died, and his own health was now failing. His kids were all fully grown, and the only thing that really mattered to him now was making his peace with God. Trying to right his own wrong. At least that was the rumor. Tavian and the prosecutor were tracking the old man down. It would be a slam dunk if the stories matched. Diaz would be granted a new trial within weeks and in all likelihood, the district attorney would decline to file a new indictment.

"Mr. Dias, we are taking your case." Joanne was gaining control over her speech again.

Estaban Diaz began crying, and Joanne couldn't help but feel touched. She had believed every word that he had told her. She had seen thousands of defendants in her career, and the one thing she learned early on was that liars, pathological liars, were really hard to pick out. They wove truth and lies like homemade afghans. They made it impossible to tell fact from fiction. She believed that the liars themselves couldn't really tell when they were lying or telling the truth. But there was something that separated the pathological from bullshitters and from honest people, that was their eyes. Those who could lie with ease had liar's eyes, cold and heartless. It was difficult to see their soul inside. Most covered it up with gregarious personalities, and charm. Those scumbags that duped women for family fortunes had liars eyes. Her ex-husband had them too. She too had been duped by his charm, and his dick. Joanne considered herself an expert in reading eyes; she had been doing it for years. The reason why it was so important to remove all emotion from death penalty law was so that she could read a convict's eyes. She had looked into Diaz' eyes, she believed she saw his soul and she hadn't seen a liar's eyes.

When their interview with Diaz ended, a guard unlocked the cage behind him and escorted Diaz out of the room. Joanne watched as Diaz shuffled next to the guard, having no idea that the nod that Diaz gave the guard was a nod that would have serious implications on her life.

After Diaz was in his cell, the corrections offi-cer who escorted him, a hulk of a man with a shaved head and barrel chest, made his way to a phone in the bullpen.

"She was high as a kite." It was the only thing the guard said before he hung up the phone.

18

Marcel dropped the kickstand to his Kawasaki and turned the front wheel into the lean. It was a little after eight on Thursday night, two days after Joanne had met with Diaz. She had arrived back in town on Wednesday morning. Marcel and Shannon met with her that afternoon to discuss their case file. First they had reviewed the materials separately, then gone over them a couple more times together. The meeting with Joanne allowed her to explain the process, what they could expect next, and what they should be doing in the meantime.

Shannon had driven over to his apartment after the meeting and they had worked on it until the wee hours of the morning. Marcel had considered inviting her to stay but thought better of it. He did not want to convey the wrong message, at least not yet. Shannon had offered to come over to his place again tonight, but he countered by offering to come to her's instead. Shannon's place in Northeast was much more convenient for him after his evening workout. Shannon had agreed.

Shannon's house was a turn of the century Queen Anne not far from the border of Columbia Heights. This was something she had shared with him in their long nights in the library during 1L. There were a lot of things she had told him. She had been living there since she moved back to Minneapolis. The house was way too big for her, and she made spending money by renting the bedrooms out to college kids. The upper level had been converted into an apartment of sorts with a separate entrance. The first two floors she kept to herself. The house was spotless; She was a meticulous neat freak just like Marcel.

Given the size with which she had to operate and the lack of possessions she owned, he thought the task of keeping the house tidy was considerably easier than his apartment.

The entryway lead into a foyer. To the left of the foyer was a den where she had a small loveseat and an enormous bean bag chair. To the right of the foyer was a small room where she had an office set up. It was the lower level of the tower. Next to the office was the grand staircase. The den gave way to a formal dining room. The two rooms were separated by gorgeous oak pocket doors. At the rear of the house was a bathroom and the kitchen.

In the kitchen, there was a servants staircase that lead up to the rear of the second floor. The servant stairs were much more narrow than the grand staircase. The second floor housed four bedrooms and a bathroom. One of the bedrooms on the second floor was Shannon's. The room next to hers contained a guest bed and dresser. The other two were completely empty.

The floor of the main level was an attractive dark wood that Marcel thought could be walnut, but he wasn't really sure. The kitchen was tiled in a handsome maroon and ivory that gave it a certain Tuscany village feel, though Marcel had never been to Tuscany.

Shannon gave him a tour of the first two levels, pointing out some of the intricate woodwork, stained glass, and the molding. It had been flawlessly restored. Marcel couldn't imagine what this house would go for on the open market even now with home values as depressed as they currently were in the Twin Cities.

After the tour, Shannon lead him into the dining room. The room was lit by a dazzling crystal chandelier. There was a large oak clawfoot table in the center of the room under the chandelier. The exterior wall was home to a large bay window that looked out to a fence and above the bay window was some marvelous leaded glass. Marcel was awed.

"This is an incredible place." Marcel was genuinely impressed when he sat down. He would certainly describe her house as a mansion.

"Thank you, I guess it's easy to do when you don't have a life." She laughed a modest laugh.

Shannon had a healthy trust fund that had been set up for her by her grandfather in an effort to avoid paying estate taxes. She had gotten access to it when she started law school; that had been his dream for her. She didn't really care about the money. The only thing she had used it for was to buy this house, otherwise it sat untouched. The income payments were put in a separate fund that she never accessed either. Marcel remembered that conversation vividly. It was the first time he knew he was out of his element here at St. Stevens and it was when his mind locked in on succeeding here.

"Is this a nice neighborhood?" He assumed, but knew that Minneapolis had its rough patches.

"Yeah, I mean it is a working class neighborhood, it's pretty quiet. There are a lot of these big old houses around. Many of them have been converted to multi family rentals, though." She pulled up a chair opposite him at the table.

"I think I saw something in one of the witness statements that was interesting." Marcel said, getting right to business.

"Want anything to drink?" Shannon said, leaving the chair and heading for the kitchen.

As she walked toward the kitchen she paused at the hutch against the wall near the door to the kitchen and adjusted a bowl that was sitting on top of it. Marcel thought the motion was odd. He didn't notice that anything was out of place in the meticulously kept house.

"What do you have?" He responded.

"Pretty much anything you can think of. Soft drinks, hard drinks, juice."

"Gatorade?"

He was incredibly dehydrated from his work-out and dying of thirst but doubted she would have Gatorade. He would have asked for water but he was feeling a little lightheaded from having such low blood sugar. He was only a couple of weeks away from his scheduled fight and still needed to cut a few pounds, so he had really been limiting his calories.

"Grape or Fruit Punch?" she asked

"Grape." He was surprised, but guessed she wasn't kidding when she said she had pretty much everything.

She left the dining room through the swinging door into the kitchen and returned a short while later with a can of diet coke and a bottle of grape Gatorade.

"Okay, so you found something interesting in a witness statement." She slid the bottle across the table to him.

They had been assigned a file review. It was the first step in the process for the Innocence Institute. Defendants would send in petitions and those petitions needed to be reviewed. This was the usual task for the Wrongful Convictions classes or student interns. They would work with Joanne to make a determination if there was really a claim for actual innocence. Ninety-nine percent of all defendants didn't fully understand the difference between guilt and innocence. There were countless petitions by guys who'd been smacked out of their minds at the scene of a robbery with their co-defendant who'd pulled the trigger who nonetheless shouted to the heavens proclaiming their innocence. Even though they took their cut of the money, helped cover up the crime, and hadn't bothered to ever tell the police, they proclaimed their innocence. When charged with the crime, they refused pleas because their ignorant assertions of innocence. Then when they were convicted and sent to the gas chamber, they acted as if they had been blindsided.

"Look, this statement from the prosecution file, Tariq Brown, states that he first met Hanshaw at the Pyramid at the Tyson fight in 2002." Marcel pointed to a highlighted passage in the text.

"Okay so?" Shannon couldn't see where he was going with a statement from an almost completely unrelated party that really had no bearing on the case.

"There is absolutely nothing in any of the defense notes, files anything about Tariq Brown." Marcel explained.

"Tariq Brown is not a material witness, and didn't provide anything of value to the defense. I read that at least five times. Everything he says relates to Hanshaw's drug use. It isn't relevant anyway." Shannon argued.

"Mike Tyson fought Lennox Lewis for the world title at the Pyramid on June eighth 2002. The victim's body was found at ten-thirty PM. She had last been seen at eight-thirty PM leaving a restaurant, Connie's Fried Chicken, in Tupelo MS. If Brown met Hanshaw at that particular fight, it would give Hanshaw an alibi." Marcel explained thoughtfully.

"Don't you think Hanshaw would have brought up the alibi, had he been at that fight?" This had been a bit of a sticking point for Marcel at first as well.

"Yeah possibly, but I was looking through the bio sheet Hanshaw sent us. Under disabilities he wrote: Traumatic Brain Injury. It's possible he forgot, or it's possible he didn't make a connection. He wasn't arrested until almost three years after the crime." The explanation had been plausible to Marcel. He was testing it on Shannon tonight to see if they could take it any further.

"I suppose he could have." Marcel could see Shannon pondering the idea. "Okay, so let's say he did meet Brown at the fight. Could he still have committed the crime?"

"Google Maps shows that it is about a two hour drive from Tupelo to the Pyramid in Memphis."

Marcel sensed Shannon's excitement growing. He himself had felt a little twinge when he came up with the theory but had tempered it prior to running it by her.

"Marcel, I have to say I am really impressed that you caught such a minute detail. I have been pouring over evidence, reading and rereading, hoping to find a break, and couldn't find anything out of the ordinary," she said in amazement.

The file had contained anonymous tips, eye witnesses, lineups, and police notes. Everything on its face appeared to be on the up and up. The devil had definitely been in the details. Marcel had found them by running through the case with a fine tooth comb. He had uncovered what just might be the key to setting an innocent man free. It would also bring him to the attention of Joanne Hart-Benson and get him involved in a shit storm the magnitude of which he hadn't seen since the old days.

19

Marcel was much better at containing his excitement than Shannon was. That was simply his nature. He knew to keep tempered about this. All they had was a theory; something to work with, nothing more. The process required them to write up their conclusions and present them for the class on Monday. Joanne had cautioned the class that most file reviews would be fruitless. The ones that weren't completely barren on their face, usually were not acceptable to the Innocence Institute after they were submitted to a heightened level of scrutiny and further analysis was done. She had told them for every five thousand file reviews completed, only one would actually get taken on by the Innocence Institute.

Joanne had been honest with them that most of the files she dished out to the Wrongful Convictions classes likely would be meritless on their face and that the purpose of the exercise was file review not freeing defendants. A way to get their feet wet. Marcel had assumed that this case was nothing more than that. They had a plausible theory, but for that theory to be proven, a lot of unknowns had to fall into place. The first unknown had to be whether Brown and Hanshaw actually met in 2002. The second was that the fight in question was actually the Tyson/Lewis fight, and so on down the line. He thought about reminding Shannon of that, but he didn't want to rain on the parade. His theory had brought an electricity to the room. He wasn't about to kill the buzz by being the voice of reason. Joanne could do that in class. Shannon made her way over to his side of the table with a stack of papers. She sat the papers down, pulled out the chair next to him, stepped up on it and sat on the table facing him.

"You are brilliant, Marcel," she complimented him." No one else could have caught that." She paused and looked at him for a long time.

Without thinking about it, he rose up and kissed her as if a force outside of his realm of control were powering him. Marcel let himself go, allowing himself to be caught in the moment.

He wished he could remain here forever. His life had been an exercise in self control. He had been an exile from connections with other people and for the first time since his brothers murder, he felt like he was no longer alone on this earth. When they finally broke the embrace, neither said anything.

Marcel's heart was racing; he wanted to kiss her again. He didn't. His mind was back from fantasy land and he knew there was too much about himself that she didn't know yet. He wasn't ready to let her that far into his life. The guarded, isolated Marcel came back into the room.

"I should probably be getting home," he finally spoke.

He wasn't sure anything in his life was more difficult than this. He doubted it, but also knew that it was for her best interest, as well as his own. After he spoke, her face changed, and he could tell that she had been caught in a dream world where common sense had no effect.

"I really like you, Marcel." She spoke

"I really like you to." He responded

Shannon walked him to the front door. This time she kissed him.

20

Ken sat on his bunk staring at the steel door to his cell. He couldn't help but let his mind drift to the permanence of his situation. He had seriously fucked up. He was an innocent man locked away in a prison out in Colorado almost a thousand miles from home. He had been working for years to get someone, anyone, to take on his plight. He had Banks, but Banks was the one who had gotten him into the shit he was currently in. Besides he was starting to feel that Banks was playing games, using him and throwing him a bone now and then to keep him working. Everything else had fallen on deaf ears until recently, and now he had fucked that all up, too.

He had gotten himself jammed up good on this one and had painted himself into a corner. Getting pinched with illegal contraband left him with very few options. The unfortunate part of the whole deal was that he didn't have a couple of pills, he had a serious stash of drugs. Enough that he was going to be charged with trafficking. What the fuck kind of irony was that? An innocent man getting arrested for something he actually did once he was in prison and thus destroying any hope of proving he hadn't committed this crime.

Ken had grown up on the Leech Lake Indian Reservation. His family could be traced back several generations and were members of the Bear Clan, which he also thought was ironic since the Bear Clan were the traditional protectors for the Ojibwe tribe. They also discovered which medicines could be used to treat the people's ailments. The thought of this made him laugh.

Ken had made a myriad of poor choices in his life, but the act that had finally landed him in one of the country's most notorious prisons hadn't been committed by him. Ken knew that his membership in a gang played a bit part in his downfall. It was what the prosecution used as motive saying: the killing was a gang related retaliation for his cousin Anton's murder. Anton had been murdered by Henry Wright at a party in Onigum a few weeks before Henry himself was murdered.

The murder of Henry Wright had gotten him sentenced to life in prison. He had been convicted on the basis of Henry's brother's testimony. Henry's brother Marcel had been there when Henry was killed. The thing that Ken couldn't understand was how the boy could have been mistaken about his identity. The man who killed Henry had walked up to him in broad daylight, pulled the trigger, and splattered his brains all over the sidewalk.

Ken mostly blamed Marcel Wright, Henry's brother, for his own predicament, and it was his desire for retribution that kept him going. He thought about the word desire, and that didn't aptly describe what he felt. No, the correct word was obsession. Every ounce of his being was devoted to getting back at Marcel Wright. It was the fire in his heart that got him through the prison nights. The problem for so long was that he had no idea how he could get Marcel into his grasp. He had no idea what became of Marcel.

After the trial, it was as if Marcel Wright had disappeared off the face of the planet. Ken had connections back at the reservation. People willing to help. They told him Marcel was a ghost, but that all changed recently. Ken had gotten word back that Marcel was in the Twin Cities. Marcel had come out of hiding. Maybe he assumed that everyone had moved on, or maybe he thought that no one was watching. That was what Ken really hoped Marcel was thinking. He hoped that Marcel didn't have the common sense to know that there was someone out there waiting for the right moment to get some payback. It had been close to him, he could taste the beautiful nectar of revenge, and then as quickly as it arrived, it vanished. All because he had been so stupid as to get caught with such a large amount of dope in his cell. Now he was out of options. There was really only one thing left he could do even though he knew it would probably be the end of his life.

21

Tess hadn't actually lied to Marcel, she just hadn't answered one of his questions. She wasn't even sure her contact with Clifford Banks would qualify as keeping in touch with anyone from the rez. Banks and Marcel hadn't even known each other back then. Tess had always felt a sense of honor in knowing the chairman of the Leech Lake band, and that her mother had worked for such a powerful figure.

He had first gotten in touch with her after her mother had passed away to share his and the tribe's condolences to Tess. Her mother had been an active member of the tribe, working in the government offices as a secretary, but people knew her best for being on the organizing committee for the Powwow and for dancing. Her mother had loved her Annishinabe heritage and her mother had always used the word Annishinabe, which meant first people. She had passed the culture to Tess, however, Tess just didn't have the interest in it her mother did. That had changed after her mother passed on. Tess had become more active in learning about her cultural traditions and practicing them more; she thought it was common for such things to come with maturity.

Tess and the Chairman had kept in contact since that time. For a while when he had traveled back and forth between St. Paul and Cass Lake, their relationship had been a whole lot more than phone calls. It was a fast and furious affair that only lasted a couple of weeks, at least until she found out about his wife, and she had assumed his wife had found out about her. The three of them had an awkward meeting at the Radisson in Minneapolis. She hadn't said anything to give it away, but the man's wife didn't seem like an idiot to her and probably suspected it. When she spoke with the Chairman about breaking off the the affair, he had acquiesced with little argument. From time to time, however, he had provided support for her. She supposed it was a function of his guilt, but either way she didn't care; it was nice to have support.

The money wasn't without strings: from time to time she had to give him a hand with minor things. Recently he had come to her looking for Marcel Wright. Tess had not thought about Marcel in years; not since he had left after Henry's murder. It was funny because Deshawn had probably mentioned his name a million times in the past, but after her most recent meeting with the Chairman when Deshawn mentioned his name, it caught her attention. Now she had confirmation with her own eyes. Marcel Wright was back.

"I need to speak with the Chairman." Her raspy voice spoke through the small prepaid mobile phone.

"May I ask who is calling?" An elderly native woman answered. Tess had no idea who worked in his office now that her mother was gone. When she was a kid, she had known everyone.

"Tess Whitebird." She was placed on hold and waited there for what seemed like a very long time. Finally the Chairman's voice came back over the line.

"Chairman Banks." He had the confident powerful voice of a leader. Tess still thought it was very sexy, even though he was married.

"Clifford, I thought you would be interested to know who I saw yesterday."

"Tess." His voice softened as if he didn't trust his secretary to actually identify his callers. "It is good to hear from you. So tell me, who did you see?"

"Marcel Wright." The words cut a silence that made it feel as though the phone were disconnected.

"You're sure?" The phone was still connected.

"I talked to him in person," She continued. A feeling of importance enveloped her. It was a foreign feeling. She hadn't been an important person to anyone in a long time. She supposed that was why she liked the Chairman as much as she did, because he had always made her feel like she was important. It reminded her of when she was sixteen and dating Henry. It was a little sad to her to think that she was more important when she was a teenager than she was now.

Henry had been someone; people had listened to him, and when she was with him, people had given her respect. When he was killed, so was her sense of self. The Chairman had given it back to her.

"Tell me all about it." She could hear that she had the Chairman's full attention and she planned to tell him the whole story.

Tess felt conflicted about the call; once upon a time Marcel had been like family, but he had abandoned her after all. He had left her with her sorrow, and no one to share her pain. She suffered more than sorrow and heartbreak. She had also been afraid. The summer Henry was killed had been a violent one on the rez and without him around to protect her, Tess had been afraid to even go to the Y-mart to pick up milk for her mom.

It wasn't simply Marcel's abandonment of her that allowed her to make the call. She also didn't feel like the Chairman had any ill will towards Marcel. She wasn't certain exactly what business the Chairman had with Marcel, but she knew he was a good man who had done much to improve the lives of the people on the reservation. Her mother had put her faith in the man and that was enough for her. The Chairman was a sheppard and Marcel was a part of the flock, even if he was a lost sheep.

22

Joanne read the write up a second time. She couldn't believe what she saw. She didn't really know Marcel, but Shannon had spoken very highly of him over the summer. Her TA had been right. Marcel was a prodigy and together they had hit a homerun with their presentation and write-up on this case. They had found something no one else on the case had seen and if they were correct it was certainly a factor that could raise a new trial on appeal. Though it was an impressive theory, it was a theory nonetheless. The likelihood of hitting pay dirt was pretty slim, but even if their theory fell apart, it was impressive. Either way, these were two students she was definitely going to keep her eye on.

She was yanked from her thought by a knock at her door. She was sitting in her office on the upper floor of the law school. It was almost eight o'clock at night and there weren't many other professors still in the building, only those who had night classes, and they were in session right now.

"It's open." She always left her door ajar when she was there.

Two men in their late twenties entered her office. She didn't recognize them as students. Both were tall and bronzed from the sun. One wore a straw cowboy hat over straight blond hair pulled back into a ponytail. The other had shaggy, long tan hair and looked like a surfer. They both wore western style shirts unbuttoned low enough to reveal chiseled pectorals. The cowboy wore a sharks tooth pendant around his neck that looked real. The surfer wore puka shells. The cowboy finished his ensemble with a belt buckle and cowboy boots. The surfer, board shorts and flip flops.

"Can I help you?" she inquired of the strangers.

The men came in and the surfer closed the door behind them. The gesture made Joanne nervous. Working with criminal defense was a relatively dangerous field of law, nothing like family law, but there were certainly unsavory characters abound.

"I think we can help each other," The cowboy responded. He had an accent maybe Australian.

"Do I know you?" Joanne was trying to formulate an escape plan but the men had the door blocked and the office was on the second floor.

"Let's just say we have a mutual friend." The man's cryptic tone didn't provide reassurance.

"Ms. Benson..." The cowboy continued but was interrupted.

"Call me Joanne." If she was going to be scared shitless, it wasn't going to be by someone calling her by her ex-husbands last name.

"Joanne" The cowboy nodded with approval. "Someone very close to us is in a real big jam right now," he continued.

"Tell me more." Joanne thought it was really odd that the men came to her office at St. Stevens seeking legal assistance.

"This person, who is close to us, is in prison for something he didn't do." The cowboy showed no emotion whatsoever.

"Has he put in an application with Innocence Institute?" Joanne asked skeptically.

"I don't know, I know he has sent hundreds of letters to everyone from the president to Santa Claus," the cowboy said.

Joanne looked from the cowboy to the surfer, who sat with an equally blank face to the left of the cowboy. He said nothing keeping his cold gaze fixed firmly on her. Joanne felt a shudder run down her spine. She was now terrified but she certainly wasn't going to show it to these two.

"Well, Mr..." She paused, realizing the men hadn't given their names.

"Cardozo." The cowboy glanced at her law degree before he spoke.

"Mr. Cardozo, I assure you that the way to handle this matter is through proper channels, fill out the paperwork..."

She was interrupted by the surfer who finally spoke up, a cold and serious tone also accented.

"There is more to the story. You had a business partner out west; he just put himself into a coma on I-90 outside of Rapid CIty." The words smashed into Joanne.

Joanne had been working with a man she met out west on a side project; something neither Frank nor Tavian knew anything about. She didn't think there was anyone else who knew about the arrangement. Obviously she was wrong.

"The man we are concerned about," the Cowboy continued, "was recently caught in prison with a considerable amount of dope." The Cowboy explained still emotionless.

Joanne's heart almost stopped. Joanne hadn't taken a case in years and the money from Court TV had run out. Her salary from St. Stevens was healthy but her drug habit and the expense of that damned house was pushing her to the brink of financial ruin, so she had agreed to help set up a corporation for some unsavory characters. The business her associate was involved in had been supplying prescription drugs to prisoners. Her partner ran the operation; she helped them hide the money. She had good insulation from any trouble. The operation was small and everything was meticulously put together, or at least she thought so. While Joanne thought she was simply supplementing her income, in reality the business had gotten involved with a major player.

Her attorney instinct told her to shut down the conversation, but the demon within her told her to keep listening.

"What can I do? I am not licensed in Colorado." This was a lie, but she thought it still pertinent to play it safe. For all she knew, the men were cops.

"Go see him, hear his story. I think you might be interested in what he has to say." The Cowboys tone softened.

"What's in it for me?" The threat in the room was beginning to evaporate. Or at least that was how Joanne was now assessing the situation and she took a calculated risk. When push came to shove, Joanne knew that she couldn't decline their offer. That didn't stop her from trying to reap some sort of benefit from the situation.

The man reached into his bag and pulled out a baggy of pills. The sight of them made Joanne's heart leap with excitement and fear. She knew exactly what was in the baggie.

"There is an unlimited supply." The cowboy slid the baggie across the table to Joanne. "These are yours simply for hearing his request tonight."

"I have no idea what this is if you are suggesting you are going to provide me illegal drugs in exchange for legal work, I am advising you right now to pack this up and get out of my office, before I call the police." Joanne wanted to dip into the bag and share a couple with her new best friends across the table, but feared a setup.

"You know exactly what that is. You know because you are a degenerate junkie." The surfer laughed.

"I would like you out of my office, now." Joanne pushed the pills towards the cowboy.

"The man's name is Ken Northbird. He is incarcerated in Florence, not the ADX, the maximum security there. He will be expecting you." Then both men got up simultaneously, looked at the pills then at Joanne. They then wheeled, leaving the pills on the table and exited her office.

Joanne wasn't sure what to do. She felt she needed to call the police to protect herself. If this was some sort of police sting, she would be in deep shit if she took these pills. On the other hand, it didn't feel like a setup. It was too close to entrapment to feel like the police. And besides, she wanted those pills.

She took out a legal pad and wrote the name Ken Northbird on it. Below the name, she scribed Florence Federal Prison. She then took several notes about the encounter, in particular all she could remember about the men. At the bottom she wrote Australian and underlined it. Before she did anything she was going to find out who the hell Mr. Cardozo was and who he was working for. She stashed the bag of pills in her desk and got on the phone with her investigator.

23

Joanne's investigator came up blank. He couldn't find anything on any local fixers from Australia. He was also unable to figure out who could be working on behalf of Ken Northbird. Ken did have a sister. It had taken the investigator less than twenty-four hours to track her down but she was clean. She had no ties to police that he could tell. He had put surveillance on her. Nothing. She didn't even mention her brother's name. The trail from the two men was ice cold once they left her office. These guys were ghosts. The only solution to figure out what the hell was going on was to go see Ken North-bird himself.

Joanne's plane touched down at 2:15PM local time in Denver. She then hopped a small plane down to Pueblo. From there, the prison was about a forty five minute drive. She had dealt with this flight like she had dealt with most flights in her life; with just a little medicine. Considerably less than she took to get to Texas, however. She didn't want to be high when she got there this time.

She felt absolute bliss when she got off the tarmac in Pueblo. Her beast was satiated. She felt no pain, and she had slept like a rock on the plane. She was still a little under the influence. It was of no consequence. She felt that she had her wits about her.

She took a quick glance in the mirror. One of the best parts of being high was that she always looked more beautiful. She had noticed in her week of sobriety that she had aged faster than she had anticipated. She felt like she was beginning to look like a junkie, her eyes looked more sunken, her skin was always dry and she was getting so thin, but this afternoon, with narco rushing through her veins, she was the stunner her ex-husband had hit on while still a waitress downtown.

Joanne was pretty sure that the drugs would completely wear off within the next forty five minutes, which would be perfect. She could sit face to face with Ken Northbird and examine his eyes just as she had looked into Diaz' eyes while at the same time not be in agonizing pain. She also felt that she was in control enough that she could slip past everyone undetected.

Her coming to Colorado presented a bit of a problem. Joanne only took A-I-I cases but she didn't want any connections between the A-I-I and Ken Northbird just yet. She also needed some deniability if she was in fact being investigated. Enter Ron Aristman.

There were two attorneys who collaborated with Joanne and the A-I-I in Colorado. One was Ron Aristman, an attorney out of Pueblo who worked for the Colorado Innocence Institute. He was an old timer; Joanne liked him. Aristman reminded Joanne of a combination of her grandfather and James Coburn. He had a powerful presence, but a charming, pleasant demeanor. The Innocence Institute had built a strong network of attorneys who were all loosely affiliated on a day to day basis. It wasn't until a case started amping up that a team would be assembled, headed by Joanne or Frank. Frank was generally responsible for the South and East Coast, Joanne for Texas and the West. The death penalty cases were their primary focus, but they took on any case where actual innocence was a claim. Joanne had been to Colorado before and worked with both Aristman and the project's other attorney Suzanne Wally. Suzanne was a kiss ass of a woman who talked too much and bugged the living shit out of Joanne. There was more to the story than just petty difference. Suzanne had a penchant for booze. When Suzanne imbibed she tended to run her mouth just a little too much. Loose lips sink ships. Well, at least that is what Joanne thought about when considering who to bring in on this particular frolic.

Joanne's revelation that the drugs had killed her looks was not the only casualty in her addiction; the drugs had also frayed her nerves. She was as cool as a cucumber when she was high, but when she started to come down her temper fuse became considerably shorter. When she was sober, she was like one of those cheap Chinese firecrackers that would take your finger off if you tried to light it in your hand. The Texas Tart knew all about that. *Christ on crutches*, If she would have had to spend an entire afternoon putting up with Wally's brand of b.s., she would likely have lost her shit and they would have all went down in flames. Jonne knew that if she were to have it out with Wally, and then Wally would get into the jug a bit, everyone in the legal community would know that Joanne was in Colorado.

Joanne was sure now that sobriety was starting to take hold; she was feeling pretty edgy. Maybe a coffee would do her some good. She asked Aristman if they could stop at a Caribou.

"Starbucks?" Aristman suggested.

Joanne had forgotten that Caribou hadn't expanded too deep into Colorado yet. Joanne begrudgingly acquiesced.

Aristman pulled the car into the lot. Joanne hopped out and hustled inside. She asked the kid behind the counter to give her something with a lot of caffeine. He hopped into action and in less than three minutes Joanne was back in Aristman's sedan. She took a big drink of the hot liquid and burned her tongue a little. She thought of the caffeine and a realization came to her. She wasn't alone; millions of Americans shared her predicament. In the legal world she saw it every day. The countless multitude that couldn't start their day without a shot of caffeine to get them going. What a load of bullshit. The same prick judges that would be quick to disbar her for her tiny narco habit couldn't start their own morning without a quick fix from their own Dr. Feelgood. It was funny to her that here, in a coffee shop in Pueblo Colorado, she came to the realization that she was seriously fucking up her life. She knew she needed to clean up, yet justified it because of coffee? The Starbuck's defense. She laughed to herself, then stopped. Was she becoming hysterical? She cleared away the fog of nonsense and decided once again that she had to get clean. Regardless of what she would learn from Ken Northbird, she had to kick the dope.

Aristman's Cadillac provided a smooth comfortable ride out to Florence. For all the beauty associated with Colorado, there was plenty of desert as well. Denver, known as the mile high city, wasn't actually in the mountains. This had always bothered Joanne. Somehow she expected more. Yet for all Denver's fraudulent advertising, it was still a hell of a lot nicer than Pueblo. Pueblo was south of Denver and was in the same high desert in Southern Colorado as Florence. Florence itself was a considerable distance from the mountains though it was still possible to see the snow capped peaks off in the horizon. Inside the Cadillac was a comfortable seventy degrees; outside was a sweltering one hundred and four. That was hot even for Colorado.

"Hot like this all summer?" Joanne asked Aristman.

"Unbearable, glad I am not one of these guys." Aristman nodded at a road crew performing construction on 115 into Florence.

The thing about Aristman that Joanne most liked was that he was able to talk about subjects other than the law. They spent the forty-five minute drive talking about his upcoming hunting trip to Aspen, the weather in Colorado, and the upcoming Broncos season. Joanne thought it was a nice reprieve to get her mind off the law for a little bit. She wasn't much of a hunter, but that was okay because Aristman was one hell of a storyteller. Joanne listened to his story, firing an obligatory question every so often to hold up her part of the conversation, but adding nothing of any true substance. The forty-five minutes flew by and before she knew it, they were pulling into the prison.

The Florence complex was bigger than she expected. It consisted of three separate facilities; a medium security, a high security where Ken was being held, and the supermax prison. It was the supermax that Florence was famous for. ADX Florence was created for the worst of the worst prisoners in the federal prison system. It opened in 1994. It was built in response to security concerns and the killing of two corrections officer at the Marion Illinois prison in 1983. The entire complex housed about two-thousand five hundred inmates, one thousand of them in the complex Ken was housed at. The facilities were ominous looking and Joanne thought they were extremely intimidating. It was her first trip to Florence, and she knew it wasn't any place she ever wanted to be. She looked at the razor wire and wondered how anyone could spend their life behind those walls. How they could make the choices they did knowing this would be their fate. Then she thought about her own choices, and began to understand. No one ever realized they were in line for this. Everyone, Joanne included, had a sense of invincibility. Everyone was aware of the consequences. It was just that no one ever thought it would happen to them. Like Joanne, they all thought they were too smart to get caught. Unlike Joanne, however, they weren't. She knew that she was smarter than all of them. But, she thought, she still better be a little bit more careful for the next couple of weeks. She was starting to play a dangerous game. Joanne wondered if places like this were in the city center of every major city in America instead of in the middle of nowhere tucked away from the majority of civilization, if it might be a better reminder for those on the edge to make wiser choices. Maybe there would be less need for them.

The security procedures at the prison were similar to the procedures at Polunsky. For some reason she had expected them to be more stringent, maybe because of the ADX although she was not entering the ADX. She had been too doped up to remember that Polunsky was on lockdown when she had visited Diaz. Florence wasn't in that same situation.

Joanne and Aristman signed in to see Ken Northbird. She had tracked down his original case file before deciding to travel to Colorado to see him. This visit, like the Diaz visit, was also not in an official attorney client capacity. The most intriguing aspect of the case next to the free bliss pills was that the prosecution's key witness was also her new superstar, Marcel Wright.

Joanne made her way through security and into the visiting room, not all that different from Polunsky. Ken was ushered in from the cell block dressed in the prison uniform, shackled at the feet and hands. He could have been Diaz or any of the other millions of men incarcerated in this country. He had two armed guards escorting him; they stayed outside. Most conversations were monitored, but conversations between attorneys and clients were excepted from that rule. Joanne, however, knew that she was still being monitored; she had not yet filed her certificate of representation. Though privilege still existed, that privilege protected Ken, not her. She needed to remain mindful of that fact.

Joanne looked at him for a long time, sizing him up, and running through the case file in her mind. She guessed he could be a gang member just as easily as he could have been a mechanic. He was a typical looking blue collar guy in his late thirties. The product of a hard life, no doubt. The physical stress of a life of manual labor many times created the same appearance as life spent in a maximum security prison. There were a million questions she wanted to ask, but knew their time was limited. Ken, however, did not allow her to speak,

"Thank you for seeing me." His words were cold and deliberate.

"Don't mention it, I am here as a favor." Joanne wanted to make clear to him that she wasn't some rube that could be pushed around.

The man in front of her chuckled over this.

He was sizing her up the same as she was to him. Joanne hoped that she made the impression that she wasn't someone to be taken lightly.

"Well, I guess you had some incentive from my friends to do this 'favor', but that's neither here nor there. The bottom line is I have an offer for you that I don't think you will be able to re-fuse." He was cagey, and Joanne didn't trust him.

"And what kind of offer is that?" She still wanted to know more.

"My friends explained my plight. I have sat in this pit of hell for ten years for a crime I didn't commit, but I made a mistake and now I am at risk to end up next door," he began.

Joanne nodded, informing him she was in the loop.

"There are a couple of things at play here. First if we get the initial conviction overturned it makes the rest a whole lot easier," he began.

"We can, but you are going to have to fill out the paperwork first," she said irritated that this asshole hadn't simply filled out the paperwork years ago.

"Second, it is of utmost importance that your student, Marcel Wright, be involved in the case." He had completely ignored her.

"Marcel Wright?" Joanne asked.

"Marcel Wright." Ken was an echo in this lit-tle shitbox.

"I am not sure that I have any control over that." She was reeling a little at this. She wasn't sure why on earth he would want the witness who sent him away involved.

"Here." he passed a note through the document slot to her. "The paperwork is in this safety deposit box, as is your motivation and everything else you are going to need to know to make this happen."

"There are ethical issues involved here, what if I can't…" she trailed off.

"Everything you need is in that safe deposit box," he spoke.

Joanne struggled to regain her footing. With Diaz it had been Chad who had been knocked for a loop by their potential client. Now it was her turn. She took the name of the bank and address and tucked it up in her briefcase. She was careful not to let the cameras see what was on the paper. She didn't want the prison authorities to know anything about this.

Ken got up and called for the guards to return him to his cell. Before he left, he turned back to Joanne.

"It's all in the box, just give it a read. I am sure you will see the logic in it all." And with that, the interview was over.

Joanne wasn't really sure what to make of the exchange. None of her questions about Ken or the two men in her office had been answered. She hoped that inside the safe deposit box she would get some, but she couldn't open it in front of Aristman. She hustled back out through the security and made her way out to the parking lot. Aristman's Cadillac was there waiting for her. She got in the car and calculated exactly what to tell Aristman. She decided to say nothing. The safe deposit box was in Fargo, North Dakota. She would retrieve it when she got back.

24

I t cost Joanne a little more than five hundred
dollars to switch her flight to Fargo, North
Dakota, but that was exactly where the note
from Ken Northbird directed her to go. The Citi-
zens Security Bank and Trust was a state of the
art facility with digitally accessible safe deposit
boxes. No need for keys, just an eight digit access code and two forms of ID. Joanne's name had
been put on the account, probably by the fixers.
She opened the box and was surprised to see a
file that appeared to belong to a Special Agent
Buckley from the FBI. There were also some

papers she recognized, as she had filed them on behalf of American Vending. She tucked the file into her briefcase and left the bank in search of a private location to dive deeper into the file. After reading the file, she made two phone calls. One to her investigator, the other to Chad.

25

C had was sitting in his hotel room in Minneapolis. He had gotten a call from Joanne who told him she was in Colorado; she wanted to meet with him and Tavian when she returned. Chad could sense that she had something big on the horizon. She had a tone; she was hurried and excited all at the same time. Chad had not heard that tone from her in quite some time and he certainly hadn't heard it down in Austin. He had been with Joanne for a long time, and he hadn't seen a meltdown like that out of her ever. She had always been a consummate professional, at least until more recently. Chad had his suspicions about why she was in the place she was in.

Chad and Tavian had flown up to Minneapolis the night before. The two men had been able to talk in private for the first time about what happened in Austin. Chad thought she was high at the prison. Part of his suspicion had come from her insistence that he be the speaker box for the trip which had gone horribly awry. This caused her to step in and when she finally did speak, her words were incredibly slurred. Tavian had voiced his fear that something like this would happen; he had known about her addiction to narcodone, but he had hoped that getting her back in the game would help. Now, the consensus they had arrived at was that she was on her way to disbarment.

Tavian had joined the A-I-I while a second year law student at Duke University. He had always been a go getter. Chad had instantly taken a liking to him. Tavian had been a star soccer player, captain of his team and a two time state track and field champion in the four hundred in high school, all the while working his way to valedictorian. Tavian's claim was that his time at Duke was a blur. When his fraternity brothers were getting drunk being stupid on Friday nights, he was building houses in Africa, getting published, and running the student government. Chad always suspected there was a small piece of Tavian that longed to have some of the college frat boy experience but he would never admit it. Tavian graduated with honors and went on to the law school at Duke as well. He had been offered full scholarships from all of the top schools, Stanford, Michigan, Harvard but had stayed at Duke because of a woman. He explained to Chad that it had been a mistake and chalked it up as a lesson learned. Because of that reason, he wasn't interested in getting involved in a relationship until he was firmly established in his career.

Tavian had made it clear to Chad that he was not a scorned man, simply a man who had a general disdain for relationships. And a love affair with upward mobility. Chad understood this. He himself was a divorcee who had decided to forgo romance in favor of pursuing his career. Chad had wanted to go to law school but didn't score well enough on the LSAT to get admitted and ended up a paralegal for Joanne.

Tavian was the type of guy who had always treated him as an equal; a lot of young attorneys didn't understand the importance of paralegals. They acted as if paralegals were glorified secretaries, but not Tavian. Chad believed it was because Tavian's law school experience had taught him that there were only two types of people in this world: those that are satisfied with mediocrity and those that will do anything to get to the top. Chad was a guy who would do anything to get to the top and Tavian recognized that. The top was the only place that either man wanted to be.

Chad and Tavian had some shared experiences growing up. Tavian had watched his parents struggle, and struggle in his mind was a relative term. Tavian's family was solidly middle class, though there were far fewer middle class black families in Henderson, North Carolina than there were poor black families. Henderson was a small town in north eastern North Carolina with a majority of its residents being black. Economically speaking, it was poorer than the rest of the state with a considerably smaller median income. Tavian wasn't satisfied with being middle class. In fact he wasn't satisfied period. He was so driven that nothing he did was ever good enough for himself. Chad's family also had its roots in the Southern working class, what many considered poor white trash. He worked his way out, dodging all the landmines placed in his path by those closest to him.

Right now they shared something beyond their personal struggles growing up. Both of them were pissed off at Joanne, but what Chad didn't know was that Tavian was pissed at himself more for trusting a junkie. That was the major difference between the two men. Chad knew that the only thing he could do was take everyone as they came to him and if others made poor decisions, it wasn't his job to protect them.

Tavian, on the other hand, expected excellence out of everyone, and if they didn't perform he blamed himself for trusting in them. They also shared the belief that Joanne's career would be over with the Diaz case, but she seemed to have one more fling left in her. The two men had made a pact to do whatever it took to prop her up. They had both been certain that they were the only ones who knew about her addiction. They were the only ones who she had let get close enough to her.

Chad had dealt with addiction his whole life. His mother had spent time in jail for drugs and his step-sister had died of an overdose. He thought he had escaped that world when he headed off to college, only to learn that his roommate freshman year had been a junkie. Joanne was no different than any of them. She exhibited all of the signs. Joanne had advanced a little farther on the social ladder than the others. His mom had been collecting disability when she died alone in her trailer house ten years ago. His step sister had been a high school drop out when she succumbed to her addiction. Chad's roommate Matt had been put into rehab and had stayed sober for a few years before finally falling off the wagon and ultimately committing suicide about five years ago. Joanne had not been to rehab yet. She had not hit rock bottom, but she was getting close. He knew it was a dangerous proposition for Tavian to put his future in the hands of a junkie, but Tavian was a big boy who could take care of himself. If Joanne started to slip, he felt Tavian was more than capable of stepping in to guide the ship. There was no doubt in either man's mind that rock bottom was coming. Visiting a client while under the influence of drugs was the rim of a very dangerous cliff.

Despite his concern about her drug use, Chad was excited about the information he had to share with Joanne. The anticipation about the meeting with Joanne made it difficult for him to sit still and wait. The more he thought, the more he came to believe that this case was going to be the one. They had tracked down the border patrol agent and confirmed the details. The old bastard had given a sworn statement and the wheels were already in motion to get Diaz a new trial.

Chad felt, however, that if Diaz did get a new trial, Tavian should be the one to take the lead. Joanne's blow up in Dallas had sealed the deal. When he had brought items to her, she had listened. He was certain she would listen to him about letting Tavian take the lead on the Diaz case, but it still made him anxious. He wondered to himself how this dynamic might play out. Joanne didn't play second fiddle. She had been first chair for a long time, but she also seemed very sensible to him and he figured that if he laid it out for her she wouldn't have any choice.

Chad was just about to head out of the hotel for an afternoon run to clear his head when the phone rang.

"Chad." His voice was professional and confident.

"Chad, Joanne. We are on the ground. I will stop and pick up Chinese on the way. Is Tavian there?" She was typically curt.

"He's in his room right now," Chad guessed.

"Okay, let him know. Does it work to meet in your room?" she asked.

"Yes, that is fine, room five-oh-seven." He was taken aback a little. He had planned to meet at St. Stevens, or even at her place on Lake Minnetonka. The group had met in hotel rooms before but those were in suites. Chad was not about to shell out any more than he had to for a hotel room. He always stayed in nice hotels, but he never would allow himself to splurge on a suite. He certainly wasn't going to put down five hundred a night like Joanne would. This meeting was going to be a lot more intimate than she was used to.

"I'll be there in about an hour." And with that she hung up the phone.

Chad hung up his receiver and looked around the room. There was only a single queen sized bed and what he assumed would be called a lounge chair, though lounging in it seemed impossible. There was a desk in the room, which was the current home of his laptop computer, and the area he planned to use as a workstation for the next couple of days. He never knew how long he would be in any location but figured a minimum two night stay in the Twin Cities.

He had unpacked right away when he got here, so the room was relatively tidy. He surveyed it quickly again and decided that the room was clean enough to host Joanne. He figured with Joanne's penchant for underestimating travel time, he had an opportunity to go for a quick run before the meeting. His plan had been to run along the Mississippi River and check out the city of St. Paul a little. He was staying at Crowne Plaza, which wasn't far at all from the river. This had been his first trip to the Twin Cities, and from what he had seen so far it seemed like a nice, clean place. He knew that winters got cold but outside of the cold, he could see himself living here someday. It had the small town feel of his home down south but with the big city perks. He loved the NHL and St. Paul was home to the Minnesota Wild. The Wild's home stadium was considered one of the best venues in pro sports. Having season tickets to a place like the Xcel Center would be pretty sweet.

Chad headed out with a quick pace. He figured he could get four miles at a six minute mile pace and easily be back in time to hop in the shower. Chad had been running five and 10K races since college. Running was something he loved more than anything, even the law. The temperature had spiked back up into the nineties and his muscles felt loose from the start. He always found it easier to get a good pace going on a warm day. Austin had been a good place for him for the last couple of years, at least running wise. He had recently competed in a 5K race and been very pleased with his performance. He had designs on a marathon but wasn't quite mentally ready for that yet.

Chad headed down Kellogg Boulevard along the Kellogg Mall. He got so caught up in taking in the city he didn't notice the Ford Taurus about a half block south of the hotel pull out from the curb, pass him and then pull into a parking spot almost out of sight in front of him again.

His smart watch let him know that he had traveled four miles running a sub six minute pace per mile and was pretty pleased with himself. The whole while the Taurus stayed at a distance where they could keep an eye on him. When Chad turned and circled around the block back to the hotel, so did the Taurus. Chad was oblivious.

Chad arrived back to his hotel with plenty of time to take a shower before Joanne arrived. After his shower, he planned to link up with Tavian and get him up to speed. The bathroom was exceptionally clean. One characteristic Chad insisted on was the cleanliness of the bathroom of a hotel. He insisted on seeing hotel rooms before signing any rental agreement and always checked the bathroom first. There needed to be a wrapped bar of soap in both the bathtub and on the sink. The grout around the tiles had to be spotless and full, he could handle age discoloration but not the discoloration caused by soap grime. There could not be any chips or dings in any of the fixtures or countertop. The mirror had to be spotless and he preferred if the toilet paper were folded neatly but if it wasn't he could live with that. There was more than one occasion he had walked out of a hotel as a result of the quality of its bathroom. This bathroom clearly fit his criteria and he had no problem climbing into the shower. He put the water on a little extra cold, it wasn't just hot outside it was also humid and he needed a little extra help cooling down.

While washing his hair, he thought he heard the door. He hadn't been in the shower that long and assumed it was Tavian; Joanne couldn't possibly have arrived yet. He and Tavian had exchanged their extra room keys just in case they needed access to anything in each other's rooms. He considered for a moment that Joanne maybe arrived early. That would be an awkward moment. He would have to walk out of the bathroom wrapped in a towel because he had failed to bring his clothes into the bathroom with him. It made him laugh to himself a little at his micro obsessions. He hated to bring his clothes with him, partly because of the steam, it made them damp, but much worse than that, it made them hot. Chad absolutely hated warm clothes. He supposed this was a symptom of living in Texas and the inescapable heat.

He finished his shower, dried and wrapped himself in the towel. He rubbed the steam off of the mirror in a tight circle and checked his facial hair. He was in need of a shave. He felt that stubble gave him a rugged look…"*white trash*"…, which he hated. He considered himself refined. He had spent his life running from his back-woods southern heritage and wanted no part of it. Facial hair reminded him of home. He turned and cracked open the door.

"Tavian?" he questioned out the crack

No response. He opened it wider and stepped out.

"Joanne?" He came out of the bathroom completely.

There was no one there. He walked into the room and looked around, then went and checked the front door. It was closed, he opened it and looked left then right, the hallway was deserted.

He walked back into the bathroom puzzled. Maybe he hadn't heard the door. He decided it must have been an adjoining room. He knew how sound carried from room to room in some hotels, but the fact that he had not heard anything else like that in this hotel yet bothered him a little. He shaved quickly and got dressed.

He wasn't certain how to dress for the occasion. Normally his hotel attire was a sweatsuit because he appreciated the comfort, however it didn't seem appropriate in this setting. He decided to go a little more formal, but not so much that he wouldn't be comfortable. Khaki pants and a polo shirt was what he settled on finally after a mental debate over blue jeans. He got dressed and sat down into the uncomfortable lounge chair. He picked the remote up off the lamp table and tuned the television to MSNBC. It wasn't long before he dozed off in the chair. He slept there until Joanne's rap on the door woke him up.

The sleep was light, and he awoke easily. He walked to the door and answered it.

Joanne stood in the doorway. She looked sober, but she also looked different to him. Joanne had always presented a strong exterior, a nothing-could-hurt-me façade, that at times was enduring. At other times it came off as self righteous. That façade was gone tonight. Standing there in the doorway to his hotel room she was the poster of vulnerability.

"Come in, Joanne." He stepped back allowing her to come through.

"Where is Tavian?" She looked around the room.

Shit! He had completely forgot about Tavian. He pulled out his BlackBerry and dialed Tavian to let him know that Joanne was back in town.

26

Tavian hadn't needed the call from Chad to know that Joanne had arrived. Tavian now had full audio access to the room, as did the agents in the truck on the street. Tavian had spent the last hour wiring up Chad's room, including the phone, and making sure that they had one hundred percent coverage throughout. He couldn't risk anything getting missed. Tavian was so thorough that when the agent in the Taurus had radioed him that Chad was on his way back, he hadn't gotten it because he was in that giant bathroom completely blocked by all the granite. He had played a nifty shell game, hiding in plain sight while Chad was going through his bathroom routine, and finally slipping out the front door while the man showered.

Tavian had been working in the Drug Enforcement Agency's deep cover unit since his hire five years prior. He was very good at what he did. The most difficult part of the job was believing the lie himself, especially the details of his life. Most people who got caught telling lies did so because they tripped up on a detail and forgot a previous lie they told. It was easy to do because there weren't real memories to recall. That wasn't the case for Tavian. When he became a character, he lived their life mentally and actually had memories to recall about the circumstances of their lives. When he told a lie, he lived it in his mind and burned it into his memory.

This case was going to be his last in the deep cover unit. Deep cover had taken its toll on him. For the last two years he had been living as Tavian Springs, a young lawyer from North Carolina. Before that he had been a gangbanger from Oakland for six months. Comparatively this was a much safer assignment, but it was much more difficult as well. His subjects were intelligent, highly educated people. He figured Joanne was the type that would skip town if she discovered his identity. The Rollin' 70s, on the other hand, would have left him in a ditch. Of course they hadn't yet gotten to the source of the drugs yet, and those people were much more likely to have violent intentions towards the authorities.

Cases like the Rollin' 70s hadn't bothered him; he could live with danger. It was a clean case that wrapped up in six months. His present assignment was a grind. He had been on this case for years with little to show for it. When it came to secrecy, the 70's had been the National Inquirer. Joanne, on the other had, was the KGB. She didn't let anyone in. Chad had been with her for years, and Tavian was able to get much closer to him. However, Chad didn't know shit. The best he could do was speculate on her drug usage.

The grind was about to come to an abrupt end. They had made a couple huge breaks in the case, and Tavian felt that they would be taking Joanne down within the next couple of weeks, all thanks to a car accident in North Dakota. After taking Joanne, it would only be a matter of time until the whole operation would fall. What was next for Tavian, he wasn't sure. The only thing he was sure of was that he wouldn't be Tavian Springs anymore.

27

Marcel hadn't seen Shannon since the kiss. Shannon had been called out of town, and he had been focused on his training. The fight was just over a week away. It was an important fight; a title fight, although only for the Minnesota middleweight title. Though it sounded important, it was really nothing more than establishing that he was the best amongst a group of mediocre young fighters and experienced journeyman. There really hadn't been a serious Minnesota middleweight since Caleb Truax, who had won the IBF title at super middle weight only to lose it in his next fight. For Marcel, this was a stepping stone to bigger things; he had to win this fight.

The current Minnesota title holder was a thirty five year old journeyman named Rico Jones. Jones was a technical fighter, nothing flashy and not a lot of power. The game plan Jarvis had devised was for Marcel to use his athleticism to move, give him different angles, and fight aggressively early. In order to accomplish this, Marcel needed to improve his conditioning. He had ten round stamina, but he didn't have the stamina to be the aggressor for all all of those ten rounds. He and Jarvis had been putting in extra sprints the last two weeks in between his sparring rounds. This afternoon they were headed out to the railroad track with a couple other guys to run forties. They used the railroad tracks to judge distances. The tracks also provided a relatively even surface, though running on the crushed rock wasn't as easy as running on a track.

Everyone took the first two sprints pretty easy to loosen up muscles and get a feel for the ground. The third one was all out. There wasn't one man among them that wanted to finish last. That was the competitive nature of a fighter. Whether it was sprints, push-ups, or simply getting their hands wrapped, everyone wanted to be first. It was a boxing mantra, but Marcel applied it to his whole life. It was part of the

Wrongful Convictions

reason he tried to be the first one in class every night, and it was certainly the reason he got his homework done without procrastination.

Shannon had beaten him in the latest homework competition. She had taken it upon herself to do the write-up and turned in the next day. Marcel felt that it was her own competitive nature that required she get the write up done since it was he who had developed the theory of the case.

He finished second in the first forty yard sprint, an eighteen year old young gun had edged him out at the very end.

"Exactly!" Jarvis gave him a cold hard stare that pissed Marcel off.

"What?" Marcel barked.

"You got pussy on your mind, and you come in second. You keep this shit up and you gone be looking up at the sky from yo fucking ass. Then you can forget about bein' world champ and concentrate on all the pussy you want."

Marcel was pissed, but he knew that Jarvis was right. Shannon had gotten him twisted. Even now running sprints, he was still not focused on the task at hand because he was thinking about her. Hell, she wasn't even in the Twin Cities right now.

Marcel won the second sprint by a nose.

"Well good, at least you beat JJ by a couple inches." Jarvis continued to mock him.

"Barely beat a slow mother fucka like JJ, he

191

can't run for shit, and you just eeking past him."
JJ really was part turtle and everyone out there
knew it. Marcel got more pissed.

On the third sprint the fire ignited in Marcel,
a fire that had been inside him his whole life. He
beat the other men by almost ten yards.

"That's my muthafucka right there!" Jarvis
grabbed him in a big bear hug "Keep THAT shit
up."

The men ran it ten more times. Marcel won
all ten. When they were done Marcel's legs and
lungs were on fire, and all he could think about
was the pain. He didn't think about Shannon. He
didn't think about class. He was singularly focused once again.

"We gotta plan, Marcel, but we can only be
successful if you want it. I can't want this shit fo
ya, you gotta want that shit." Jarvis put his arm
around Marcel.

Marcel knew he was right; he had to make a
choice. If he was going to be a fighter, he needed
to be a fighter. If he was going to be a student and
a boyfriend, then he needed to be that. For him
the choice was easy. Marcel was a fighter. What
Marcel didn't know was that there were a lot of
other people with a lot of other plans for him.

28

J oanne pulled a chair from the desk and sat down. Moments later, Tavian appeared in the door. The sight of seeing Tavian here, in this particular setting, turned her on a little. It somehow felt a little wrong being here with the two men in such an intimate setting. It was visceral and maybe that was what sparked her interest. It was that same feeling why she got into defense work in the first place. Somewhere deep down she acknowledged that long ago. Working defense allowed her to live at the edge of society in some grey no man's land between the criminal world and the rest of the squares in society. She was also certain that feeling was why she married her ex. It was why she did her first line of coke. All of those things were wrong. The drugs were wrong. But she was done with the drugs; now her brain searched for other avenues of wrong.

Her conversation with Northbird jolted her to the realization that being high during this case could have damning consequences. If she was going to play through this little game, she realized she better damn well be straight. Northbird was going to make it worth her while; she would be able to retire and disappear. She wasn't sure where she would disappear to, Montana, maybe? Montana seemed like a place where people disappeared. Disappearing clean was an added bonus. The money, her sobriety, and a whole new life were the incentives for getting straight right here and now. She wished that she had gotten rid of the drugs Nortbird's "friends" had given her. As strong as she thought she was, the animal within her still called out for them and she hoped to God that she was strong enough to fight the animal these next few weeks.

Tavian sat down. He looked at her, and she knew two things at that moment. One, this would be the last stand; her career in law would be over after the Northbird case. The second, she was going to have to heavily rely on Tavian to carry her through this case because if she stayed sober, she was going to be a mental mess in only a couple of days.

Joanne relied heavily on her abilities to read people. Along with her talent to read liar's eyes, she had also considered herself an excellent talent evaluator. Shannon and Marcel were her two newest finds, but before they came along it was Tavian who had been her star. It was him she trusted as an attorney above all others. Because he was her star, she decided she was going to place her hopes in his hands.

"Will we need a conference room?" Chad asked.

Joanne thought over his question for a second. Once the team rolled into town, they would certainly have to do something different. For now she thought this would suffice.

"No, this works. When the others come, we will set up a war room. That's later." Joanne answered.

"How was your flight?" Tavian asked her with obvious concern.

"Not much different than any other flight. To be honest, Tavian, I am tired of the flying and the travel." She looked out the window at the St. Paul skyline and she realized she was tired of cities in general. Her mind wandered off to the mountains of Montana again. Then she thought about Grand Marais. She had traveled there before. It was secluded, on the water, and quiet. Quiet is what she wanted more than anything in the world.

"Are you okay, Joanne?" Now it was Chad's turn for concern.

Joanne could tell Chad was afraid that she was losing it right in front of their eyes. She knew he was afraid they wouldn't even be able to get this project off the ground. She saw his glances at Tavian and the look he got in return. She knew Tavian was thinking the same thing.

"Guys, we have one hell of a situation. This is a once in a lifetime case, but there is something you should know about me first before we talk anymore about the case."

She took her eyes from the window and looked at Tavian. She could tell he already knew, but she could also tell that he was willing to help.

"I am an addict," she admitted.

"To be honest, Joanne, I have suspected that for a while." Tavian's tone was full of compassion.

She looked at Tavian. He was brimming with compassion. Then she turned to Chad. She could tell that he too knew. Her words hadn't surprised him. Sweet Joseph, she thought to herself. She wasn't as guarded as she thought; did everyone know? She doubted it. These two were her closest confidants and knew her best. If her addiction had been that out of control, others would have said something.

That was the extent of her conversation

about her personal demons. Everyone in the room was on the same page and it was time to move forward.

29

"Esteban Diaz is an innocent man?" Chad's mind couldn't pivot that fast.

"Yeah, we found the border patrol agent," Chad answered reactively. He never expected Joanne to admit her addiction and was thrown for a pretty big loop when she did. Her decision to not dwell on the subject, however, did not surprise him one bit.

"Good. Tavian, you are going to take the lead on Diaz. I am going to step away."

Joanne's revelation was a welcome relief to

Chad.

What he didn't know yet was that it created a whole

other set of problem circumstances for Tavian.

"I believe we have another case worthy of our attention," Joanne continued.

This new prospective case was what had drawn Chad to this meeting in the first place. Joanne was always cryptic; more so recently with the drugs. This was different.

"I met with a prisoner named Ken Northbird out in Colorado. He is innocent. I believe this a hundred percent, but this is a case that is in our own backyard." It was strange the way she said this. It wasn't strange that it was in their own backyard, but it was strange that Joanne had completely broken protocol, and she was making an ex parte decision that the guy was innocent without any research.

"Joanne, what are you talking about?" Chad sounded confused.

"Well--" He could tell she was on the defensive, "The eyewitness who testified against Northbird and put him away, is a student in my Wrongful Convictions class."

Chad watched Tavian's jaw drop so quickly he thought that the ligaments holding it together were going to snap right off. There was a long silence in the room. Chad got up and walked to the window and looked out. He was stunned. He completely forgot about the deviation from protocol and Joanne's admission. This was something he couldn't really wrap his head around. Joanne waited for him to speak before continuing.

"Holy shit." It was the best Chad could come up with under the circumstances.

"Tavian, this could be the case of the century. Think about the press on this one. The man who put away the accused helps to free him years later upon learning of his innocence."

"Wow." Chad wondered if Tavian could see the shit storm coming. He assumed that Tavian could and could not understand why Joanne was overlooking it.

"No fucking way." Chad finally got a footing in the conversation.

"There are going to be some ethical concerns getting the ball rolling on this one." Joanne wasn't talking about legal ethics, though they all knew those would come into play in this at some point.

"Ken would like to have the student involved." Chad couldn't believe that Joanne was actually considering this.

"Who is the student?" Tavian's tone was a clue. Chad knew that he was thinking the same thing he was right now. *How in the hell could Ken know the witness was now a student!*

"His name is Marcel Wright. He is an up and coming star, and if we can convince him to get on board there is no problem. This would garner so much press for the Innocence Institute." Chad could see Joanne was almost salivating at the thought.

"What do we know about Wright? Any idea how he is going to take all this?" Tavian followed up.

"We have to sit down with him; take his temperature," Tavian continued.

Chad looked at Tavian incredulously. Joanne was falling apart. Tavian knew that, yet Tavian wasn't putting a stop to this. Chad felt he had to say something, but he had no idea what to say. Chad's head was spinning again. He was oblivious to the hidden agendas in the room. Joanne had only shared a fraction of the big picture with them. Tavian was waiting for his moment. Chad's only option was to lay in wait for the right moment to make his play.

30

"Good greatness! This operation has just become a clusterfuck." Special Agent in Charge Kevin Josef said slamming down his headphones. He had been listening to Joanne Hart-Benson, her lacky Chad Hunt, and Agent Tavian Springs, discuss their upcoming plans in a hotel room in St. Paul. The conversation was courtesy of devices concealed in the room by Agent Springs in an operation that was more akin to a monkey humping a football than it was to a special-op conducted by highly trained professionals. Tavian had recounted the events that took place, being in the palatial granite bathroom when the mobile team attempted to notify him of Hunt's return. He had played a human shell game, eventually hiding under the bed before making his way out of the man's room.

The investigation into Joanne Hart-Benson had been open for a little over two years. They had been working on the illegal prescription drug ring for almost three years now and they kept opening new rabbit holes. Joanne had been an unknown until a prisoner at Florence Federal complex had been found with a shitload of pills in his cell.

They had learned that Joanne had been the attorney for a front that was brokering deals all over the country. Tavian had uncovered operations in fifteen different prisons in ten states across the US. Joanne was the linchpin of the whole thing concealing the money and covering every detail, and she did an impeccable job of insulating herself from anything that could tie her to the deals.

They were now all in place, poised to take her down. Once they had her, they were certain that she would roll on her supplier. Whoever this big fish was, they were moving major weight. The agencies theory was that her supplier was probably manufacturing the stuff. The pills that turned up in Florence were a completely synthetic opioid that no major manufacturer was producing right now.

Some of the honchos had wanted to take her down and try to flip her; Josef knew better. Joanne was too high profile and she understood the system too well to give anything up. The gamble would have amounted to a high stakes bluff with all their chips in the middle and Joanne would have called it without batting an eye. She had the top hand. Everyone knew it. No one wanted this one to get away from them. Too many resources had been put into this. Josef had won out. Joanne was the central figure in the largest smuggling operation inside the U.S. prison system; Ms. Hart-Benson and her associates were responsible for over one hundred million dollars worth of drugs moved in the last five years. The number of murders associated with the ring was somewhere over one hundred and counting. Josef was going to take this thing down. Josef didn't care that it was an underground op. On the outside, the public had no idea. That was the genius of network; it existed only within the walls of correctional facilities. Dealers and gangs weren't shooting it out on the streets of places like Detroit and Washington DC. Innocent people weren't being gunned down and kids weren't getting hooked on free samples. There were no headlines about this epidemic; everything had taken place hidden away from society at large and more importantly, politicians didn't give a shit about these things that didn't carry political capital. It mattered to Josef, though.

They had proof Joanne's associates had delivered drugs to some of the most secure facilities in the nation. Sometimes it was delivered to crooked CO's, who in turn delivered to the inmates for a nice little bonus every month. Sometimes it was brought in by lawyers, family members, and Joanne's associates, all of them unwitting accomplices having no idea that the documents and care packages they delivered were concealing pills. She had used her status to cozy up to wardens and rig vending contracts, so that vending machines would be operated by her business partners' shell corporation. The vending machine always contained an obscure item that normal inmates had little interest in. Joanne's clients, however, always asked visitors for the item, and it was delivered with the supervising guards none the wiser. Joanne herself never touched a thing. Nothing in her conversations could tie her to the crime. There was no paper trail, either. Josef had listened to hundreds of hours of recordings made from wire taps on her phones, there was nothing. They were all at a loss for where she was getting the drugs. The inmate at Florence had no idea.

They had came close with a man named Milton Bosch. Bosch was a delivery driver who had been stocking the vending machines. They had been tracking Bosch, waiting for him to slip when he flipped his H2 in the Black Hills. He was on life support in a hospital in Rapid City with little hope for recovery. It was another dead end. Drug dogs had been searching all of the latest vending machine deliveries and they were clean. Drugs were not getting in through the vending machines anymore, but they were still getting it.

Less than a month ago, a corrections officer at a prison in Montana found a healthy supply of pills in a cell that belonged to an ex-state senator. The senator was serving time on an embezzlement charge. He was about to turn state's evidence on an unrelated case when he ended up hanging from a makeshift noose in his cell. The investigators began looking into the ex-senator's visitors. The senator's wife and daughter were his only visitors. The daughter was a bible thumper who had been trying to start a ministry at the prison. The wife, on the other hand, was a drunk who had taken too many pills along with a half bottle of scotch and ended up in a cemetery plot next to her husband. Every time they got close to a key player, they ended up dead. It made for a more cumbersome investigation. The break that got the ball rolling, however was the wife's attorney. It turned out that the wife's attorney was none other than Joanne Benson. The pills in the cell were an exact chemical match with the ones found at Florence. There was a connection. With Bosch in the hospital and the senator and his wife fertilizing the lawn in Mountain View Cemetery, the investigation now turned to deep cover.

What they heard today in that hotel room made that responsibility all the more difficult. It was the worst case scenario; a media circus like this one was dangerous for his agent. Now Joanne needed his agent to take the lead because she couldn't stay sober long enough to get out of bed in the morning. He knew there was no way he could allow Tavian to appear before a judge as Tavian Springs. The honchos would have his ass for that one back in DC. This whole scenario pushed their hand. They would have to make a move much sooner. Damn it, he needed a break, and he needed it in a hurry.

31

Marcel had just finished a grueling work-out about the same time SAC Josef was listening in on the conversation in Chad Hunt's apartment. The heat had gotten more oppressive this afternoon than any day in the last couple weeks, and he had sweat like a madman. This was important because he was having a hard time losing the last couple pounds he needed to make weight for the fight. He had showered and was sitting on a bench next to the ring when his phone rang. He didn't recognize the number and let it go to voicemail. After it chimed, signaling he had new voicemail, he punched in the numbers and listened to the digitally recorded message.

Marcel, now only days away from the fight, had barricaded himself off from the rest of the world to prepare. Marcel had left a message for Shannon explaining that he wasn't going to be at school until after the fight and he hadn't heard back from her. He had talked to all of his professors briefly to get his course work and made the necessary arrangements. He was not able to get a hold of Joanne; she hadn't been at her office. He had no way to track her down. However, he and Shannon had gotten their assignment done and he knew there wouldn't be anything more until after the fight, so he wasn't too concerned.

"Marcel, this is Joanne Hart-Benson from St. Stevens. I would like to sit down with you and talk about the next assignment. I would also like you to meet with my associate, Tavian Springs, who will be assisting on the case. Please call me back at your convenience. My number is six-five-one..." The voice on his voicemail spoke through the loudspeaker on his cell.

He hit the save button. He had no plans of calling her until after Saturday anyway.

He walked to the scales at the front of the gym by the large garage door. The door was open allowing the scorching heat in, but it was also allowing the stagnant air of the old warehouse to escape. One hundred fifty eight and a half, al-

209

most two pounds under. He was excited. He had made weight, and there was little time to spare. He and Jarvis were leaving for Grand Casino that night. They were going to check into their rooms, and then it was on to an interview scheduled that evening with a sports radio station out of the Twin Cities. It was a pre-recorded piece that would air on tomorrow's show with Don Colt, the stations boxing aficionado, and one of the few knowledgeable fight fans in the local media.

Tomorrow night would be the weigh-in, and a meet and greet with any fans that were around. It was Marcel's least favorite part of big fights; he couldn't imagine the world title fights in Vegas. Marcel wasn't very good at schmoozing. Local fights were very small time in that respect. A few wealthy fight fans, folks from the commission, and a couple of reporters. There would be a decent buffet, and he was planning on making use of that for sure. He had been starving since training camp started.

32

arcel sat in his dressing room waiting for a member of the commission to sign off on his hand wraps. This was done to ensure the fighters didn't have illegal substances in the wraps; plaster or metal something to make the punches harder. The commission member would then watch the fighters glove up and check the gloves. It wasn't beyond fighters; managers and promoters to pull these shenanigans to get themselves to the top.

Marcel had always been a student of the fight game, he knew the story of how Billy Collins' life had been irreversibly altered when Luis Resto's pads had been altered in his gloves in 1983 when the two men fought on the undercard of the Roberto Duran, Davey Moore fight. Collin's ended up with a torn iris and permanently blurred vision; he never boxed again. He died a short time later in a car accident his family believed was tied directly to the fight. Luis Resto spent two and a half years in prison for assault because of the fight.

Marcel also knew about Antonio Margarito, In February he had his license suspended when he was caught with an illegal substance on his hand wraps before his fight with Shane Mosely. There were persistent rumors that he got away with using illegal hand wraps against Miguel Cotto, who took a savage beating in their fight prior to the Mosely incident.

Marcel closed his eyes. In the darkness of his mind, he pictured himself in the ring. He was fast. He moved fluidly and with grace. His punches were hard and accurate. He opened his eyes and looked around the small dressing room. Jarvis was talking with a man from the commission. A couple other fighters from his gym were there fidgeting with some equipment. He was ready to go. The heat of the dressing room was getting close to overtaking him. Right now he felt good, but if he was here much longer he would not. He looked at the guy from the commission and wanted to shout at him to get this thing going but didn't. Marcel knew he needed to relax himself again right now. He dropped the hood of his sweatshirt and took two deep calming breaths. He knew it wouldn't be long before Jarvis started giving him shit about the hood. Jarvis was in the shit giving business, and business was always good when Marcel was around. Marcel breathed and waited for Jarvis to say something.

As a challenger he was to be introduced first. The director of the arena came in and told him it was time. His entrance music was "Justice " by Lil Pop. The song had a deep personal meaning to him; it had a desperate tone. In Marcel's experience justice always had a tragic undercurrent. Lil Pop was an artist from Red Lake who had been close with his brother. He was a success story and a man that Marcel admired, plus the beat of the song got him going.

He left the dressing room. The base pounding from the arena's sound system shot adrenaline through his entire body. In that moment he hated everyone.

"They say justice is blind, I say there is no justice," Lil Pop's voice announced to the crowd. Back in the dressing room it was muffled. Marcel listened waiting for his moment.

"Son you can't escape, that game called fate?" The song opened, Marcel pulled the towel over his head and let the music sink into him. He knew he was ready for this fight and there wasn't anything Rico Jones could do to slow him down.

"It's too late on the judgment you must await." His cue from Lil Pop to exit the dressing room. He entered the arena. The crowd erupted. It was a very good crowd. He had fought in front of smaller, that was for sure. Tonight the arena was packed; The radio station had done a very good job of hyping the fight and more importantly, the co-main event featured a member of the Minnesota Vikings who was fighting in his first professional fight. That had garnered a lot of interest. The fight ended in a knockout; a bloodlust surged through the crowd.

"Against the ropes, drownin, your lost, there's no hope." Lil Pop droned over the the crowd.

"Sins of the past, creepin fast, This ain't no joke."

Marcel moved closer to the ring, head down a towel draped over it to cover his eyes, no distractions.

"You'll soon be lost, all for not, you be left to rot." Marcel nodded his head to the beat willing himself into the zone. That unknown dimension where anything but peak performance was impossible.

"What's done is done, on the run, forget number one" He was there now, the crowd was gone everything was gone. All that remained was the ring and Lil Pop.

"We bleedin for the rez make no mistake, believe no one finds justice at Red Lake." He was in the ring, bobbing slightly left to right to the beat of the song, eyes closed head down.

Lil Pop was silenced replaced with Three Six Mafia as the lights when completely out in the arena.

The lyrics to *It's a Fight* opened and invigorated the segment of the crowd that was there to support Marcel's opponent. A spotlight lit up the walkway from the dressing room where Rico Jones bounced and shadow boxed. He was much more of a showman than Marcel. Marcel's crowd appeal was solely a result of his actions in the ring.

Jones, the defending champ, had what seemed like twenty-five men and women in his entourage as he came to the ring. He was dressed in a flashy robe and wore a stocking hat with the logo of one of his sponsors on it. Sponsors for local fighters gave them just about enough to buy the stocking hat on it with the logo, and Jarvis hadn't bothered yet to find sponsors for Marcel. He would if Marcel won this title and got a shot on an undercard in Vegas.

Marcel fought out of the red corner. As usual, he wore all black; black trunks, black shoes with black socks. Jones had much more pizzazz in his ensemble as well. He wore camouflage trunks with frills that matched his ring shoes.

Jones was a conventional fighter. Marcel a southpaw. Marcel was the taller of the two men at just over six feet. Jones was three inches shorter. Both had weighed in at exactly one sixty last night, this morning Jones was an un-official one sixty-eight, Marcel one sixty-five.

Marcel watched Jones intently as he bounced around the ring during introductions, never tak-ing his eyes off his opponent. Marcel couldn't stand his opponent moving around so much. When the two men met, Jones continued his show, pounding his chest several times with his glove. All the while Marcel stood pat watching the man thinking how scared the man had to be to put on this show. Marcel had learned long ago that the guys who made the most noise were the most afraid. Like the birds that puff them-selves to seem bigger and more ferocious when in reality they were just songbirds about to get pounced on. Marcel saw himself as that pred-ator. He almost laughed when he pictured him-self leaping from the corner onto this chump. They touched gloves and headed for their re-spective corners.

Bing. The bell rang and the two men came out. Jones confirmed Marcel's impression of him by throwing a couple wild haymakers, trying to end the fight with each swing. Marcel stayed calm. He held back in the disciplined style that Jarvis preached; waiting to pick his spot. He landed a jab, then another, moving to his right cutting the ring off for Jones. He kept Jones in his power alley. Marcel threw a lead left cross that glanced off Jones' forehead. Jones countered with a jab cross combination; Jones threw the cross hard. Marcel believed it was everything Jones had, and smiled. The punch didn't phase him. Jones, not known for having heavy hands, was actually a much lighter puncher than Marcel had anticipated. Marcel thought, *he can't hurt me. I just took this guy's best. He has nothing.*

Confidence began to grow in him exponentially like cells splitting and resplitting. Marcel decided to make a move quicker than he planned. He threw a jab and quickly followed with a cross that was blocked by Jones' gloves. That punch set up the next. Jones never saw it coming; a right uppercut that split Jones' gloves and picked his chin up. The uppercut itself wasn't enough to hurt Jones, but the right hook that followed buckled Jones' legs and sent him tumbling to the canvas.

Jones took his standing eight count and took a step forward on shaky legs. Marcel looked at Jarvis, asking him if he should finish the fight now. Jarvis nodded. There was always a danger in boxing, that if you knocked a guy down in the first round and it was only a flash knockdown, that you could punch yourself out. That would make it a very long night. When Jarvis nodded Marcel knew the gospel truth that he could put down Jones right now. There was zero chance he would punch himself out. Marcel trusted Jarvis to make the right call, and Jarvis had let him know this was no flash knock down. Marcel went on the offensive. Leading with a jab, then throwing a shovel punch to open up his gloves again allowed him to land a cross on the bridge of Jones' nose that opened a floodgate. Marcel followed up with two front hooks to the body, the second one catching Jones on the liver and sending him to the canvas for good.

Marcel had just won the Minnesota middleweight championship in the first round. He was now ten and oh as a pro with ten knockouts. For the first time since Jarvis had dressed him down on the railroad tracks his mind wandered off. He started to think about Las Vegas. Though he had never been there, his mind appropriated images he had seen in pictures or on television. He allowed himself a level of excitement he had never felt before. His dreams were coming together, and if the right people saw this fight, it might be his ticket to Vegas. His first thought was that St. Stevens might have to be put on hold.

Marcel let the euphoria drain off a bit and forced his mind back to the present. For the first time tonight he fully appreciated the size of the crowd. He could hear them now; it was electric and a bit intoxicating. He looked into the ring, and he saw that Jones was on his back. He was a bit horrified. Before the fight, he was filled with hatred. He had been annoyed by everything Jones had done. Those emotions weren't real; figments of a mind preparing to fight. Now he was concerned for his opponent who had provided him this opportunity. He knifed through the growing crowd in the ring to get to Jones. Jones was conscious but not what he would describe as lucid. The ringside physician was already in, giving him a battery of tests.

"Thanks for the opportunity, hell of a fight bro." Marcel extended a glove.

"The fuck outta here." Some goon from his corner slapped away Marcel's glove. Marcel paid him no mind.

Jones' trainer stepped to Marcel and put his arms around him.

"He'll be alright, you're a hell of a fighter kid. Take this shit to the top. Be a champ."

"Thank you." Marcel nodded and turned to find Jarvis.

This was far and away the largest crowd he had ever fought in front of. His corner was making a frantic search for the belt. They found it and presented it to Marcel.

This was some chaotic shit, thought Marcel. It was almost overwhelming. There were so many people all over, a mass of humanity, that he thought he would never find Jarvis.

Much to Marcel's surprise there were two familiar faces sitting on opposite sides of the ring. One belonged to Shannon McCarthy. A lightning bolt of shock rocketed through his body. She was stunningly dressed in a full length black evening gown that was cut low enough to start a man's imagination running but not so low that no imagination was required. Her hair looked professionally done, pulled up and to the side with elegant curls. The idea of dressing up for a boxing match had always seemed a bit odd to Marcel, but it was commonplace. Shannon was with some of Jarvis' crew and he had no doubt that Jarvis had invited her to come. That wasn't a surprise; Jarvis talked tough during training, but outside of camp, Jarvis was constantly hounding him about finding a woman.

On the other side of the ring was Tess. She was not dressed at all the way Shannon was. Tess was in a pair of blue jean's and t-shirt that fit snuggly revealing her curves and giving her a certain girl next door look. She was with an older man that he didn't recognize at all. He was native and had a very dignified look about him. Marcel didn't pay him much mind.

Both women waved and he acknowledged them, first Shannon, then Tess. He wondered if either of them would be staying for the after fight party. The after fight party was another portion of boxing that he disliked, but it was also an important part as far as building a fan base. He needed a fan base to get to Vegas. He was terrified that both Tess and Shannon might come. His old and new world colliding in person not just in his mind.

33

The after fight party was in the ballroom of the Casino. The promoters put it together as a way to reward the folks who bought the five hundred dollar ringside VIP tickets. There was a real nice buffet, and a DJ was spinning music that started quiet but gradually got louder as the booze was poured.

Marcel took a moment in the dressing room to savor the win with Jarvis after it cleared out.

"Your grandfather would be proud of you tonight, son." Jarvis spoke giving him a big hug.

"Yeah, I know." Marcel held back tears.

"This is just a stepping stone. This ain't the end, though." Jarvis knew he didn't have to temper the mood, but did so anyway.

"When are we going to Vegas?" Marcel smiled.

"As a matter of fact." Jarvis had a shit eating grin on his face the likes Marcel had never seen. He was certain Jarvis had something up his sleeve and couldn't wait.

"Come on man, stop fucking with me, what we got?" Marcel was beaming.

"Rafeal Lopez at Mandalay Bay next June." Jarvis was beaming.

Marcel couldn't believe his ears. Rafeal Lopez was one of the best fighters in the world! Fighting at Mandalay Bay was huge; it wasn't the MGM, but this wasn't a title fight either. It would, however, be the main event on ESPN Friday Night Fights. Marcel couldn't believe it. He was so close to his dreams that he allowed them to be real for the first time ever. The emotion overtook him. A couple of tears again welled up in his eyes. He wasn't trying to let Jarvis see them. He fought them back the best he could, but both men knew they were there. Jarvis gave him a big hug.

"You earned it son; you worked hard." Jarvis sounded like a proud parent.

"Thanks, man. I love you, Jarvis."

"Get cleaned up, we got some celebrating to do." Jarvis slapped him on the back and exited the dressing room, leaving Marcel alone to shower up and get dressed. Marcel thought that maybe, just maybe his penance for all the bad things he had done in his life was over and that finally he would get some of the good that was out there in the world. He was alone with his thoughts in the locker room. For the first time in a long long time he didn't think about his brother or his childhood. Right now he was thinking only about his future and leaving his mark on the world of boxing.

Marcel took a long shower. Letting the water wash over him. He didn't hurt from the fight, but he was tired from the training leading up to the fight. In this moment he was alone and happy. It was the first time in his whole life that he had ever allowed himself to be happy when he was by himself.

34

Shannon was waiting for him when he entered the casino's ballroom. The music, as Marcel had suspected, whas bumping, but it wasn't banging loud enough that he had to shout over it. The booze hadn't been flowing long enough.

"You were amazing." Shannon hugged him.

Not far from them stood Tess. She was with the older gentlemen still, Marcel could tell that she was watching them.

"Thank you," Marcel answered before the crowds descended on him.

Marcel could sense that Shannon wanted to say more but wasn't able to. When the people at the party saw him, they flocked to him. They all coveted some of his greatness. They masked their sin with congratulatory tones, but Marcel knew it was bullshit. The older gentlemen with Tess was one of the first.

"Congratulations. It's good to see one of our own representing us in such a formidable manner." Marcel guessed him to be in his sixties. He wore his hair traditionally long, pulled back into a ponytail. A few hints of gray were creeping in.

"Thank you." Marcel extended his hand to the man.

"Marcel, let me introduce you to Chairman Clifford Banks of the Leech Lake Band of Ojibwe." Tess spoke with an air of pride in her voice. She too leaned in and hugged him.

"I am honored to meet you sir," Marcel directed this at the chairman, though honor was not what he felt. Horror more aptly described it. Now his fears had been realized, but he had expected it and had been braced for its eventuality. His face showed nothing.

"Nonsense, I am a mere civil servant. It is I who am honored. Though I have never been a fighter myself, I know how difficult a sport it is. How much discipline it takes, and how much work you have to put in. That is admirable. You could provide a tremendous example back home." Banks was in full politician mode.

Shannon watched the exchange, listening intently. Marcel shot her a look and thought that he saw recognition, but he couldn't be sure. Maybe he was just mistaking her curiosity for something it wasn't.

"I guess I don't really know what to say. I have never thought of myself as any kind of role model. Just a regular guy having the opportunity to live out his dream," Marcel answered sheepishly. He was not used to this type of praise.

"How's about coming back for a small celebration at Cass Lake high school? You know on the Rez; there aren't a lot of kids who believe they will get to live their dreams. Seeing one of their own living your dream will certainly be a very big event in their eyes. Who knows, you may get the opportunity to change a life," The Chairman continued.

It wasn't out of the ordinary for a fighter to get asked to make appearances here and there. Marcel had made a couple for some local bars as a favor to Jarvis, but he wasn't really known enough to get asked to do much more, until tonight. This time he shot Tess a look. The look was much different than the one he gave Shannon. With Shannon, he was trying to gauge her opinion on the events taking place. The look he gave Tess, however, was a look that was more telling than investigating. He was asking for her help in the most non-verbal way possible.

"Mr. Banks, I will work on getting it set up. I am sure that Marcel has a lot of people to meet right now, and I need a drink." Tess sounded like an old pro at handling politicians, though Marcel thought she was probably making it up as she went. Marcel didn't care. He wanted to get the hell out of there before he was committed to traveling to the Leech Lake Reservation a place he swore he would never go again. He had no intention of getting caught up in the vortex of that black hole. Marcel was disappointed to see that Tess' words had little effect on the Chairman. He wasn't going to let the eye candy run his night. However, when the "Average Man" Don Colt, a local radio personality and fight announcer, came over to congratulate Marcel, the chairman knew that he no longer had Marcel's ear and agreed to Tess' proposal.

"This would be good for everyone, Champ." The chairman gave one last encouragement before walking away. Tess gave him another look and a smile as they walked away. Marcel smiled back, then turned back to Shannon who was still waiting for him.

"Important friends?" There was something in her tone that Marcel took for jealousy.

"I guess, win a fight and you have more friends that you did before the fight." Marcel didn't really want to get into his relationship with Tess right now. It was far too complex and he was ready to celebrate.

"I guess." She smiled. It may not have been genuine, Marcel couldn't tell.

"Wanna meet some of my new friends?" Marcel extended his arm to Shannon and she took it. He lead her deeper into the heart of the party. There were all walks of society in the crowd. Businessmen, sports writers, other fighters, doctors, and politicians. Fight fans came from a more diverse cross section of the population than any other sport. The ones who were able to afford this party came mostly from the top of the food chain. Had Marcel not been the center of attention he certainly wouldn't have been welcome there. Shannon, on the other hand, well that was a whole other story.

Marcel thought she seemed at home with the wealthy, and she certainly played the role of a fighter's lady to perfection. If Marcel had to bet, he would have put the smart money on Shannon being involved in theater at some point during her undergraduate career. He knew she hated socializing in these circles as much as he did, but she was only a supporting actor in this farce. However, she stayed by his side until the wee hours of the morning, schmoozing and dancing. It was a fun night. Not romantic so much as it was an opportunity for them both to get to know each other in roles they were completely unaccustomed to seeing each other. Marcel started realizing that Shannon was something special to him.

35

Marcel hadn't seen Shannon since the fight. He had no idea how exhilarating an experience it was for her to watch him move with such speed and precision in the ring. He also had no idea the torment she was going through, either. Marcel hoped that their kiss had stirred her as much as it stirred him. He hoped that she figured out her emotions. He was right, in a sense. She had been jolted, but she didn't need to figure anything out.

Marcel was nervous walking up to the office for the meeting tonight. Not knowing quite how

Shannon would respond was part of his unease. The rest was a result of not knowing what Joanne had in store for them. They had made a big splash with their last assignment, and now here he was fighting an inner battle with himself whether to continue at St. Stevens or put all of his focus on Vegas.

He entered Joanne's office. Joanne was accompanied by a well dressed black man. Marcel assumed the man was her associate, Tavian Springs. He was greeted and guided to a seat in front of her desk. Behind Joanne were windows that looked out on the parking lot and the surrounding neighborhood. They were nice windows, and overall Marcel was impressed with the office. He thought it was squared away. He hadn't anticipated that from Joanne, who he believed to be a little disheveled. He sized up Tavian and didn't like what he saw. Marcel felt he could spot a phony a mile away and Tavian had the make of a poser. Marcel decided that Tavian would likely be a tough challenge for him in a fight. He was built well and the way he leaned on the sill of the window was in such a manner that he could quickly get to his feet and be in a ready position if something went down. The way he stood made Marcel uneasy. It wasn't just the way he stood. Marcel didn't like what he saw in Tavian; there was a smell of arrogance that emanated from the man. Marcel assumed this was how he approached a courtroom, like a pitbull. Marcel knew that if they were to battle for supremacy of the room he would be in for a hell of a fight.

"Hi Marcel, let me introduce you to Tavian Springs, my associate." She pointed in the direction of the man leaning on the sill.

Tavian didn't offer his hand and Marcel was certainly not going to offer his. Instead Tavian nodded in acknowledgment, and Marcel gave him a reverse nod. On the rez this was an anti-establishment gesture, not quite disrespect but not quite friendly either. Neither said a word.

"Let's get right to it, Marcel, we were really impressed with your write up on the last assignment. That was some brilliant work." Marcel could recognize that Joanne was trying to soften him up before dropping a bomb on him.

"Thank you," Marcel said, accepting the shit she was shoveling.

"Shannon has been telling me for a while that you are a rising star, and I am starting to see that myself." Marcel wondered how all those juries in the past could have bought her snake oil.

"Shannon played a very big role in the last project." Marcel stood up for his partner.

"Bullshit," Tavian spoke.

Marcel gave him a hard look. Tavian gave it right back.

"Marcel, Shannon has already told us all about the project, this is no time to be modest." Joanne took a sip from her coffee and continued,

"Marcel, the case we have now might be the biggest case the A-I-I has ever happened upon, and we need you to be a part of it."

"Why me?" he asked.

"The defendant requested you," Joanne said.

Marcel had no idea how a defendant could have requested him. Who would have known he was even an option?

"Who is the defendant?" he asked.

"Ken Northbird," She said, after a few seconds of silence.

It was the left hook to the kidney that he had been dreading his whole life. It sucked all of the air and energy out of him. The room spun around him and he felt like he was going to go down for the first time in his career. There were so many questions in his head. None of them could get formulated into clear and concise words. His skin was tingling, and he couldn't feel his face. He wondered what he looked like from the outside. He envisioned watching himself turn into a puddle right there on his chair. No form to his body, simply a hideous blob in front of them.

Marcel couldn't hear the door open to the main hall of the professor's offices. Shannon had taken the staircase and was in the middle of the building. She had passed the atrium and the first two big lecture halls. She had started up but hadn't made it to the office yet. The second floor housed the library to the right of the stairwell and the professors' offices on the left side. They had all disappeared in Marcel's mind. Joanne's office was at the end of the hallway on the south side of the building. With the door open, Marcel was able to be heard by anyone in the hall, though he had no concept of anyone else in the world for the time being.

"I am going to need some time on this," Marcel said, getting up and walking out of the room. He was so deep in his world that he didn't even notice that Shannon was standing there in the hall. He was oblivious to the fact that she stood there deciding whether to chase after him or enter Joanne's office. He was gone by the time she eventually decided to check in with Joanne.

Marcel got out into the parking lot and jumped on his bike. He hit the electric start and the machine roared to life. Marcel twisted the throttle a couple of times before kicking the bike into gear and pulling out of the parking lot, not bothering to check for traffic. He got out to Snelling and headed south. He continued to accelerate as he drove, paying no mind to neither traffic nor stop lights. By the time he got to 94 he was traveling eighty-five miles an hour.

He slowed enough to make the hard right turn onto 94 West, and in seconds had surpassed ninety and was quickly approaching one hundred. Through downtown Minneapolis the needle buried at one seventy-five and everything became a blur, including the highway patrol officer, who knew better than to even try and pursue him. A call was put in, but it was no use. By the time the patrol was in a position to cut him off, he had long since passed. At the speed he traveled, it only took him thirty minutes to get to St. Cloud. He exited into downtown and pulled into Burger King. He couldn't remember ever having fast food; he thought it was possible when he lived with his grandfather but he wasn't sure. He went in and ordered a bacon cheeseburger and fries.

He dug out his phone and sent a text.

FEEL LIKE TAKING A DRIVE" the message appeared on his phone.

SURE WHERE? was the response.

NORTH He hit enter then added a follow up MEET ME IN ST CLOUD.

36

"Shannon, there is a whole lot about me you don't know." Marcel spoke first.

It took Shannon about about an hour to make it to St. Cloud. Marcel had sat at Burger King contemplating his life thus far, and where it was going to go from here. He came to no clear answers.

"I kind of gathered that from the fight," She responded.

"Yeah, what did you gather?" Marcel was curious, he assumed that she was talking about his ink, but wanted to be sure.

"So the tattoos...," she trailed off not knowing quite how to put it.

"Are gang tattoos." The honesty was cathartic.

"I grew up on the Leech Lake Reservation. My dad went to prison for killing my mom. All I had growing up was my brother, Henry, who was a member of the Native Mob Vice Lords. I never really knew anything else." Admitting it felt strange to him. He had never said those words out loud. This made it real which is probably why he hadn't ever said any of this before. He was ashamed.

"And now?" Shannon continued the questioning.

"My brother was murdered when I was fourteen years old. I didn't have anyone left in Minnesota, so I was put on a bus and sent to live with my grandfather in Colorado. He died a few years later, and Jarvis took me in. Jarvis and my grandfather were pretty close through the gym." It wasn't really an answer to the question.

Marcel didn't really know the answer to her question. It was his belief that once you were part of the crew you were part of the crew for life. Now, however, there was no crew, there was only Marcel and Tess. There were several cemetery plots up north that were the final resting places for the crew. They were all gone now. If they were all gone, was it still possible to be one of them? That being said, he would never deny his brother. His brother, who had been dead for more than a decade. His brother, who he missed so badly and held so dear.

Shannon remained silent.

"Jarvis was from Minneapolis. When I got accepted to law school, he suggested we move back together. I could continue training while I went to school, but that isn't very interesting. What you want to hear about is what happened in Joanne's office." Marcel was getting uncomfortable with narrating his life.

"My brother was my whole world, but he made all kinds of bad decisions. The gang was just one of them. The gang wasn't like the Trey-Trey crips or anything; we weren't a criminal syndicate. We were a family. We looked out for each other, sold some weed to make money, partied, and didn't allow anyone to fuck with us. It was pretty unorganized stuff, but I guess that made us all more dangerous." Marcel wondered if this was a lie of omission. He thought it was and thought it was best to be honest now and not have his integrity questioned later.

"At least it made my brother more dangerous. He was involved in a stabbing at a party where a kid was killed. My brother did it; I wasn't there but I knew he did it. The next day he got out of town to let things cool off. Everyone thought he was in Minneapolis, but he wasn't. He was staying with some of our people in Duluth. He should have stayed longer. No one knew he was there. He was putting together some cash to get me and him out of Minnesota for good. He came up to get me, but before we could leave, he was murdered. He was outside our trailer when this guy came up and shot him in the head. I didn't see it actually happen. When I heard the shot, I came running and saw my brother laying on the sidewalk. He was bleeding all over the place. There was so much blood, and it looked like half his head was missing. I will never forget that sight. There was a man, or I guess a teenager running away with a gun in his hand. I didn't think I would ever forget that face, either. I picked a man out of a lineup; I was sure that he was the guy I saw. I testified at trial, and the guy was convicted. His name was Ken Northbird."

Marcel paused and took a deep breath. He was keeping it together a lot better than he thought he would. The story he had told was mostly true. He left out a few things that he was never going to tell anyone, but the gist of the story was the best he could remember it.

The lights on the side of the road were mostly gone. They had passed a train just out of Little Falls and now darkness enveloped the countryside. Shannon drove and said nothing the whole trip. Marcel had talked because he had something to say. Now it was time for him to finish the tale.

"Ken Northbird is the client who Joanne asked us to work on next." Marcel looked at

Shannon. In the darkness he couldn't guage her response.

Shannon didn't speak and Marcel figured she didn't know what to say. They sat in silence for the next twenty miles.

"Wow." Shannon finally spoke, breaking the silence.

"Yeah, I guess that says it all."

"Marcel, I am sorry that happened to your brother. I am also sorry that you had to go through that, and I am sorry that you have to deal with all this again." Shannon's voice had changed. It sounded real? Did that mean other things she said weren't real? A warning beacon went off in Marcel's head but quickly faded out. Compassion. That is what he heard. That is what he wanted to hear.

"Thanks." But gratitude wasn't what he was experiencing.

"So Northbird is claiming to be innocent?" Shannon asked.

"Yeah, and Joanne said he wants me on board with it." Marcel answered.

"Could you have been wrong about the ID of the killer?" It was a valid question given everything that had transpired in the last four hours.

"I don't know." Though he did know, he knew for sure. If he closed his eyes right now he could see the picture in his head. The scene was like a movie playing in the highest definition possible.

"I mean, for sixteen years I have lived in a

world where Ken Northbird was the guy that killed my brother; I went from confusion, to hatred, to forgiveness and now this gets sprung on me. My initial reaction is remorse. I mean shit, it's entirely possible that I am the reason an innocent man has spent the better part of his life in a maximum security prison hundreds of miles away from his family, and that is really the hard part to get a hold on."

This was Marcel at his most vulnerable. Here he was a former gang member, a pro boxer, who only a week ago had pummeled a man in short order in front of a few thousand people, and here he was conflicted about a piece of trash like Ken Northbird rotting in a cell. He had changed, though. He was not the same person he was all those years ago. He had moved passed vengeance. He was a better person, wasn't he? But didn't he build up a hatred for his opponents in the moments leading up to a fight? Wasn't that the same thing he did back then? There were two parts of him tearing each other apart. There was the old Marcel, angry and violent, and there was the new man he wanted so desperately to be. Which one was the fraud?

"How convincing is the evidence?"

"Shannon, I was an angry kid filled with rage; Ken was a rival gang member. I was fourteen years old when my brother's murder took place right before my eyes. I had lived a short, violent life at that point. I didn't know right from wrong. The person I was..." He trailed off.

He hadn't stuck around to hear Joanne lay out her case. He had enough evidence within himself to know that Ken Northbird had a valid claim that he was innocent of the crime he was convicted of. That didn't make Ken Northbird innocent, but perhaps if Marcel allowed himself to let go of everything from his past the man he wanted to be could win the war going on inside him.

There was another long silence in the car. They were deep in the Chippewa forest north of Brainerd now and it was very dark. Over the last two hours he had come to terms with his past, and now he feared what would happen next.

37

Joanne had never actually brokered a drug deal before. She knew that Milton had been using their company to launder money for a drug business but she herself had never gotten any deeper than white collar criminal. The closest she got was putting clients in touch with sellers. She hadn't been in touch with her own supplier in quite a while. She had stashed enough pills to where she was able to get by for quite a while. That stash was gone; she had taken the last couple pills before her trip to Texas. Now she had a lot of fish to fry. First she needed to get back in touch with her supplier, then she had to find a way to get the drugs to Colorado without getting pinched by any local cops.

Ken Northbird was in a hell of a predicament. He was being squeezed by a crooked C.O. over his last pinch, which just so happened to be dope out of her vending machines. The C.O. would give Ken up unless Ken turned his business over to the C.O. If Ken refused, his chance at a new trial was gone. The vending machines were a problem personally for Joanne. Somehow Ken had gotten information on her as well. A shitstorm could be prevented though. All she had to do was get the drugs to the corrections officer. Joanne, however, was not about to pack them in a bag and take them on a plane or put them in the trunk of a car and drive them out there. Joanne could not be caught by any local yocals; she needed insolation. Ken had offered her a solution. That was where up and comer Marcel came in. It was a brilliant plan, really. She would maintain her distance to the whole operation. She would set Marcel up in a hotel paid for by the A-I-I. Marcel would then be responsible for delivering the package. If the package was intercepted, she would have no connection to it. Marcel would be the fall guy, and his prior connection with Ken would be enough to keep any suspicious eyes off her. The C.O. would never have to know who she was. Marcel would be an unknowing front man for the whole operation.

The challenge would be getting Marcel to bring the package to the C.O. no questions asked. She would cross that bridge when she came to it. For now, she had another issue to deal with.

Her first order of business was to reconnect with her supplier. It was a fairly innocuous process. Anyone watching on the outside would have no idea what she was doing. Her contact was a bartender in Dinkytown. He had a permanent ad on Craigslist selling all sorts of stuff, from furniture to used cars. Joanne would go into the bar, order a drink, and tell the man she was interested in one of the items depending on how much she needed. He would ask her how much she was willing to pay, and the deal would be done. The whole process was basic 1L contracts, offer and acceptance. The second part of the process was for her to stop somewhere to pick up the package. With the amount of weight she needed, she was in the market for a used car. The location was a dealership up in Blaine where she would deliver the payment. The car would then be delivered to a location after she left it at the dealership. It was a process Milton had used with American Vending out of Rapid City, SD. American Vending would package the dope and deliver it to the vending machines at the prisons they serviced. This deal would be slightly different. With Milton clinging to life in some hospital out west, American Vending was no longer viable. Did she dare having the dope delivered to her house? She thought maybe she should have it addressed to Dr. Cockslinger at her address. That way if anything went down she could plead ignorance and put it on her ex-husband. This made her laugh.

She went into her kitchen, this time not even considering her ex-husband's past indiscretions. Instead she was solely focused on her keys; she couldn't remember where she had put them when she had gotten home from her meeting with Tavian and Marcel. They weren't on the granite countertop where she had anticipated them being.

"Shit," She muttered to the empty house

Oh hell, I came in through the garage. Is my brain that polluted? she thought, remembering she had entered the house through the attached garage and likely left them on the stand right by the entrance from said garage. She headed to the back of the house and sure as shit, there where the keys. Praise the Lord.

She opened the door that lead down to the garage. The garage was below the house. There were spaces for ten cars in the underground bunker. Her ex had been a car collector. Now that he was gone, the garage sat mostly empty. Joanne usually parked her Lexus in front of the house in the driveway. She had no idea why she had parked in the garage last night. Things like that were happening more and more to her. Unusual acts without motive. She knew that this was part and parcel to the drug abuse. Her brain was becoming rewired. Or fried.

She pulled the Lexus out of the driveway and headed into Minneapolis. She was so preoccupied that she didn't see the Ford Taurus two driveways down from her own. In the driver's seat was Tavian; he had been waiting for her. When she drove passed, he pulled out and followed.

It took her about twenty minutes to make it over to Dinkytown, which was in the northwest part of Minneapolis, and made up of the businesses that surround the U of M. School was in session so parking was difficult. She did find a lot north of the football stadium about nine blocks from the bar and parked. Tavian circled the block. He kept an eye on her from the car, and found a meter considerably closer. Joanne continued walking, oblivious to the fact she was being watched.

She entered the bar and was not surprised to see she was the only patron; it was only 10:30AM. The bartender was a familiar face. It was the man she had dealt with in the past, and he certainly recognized her.

"Hillary, good seeing you again. What can I get for you?" He called her by the alias she used. No sense putting her real name out there for this guy to know.

"Greyhound." She wasn't a drinker but the unusual drink was part of the deal.

"Like to see a menu?" He set the drink in front of her.

"Umm no, I am interested in your car that's for sale."

"What are you looking to spend?" The man spoke with a thick Welsh accent.

"One hundred"

The barkeep shot her a puzzled look. Joanne had been a good customer but no high roller. Usually putting down between five hundred and a thousand dollars at a purchase. Joanne knew he was trying to determine if she meant one hundred or one hundred thousand. She was too small to be buying a hundred thousand and was much too big a fiend to only be buying one hundred.

"I am looking for a big car."

His look changed from confusion to concern just like that. A number that big was out of the ordinary. In this game, anything out of the ordinary was suspicious.

"That's a lot of car, sure you don't want something a little smaller?" he responded

"I am retiring. This will be the last car I am going to buy. I want to make sure I get exactly what I need." Good grief, she thought. in what other business would you have to beg someone to take your damn money?

"I got something up at Blaine Auto. Stop by this afternoon, they will take care of you." The Welsh bartender surrendered his suspicion only because Joanne had been their biggest customer for years.

"That'll be four-fifty for the drink." He nodded to the untouched drink in front of her.

She pulled out a five dollar bill and left it on the bar, got up and left. She never noticed Tavian, who was now outside the bar surveilling her.

"Car's that big can be dangerous. You don't operate them right, anything can happen," The Welshmen warned as she left.

Fuck yourself, she thought.

249

38

Marcel and Shannon spent the night in Walker. The next morning they got up early and drove out to Onigum to see some of the places Marcel used to run around as a kid. The trailer he lived in was still there, but it had pretty much fallen in on itself. They visited the spot where his brother had been murdered. Marcel recreated the event, looking down the street at his brother's killer. He could remember it so vividly though all the trees were now bigger. Some of the trees he remembered were gone, and some new ones had popped up. The cycle of life continuing as if he had never existed.

Marcel took off on a jog about the same pace as the killer while Shannon stood where he had been all those years ago. At one point he turned, as the killer had done. Marcel believed the shooter wanted to check and see if the man he shot was moving. Marcel circled back to Shannon, and they compared notes discussing what was and was not visible.

The morning was mentally and emotionally draining for Marcel. Inside he was a mixture of sadness, anger, fear and regret. Though everything that was running through his mind was deeply personal, he couldn't help but wonder what was going on in Shannon's head through all this. Here she was watching him relive the worst moment of his life and she stood there holding back whatever emotion was inside of her. The way she talked, the way she carried herself it was like it was just another day at the office. Marcel couldn't help but wonder if she was putting on this display of strength to help him to be stronger. Maybe, he thought it had to do with upbringing. Maybe the security of a good family provided her with the tools to control her emotions in a way that he never could. He wondered, but wasn't ready to ask.

After their reenactment they headed into town and split a pizza at Benson's Eating and Drinking Emporium. A cold front had blown through, and the temperature had dropped about twenty degrees. A cold wind blew off the lake. It was the first pizza Marcel had eaten in a long long time. He pondered it a moment, for sure the first pizza he had since moving to Minnesota. Jarvis strictly forbid it, but now that he was the Champion he could take some liberties. And besides, he wouldn't be fighting for at least six months. First he had indulged on a bacon cheeseburger from Burger King for lunch and now pizza for dinner. Damn, he thought. This is complacency creeping in. Tomorrow I am back to work.

While they ate neither of them noticed the short stocky Native with the thick mustache come in and take a seat at the bar.

"So what do you think?" Marcel asked Shannon. Pausing from the pizza to take a drink.

"I think the pizza is really good." Shannon said with a smile.

Marcel appreciated how she was trying to keep it as light as she could.

"Seriously though, I think it would have been really easy for a fourteen year old kid to mis-identify someone in that scenario," Shannon admitted.

Marcel nodded his head, though inside he had mixed emotions about her response.

"So why is it you thought it was Ken all those years ago?" Shannon asked, stretching her back.

"I think we have to go back and talk to Joanne and figure out what other info she might have on this whole thing. I mean, this is a lot of history and I am not sure I want to be a part of this. To be honest I am not sure I am even going to continue at St. Stevens." Marcel intentionally ducked her question. He wondered what she was thinking when he dodged these questions. She never pressed, and he assumed she was being polite, not wanting to open old wounds any deeper.

The mustached man had moved from the bar to a table near enough to hear their conversation. But neither Shannon nor Marcel noticed.

"That makes sense, I guess. Anything more you need to do here?" Shannon took a drink of her beer.

"Leech Lake is a small place, everyone knows everyone else. No one ever talked about Ken being innocent and more importantly, no one ever talked about someone else pulling the trigger." This bothered him as much as his own conscience did.

"Maybe an out of towner?" Shannon suggested.

"I think I know the man to talk to." Marcel looked at her.

He thought about the Chairman. He seemed like a big windbag but he also had his finger on the pulse around here.

"The Chairman?" Shannon asked.

"That's right." He pulled out his phone and rang Tess' number.

"Tess? Hey, this is Marcel," He spoke into the

phone.

He could feel Shannon's eyes digging into him. He shrugged his shoulders. He didn't spend a lot of time making small talk with Tess. She agreed to put the Chairman in touch with Marcel.

"By the way, who is this Tess woman?" Wow, is she jealous? Marcel thought.

"My brother's girlfriend, or ex girlfriend?" Marcel answered earnestly.

"Oh, I see."

Marcel could tell that Shannon was now very interested in meeting Tess.

The pizza was a decadent feast Marcel hadn't indulged in for years. Shannon's half was all vegetable, Marcel's was loaded with meat. Though he was splurging, he still opted for the thin crust as opposed to the deep dish. This was the first step to battling his own complacency.

Midway through dinner Marcel's phone rang. It was the Chairman. He invited them to his home on First Point Drive just outside Walker. Marcel quickly waved for a waitress who came over and boxed up the remaining slices of pizza. Shannon picked up the tab, and the duo hurried out to Shannon's car. They still had not noticed the mustached man who had taken the sudden interest in them. He too left the restaurant and followed them out. His Jeep Cherokee was parked across the street by the car wash.

They were hit with yet another cold blast

when they walked outside. This one was mixed with a drizzle only slightly above freezing. It was typical Minnesota weather. It had gone from sweltering to freezing in a matter of days.

39

The Chairman knew for a fact that Marcel and his squeeze were both full of shit. They had come to him about the school appearance but ended up talking about Ken Northbird. The guy they were looking for was named Travis Jackson. As far as Clifford was willing to tell them, no such man existed he and his friends in high places made sure of that. Marcel hadn't mentioned his brother or drugs and that was telling. Their lie hadn't been particularly well crafted, and he saw through it. For some reason Marcel was holding his cards close to his chest and the Chairman didn't like it.

Ken Northbird was a piece of shit as far as Bank's was concerned, but a dangerous piece of shit. Ken knew things that could hurt Banks and the reservation. Banks wasn't going to allow that to happen. Northbird was a loose end, and Banks liked things tidy. This asshole Northbird had been locked away for years, and he hadn't really caused any problems. Northbird's focus had been on screaming to the high heavens, and to anyone who had listened, that he was innocent. Banks had used some of his considerable influence to get more than one of his petitions for a new trial dismissed. As long as Northbird was chasing a new trial, he would keep his mouth shut about Banks. However now that Marcel Wright was digging around Northbird, Banks wondered if maybe Northbird had given up and was starting to run his mouth. If he was, Banks would have to solve that problem.

Banks wasn't a reactionary, though. He was a planner. He was the type of guy who wouldn't go outside to take a leak without a plan. He needed more information. Bank's needed to know exactly what Wright was doing and what he knew. Bank's thought if it came down to it, Marcel Wright might be a problem that needed to be solved as well. Luckily he had just the man for the job.

40

The next morning Marcel awoke just before sunrise and headed out for a run
along the lake down to the city park. The
Chairman wasn't able to help them much. He
had no information about the shooting, hadn't
heard any sort of rumors, and seemed sure of
Northbird's guilt. The only thing that really
came out of the meeting was that Marcel had
agreed to return in a couple days to meet with
students at Cass Lake High School as well as
Chief Bug-O-Ne-Ge Shig School.

Marcel figured the best thing they could do

was get their hands on the original case file and find out exactly what went on from the perspective of the original players. To accomplish that, they would have to head over to Duluth to the see the U.S. Attorney and public defenders who handled the case. Duluth was two hours east of Walker, and if Shannon was up, they would be able to get there before lunch, which would give them plenty of time to dig into the casefiles. Joanne would be able to get them access.

41

They made the drive in just a little over two hours. It was Marcel's first trip to the Port City since he had testified in Northbird's original trial. He didn't remember much about the city or the lake. Entering the city now, Marcel was impressed by the size of Lake Superior. He thought the city itself was a really cool place, filled with character and charm. He sort of wished they had some time to just tool around and see the sights, but they had business to attend to.

Marcel and Shannon agreed they would split

up; Marcel would go to the U.S. attorney's office, and Shannon to the public defender's office. Ken had been represented by a public defender in the original case. Marcel thought it was important to compare notes. The public defender should have everything that the prosecutor had through the discovery process. If they didn't, that would be one indication that something foul may be afoot.

The office for the United States Attorney in Minnesota was housed in Minneapolis.

However, an office staffed by a skeleton crew was kept in Duluth where the local files were stored. The office was in the Gerald H. Heaney Federal building off First Street in a plaza that was home to three government buildings. The central building was the St. Louis County Courthouse. The building to the right was City Hall, and the building on the left was the Federal Building. Marcel went into the building and filled out a request to see the file for US v Ken Northbird.

It took awhile for the woman working the front desk to retrieve the file. Once he got into it, what he found amazed him. There were several statements from witnesses that he had never seen before. He was surprised that he hadn't considered there being other witnesses, as sophisticated as he thought of himself. He had always assumed he was the only one, which now seemed incredibly naive.

One statement he read was from Travis Jackson. He hadn't known Jackson. Jackson was another member of Ken Northbird's Bloods gang. There was more in the statement than Marcel thought he would find. It turned out that the police had been quite interested in a man named Antonio Eagle, but had been steered away by Special Agent Buckley's star witness, Marcel Wright.

There were several other statements from witnesses that had never testified. He wondered if the same statements were in the public defender's file. Even with all this new information, he found there was no mention of Agent Buckley anywhere else in the file. The more he read however, the less concerned he was about Agent Buckley because there were enough other avenues to look at. First and foremost was the original attorney assigned to the case, the one who had taken Marcel's original statement and had steered police away from Eagle.

The United States Attorney responsible for taking Jackson's statement had been Walter Carmody. Marcel didn't recognize that name; he was certain Carmody hadn't dealt with him, though he couldn't remember the man who had. Marcel decided to check and see if Walter would speak to him about the case, if he was still with the US Attorney's office. He photo copied several documents and put them into his file. He then headed for the area of the office that housed the support staff.

The U.S. Attorney's office itself was much smaller than was the Hennepin County Attorney's Office. It was home to only two attorneys and five support staff. This was the specific division assigned to prosecuting major crimes from the reservation. They handled other federal cases from Northern Minnesota as well. He found the secretary for the attorney that handled cases under the major crimes act; she was busy at work transcribing some document.

"Excuse me," he said making sure not to startle her but at the same time get her attention.

The secretary was a heavier set, yet pretty woman, about his age. She had short blond hair. Marcel thought she looked trendy and professional all at the same time.

"Hi there." She turned from her work to him. He couldn't help but think she had a pleasant smile.

"Can I help you with something?" she continued

"I am looking for Walter Carmody." Marcel attempted to smile back but felt goofy doing it.

"Who is Walter Carmody?" She asked politely and Marcel was certain she really didn't know.

"He was a U.S. Attorney who worked on major crimes cases in this office fifteen to twenty years ago." *Someone around here has to know what happened to this guy don't they*? he thought.

"I have only been here for a little over a year, so I haven't heard of any Carmody." She looked apologetic

"Well is there anyone who might know what happened to him?" Marcel questioned.

"Maybe Marcy, she has been here with the office for twenty years. Let me call her." The woman picked up her phone and pushed a couple of buttons. Marcel could hear the phone ring and someone pick up on the other end.

"Marcy, this is Jamie." She paused and the jabber voice on the other end responded.

"Well I am doing just fine, thank you for asking." She looked up at Marcel and made a face.

"No it's good," she spoke as some more jabber voice came through the phone.

"No," she went on.

Seriously, woman let's get to it here. Small talk was maddening to Marcel in the first place and even more so when he was on a mission.

"Look Marcy, the reason I am calling is because I have a gentlemen here that is looking for information about Walter Carmody, do you know..." She was again interrupted by more jabber voice.

"Okay, I will bring him up." She shot a smile at Marcel, and hung up the phone.

Marcel didn't think he needed an escort through the public hallway to see another secretary and was beginning to think that Jamie might have an extra-curricular interest in him.

"Well it seems like Mr. Carmody is a bit of a skeleton in the closet." She unlocked the door and came outside. He was instantly drawn to her disproportionately large hips, when she got around to the front of him he noticed she had a back side to match.

"Why do you say that he was a skeleton in the closet?" It was an odd statement and he wanted to know more.

"You know how old people are about dirty laundry." She turned to him, and he quickly raised his eyes off her enormous back side and nodded his acquiescence.

"They use whispers when no one else is around, but would tell anyone who asks." She laughed. Marcel thought it was comical as well, he had known a few old timers that did this.

They walked through the corridors of the office, finally reaching a bank of elevators. The girl named Jamie pushed the up button and they stood there waiting in the uncomfortable silence that ensued.

"What is it that you are working on?" She finally broke the silence after what felt like five minutes but in reality was probably closer to fifteen seconds.

"I am investigating an old case for the American Innocent Institute." Marcel was not really sure how much he should be telling this woman. He had held his cards close with Banks, and felt he should do the same here to. At least until he spoke with Joanne.

"Really? Why?" She didn't really sound like she cared that much.

"Claims to be innocent." He hoped that this would be enough. He was ready to be away from this woman now.

"Don't they all." Her flippant response assured him he wouldn't have to explain himself any further.

"You're a lawyer then?" Aha, now she was starting to move her feelers into his personal life

"No I am a law student, at St. Stevens, but I am working for the Innocence Institute"

"I've heard of that. You guys use DNA to get people off death row. We haven't prosecuted a death penalty case up here ever." Marcel thought she sounded a little suspicious.

"We don't just do death penalty cases. We take any cases where there is evidence of actual innocence." He realized his words were making himself sound bigger than he was. He wasn't really a part of the Innocence Institute. He guessed he liked the feeling of a strange woman showing some interest in him.

"St. Stevens, is that in Superior?" She redirected him back to personal information.

"No. St. Paul, this is my first trip to Duluth." He lied omitting his trip to testify at trial.

The elevator dinged and opened on the third floor. There was nothing particularly special about the third floor. There were three offices that surrounded a short hallway. At the end of the hall was a law library that was shared with the county. There was one office on the left of the hallway that belonged to Marcia Olafson, or Marcy as the woman with the enormous back side called her, what was her name? Jaime?

The woman with the enormous backside knocked on the door jamb as the door was wide open.

"Marcy, I have Mr. Wright here from St. Stevens University, he has some questions about Mr. Carmody."

"Send him in." The voice sounded pleasant from around the corner.

42

A few blocks away Shannon was making little headway at the public defender's office. The system in use for tracking files had changed drastically in the last few years and finding old closed files was a painstaking progress. What she had learned was that the attorney handling the file for the PD still worked with the office, but he wasn't in today. She also learned that there had always been a suspicion around the office that the original prosecutor had been involved in some shady business. They had a ton of trouble with discovery early on then that attorney had disappeared under some odd circumstances. That was the extent of what she could glean from the PD file.

Fran, a lovely older woman with a lot of fire, came up and introduced herself.

"Hi, I am Fran Hinkmeier, you can call me Fran. I hear you are a law student looking into some old cases?" She was direct and to the point.

Fran was smartly dressed; clearly an attorney and a lifer at the PD's office. For most attorneys life in the PD's office would be depressing, but Fran saw it as a calling. Where public defense wore down others half her age, she was energized by it.

"Yes, Shannon McCarthy, nice to meet you." Shannon replied.

"Come with me." She wheeled on her short heel and quickly walked down a corridor to a locked office room. The name "Andersen" was stamped on the glass. Shannon instantly recognized Anderson as the attorney who represented Ken Northbird.

"Charles has been out for sometime. I have been handling his caseload; he has some medical issues to take care of. I doubt he will be back," Fran said, unlocking the office.

Fran guided Shannon through the door. The office was in utter disarray. There were files stacked and strewn in every corner. There was only one area of the room that had any semblance of order, a locked filing cabinet against the rear wall.

"We are using the office for overflow storage for the time being. All of these files are closed; it may appear unorganized, but there is a delicate system in place until these get shipped to the vault." Fran smiled a wiley smile. Shannon knew that she was full of shit. There was no system. With virtually no money for support staff, filing closed files was not a huge priority for the public defender's office.

"That cabinet back there is a cache of files that we have 'suspicions' about. I think your case is one of them." Fran walked to the filing cabinet and unlocked it.

"What do you mean by 'suspicions'?" Shannon asked the woman who had already started for the door.

"Well, we think there were some cases not handled properly. Most of the cases were clients prosecuted by Carmody."

"Mind if I go through these?" Shannon pointed at the file cabinet.

"Be my guest. I have a ton of work, but if you need anything don't hesitate to ask." With that she was gone from the office, leaving Shannon to the cabinet full of files.

Shannon quickly found the file and began to scan documents for new information. There were several notes, presumably written by Andersen, most of which were his thoughts about holes in the story, questions about witness veracity, and misconduct by the prosecutor, Mr. Carmody. There was one strange note that she saw at the corner of one of the pages. It read "Carmody" with an arrow drawn to another hand scrawled name: "Banks".

Shannon selected five files to compare. Not one of them was Andersen; they were from all different PD's. The common thread in each was Walter Carmody. Apart from the notes on Carmody, there was little else of interest in the file, especially for a murder case. There was nothing in the section labeled exculpatory evidence. There were two avenues to obtaining a new trial in this case. The first was a half ass public defender. The other was prosecutorial misconduct. What Shannon was really looking for was more information on Marcel, or at least something she could use to get more information from him.

Shannon attempted to call Marcel, however she was unable to get reception in the crypt like office. The walls were solid granite. The only way to get through to him was to escape the dingy office and get out into the sunshine. It had been a beautiful day in Duluth when she went in. The sun was warm, and the wind had not shifted to the North. When the wind shifted from the North, Duluth became a sitting duck for ferocious weather.

Shannon stepped outside to find the sun had vanished behind a thick covering of grey clouds, and the wind had in fact shifted to the North. It was cold. She was glad she had brought a sweatshirt with her. She took out her phone and punched in Marcel's number. It went straight to voicemail; he was apparently still about his work.

She figured it would make sense to learn a little bit more about Walter Carmody. The library seemed like the perfect place to do so. It was only two blocks down on Superior Street, so she started to walk to the east in the direction of the library. She nearly jumped out of her skin when a voice cut through the silence directly behind her. She wheeled quickly to ascertain where the voice came from. There was a man directly behind her.

"Who the hell are you!" Shannon said, a little exacerbated.

"Maybe I should be asking you that. After all, you were the one in my father's office, and I am sure he didn't give you permission to be there." The man who spoke was short and stocky. He wore a thick mustache that covered his upper lip, and he was balding a little on the top of his head. His voice was fairly high pitched and he had a thick accent that Shannon couldn't place.

"I had permission from Fran." Shannon had calmed a little and had gained control of the quiver in her voice.

"For what?" He took a step toward her, and she retreated a little.

"That's not really any of your business." Shannon did not trust this man one bit and doubted he was really Anderson's son. The man looked more like a hired thug, and she had seen him before but couldn't connect that he was the same man who was eavesdropping into her and Marcel's conversation over dinner at Bensons.

"Let me give you some advice," he said coming closer still. "Dead lawyers should stay dead. Keeps everyone healthy."

"Is that some sort of a threat?" Shannon did her best to feign fear.

"Like I said it is some friendly advice. Pretty girl like you should stay away from a dirty business like this," he said, though they both knew this wasn't advice at all.

Shannon backpedaled to get away from him, but he continued to move forward at her. Her training taught her that it was time to get the hell out of the situation. She turned and ran.

"Hey, come back here," the man said from behind her, but not very loudly. Shannon hoped the man had felt she was truly afraid. His tone was the tone of a man who did not want to be heard by anyone else on the street. She needed to play the part.

Shannon wasn't the most fleet of foot to begin with, and in the shoes she was wearing, no one would mistake her for a track star. She knew that if he sprinted after her she would be caught in no time. What she needed to do was make a scene. The downtown area was fairly busy with foot traffic and a woman running from a man down here was bound to garner some sort of attention.

She took a peek behind her. Her stalker wasn't running, but he was still moving in her direction. She took out her phone again to call Marcel, but now her battery was dead. She continued running for another block until she was comfortable with the distance between them then slowed to a hustle. The rain started to fall before she got to the library. She maneuvered to the circulation desk all the while keeping a keen eye on the front door.

"Do you have a phone I can use?" She raised her cell as if to show it was dead.

The woman behind the desk pointed to phone at the end of a row of computers, there was a sign over it that read "local calls only."

Shannon punched in 4-1-1 and got an operator.

"Fran Hinkmeir in the public defender's office." She spoke in a robotic tone.

An equally robotic voice responded "One moment."

The terse voice that picked up on the other end was instantly recognizable to Shannon.

"Fran, this is Shannon McCarthy. Thanks again for your help. I have a question for you." Her voice was cold and emotionless.

"Shoot," the older woman responded.

"You got a guy in your office about 5'5 220 pounds, balding a little, with a thick mustache, looks kind of like a wrestler?" She described her assailant to the best of her ability.

"Nope, doesn't sound familiar." The lady didn't need much time to think about it.

"What about Anderson, does he have a son, dark black hair, mid fourties?" She added a couple more details to assist Fran in identifying the man.

"Anderson? Hell no, Anderson is a bachelor, never married no kids." Shannon loved the woman's short and sweet approach; her answer, however, was exactly as she expected, and Shannon wondered who the hell this thug was. She continued to keep her eye on the door, but the man never materialized . She doubted very much that he was standing out in the rain waiting for her. It was a regular down pour out there and she could hear thunder off in the distance.

43

United States vs. Arlen A. Fossum was the case that Shannon was reading when she finally got a call from Marcel at ten minutes after six. Fossum was a case prosecuted by Carmody from the Red Lake Reservation. He had secured a conviction that was later overturned on appeal. It was Carmody's last case. According to the Duluth News Tribune, Carmody's car had been discovered in a wooded area outside of Bena near Cass Lake on the Leech Lake Reservation. There were no clues to his disappearance, no suicide note, no body ever turned up, nothing. He had simply walked into the woods one night and slipped into a black hole.

Marcel had a lot to tell Shannon, information she was not privy to because it wasn't in the file at the public defender's office. Shannon wanted to tell him about the strange encounter with the heavy set man, but she didn't want to do it over the phone. She needed to see his reaction.

Marcel instructed her to hang tight; he would come down to the library and meet her. They could walk to the parking lot to get her car together, and then head to the canal for a bite to eat. Shannon hadn't eaten all day and now realized she was starving. She was glad that he was coming to her. Even with the rain she didn't really want to walk to her car by herself.

44

L ittle Angie's Cantina was a Mexican restaurant in the Canal area of Duluth. Duluth was an area that had been inhabited
by Native peoples since the Paleo Indians first
came to North America. Various Native Tribes
called the area home until the Ojibwe drove
the Sioux out in the middle of the 1600's.
The Ojibwe existed there along with French fur
traders until 1854, when the Treaty of Washington relocated them north to Fond Du Lac. The
relocation was due in large part to the interest
in possible copper deposits in Northern Minne-

sota. As it turned out, copper was scarce. What wasn't scarce were the iron ore deposits northwest of Duluth.

At the turn of the century, Duluth was home to more millionaires per capita than any other city in the world. The reason: iron ore. Duluth's port surpassed New York and Chicago in raw tonnage to make it the largest port in the U.S. The economic boom in Duluth lasted until 1960, when the city's population peaked at 106,000 people. The high grade iron ore mines gave out and along with foreign competition in the steel market, created a domino effect of plant closings that sent unemployment rates soaring to fifteen percent.

Duluth had to adjust to the downturn and did so through promotion of tourism. The hub of Duluth's tourism was the Canal Park area east of downtown. The Canal Park was home to the Aerial lift Bridge, a rare vertical lift that connected Canal Park with Park Point. The bridge was originally constructed as a transporter bridge, of which there were only two in the world.

Little Angie's Cantina was a Tex-Mex restaurant located at the corner of Buchanan and Lake in the heart of the canal. The atmosphere of the restaurant was phenomenal and the food and service were excellent.

Shannon and Marcel were seated at a window booth normally looking out at the bustle of the canal, though seeing outside today was impossible because of the rain. Their waiter had brought them a basket of chips and salsa. Shannon began snacking but Marcel left it alone.

While Shannon ate chips and salsa, Marcel started putting the pieces of the puzzle together. Carmody had prosecuted a case out of Red Lake in which he had won a conviction. It was a manslaughter case. A drunken brawl that had ended with the victim falling after a punch and splitting his head open. Nothing special about it that Marcel could tell.

Not long afterward, Henry Wright's murder case came across his desk. The police had originally suspected Antonio Eagle until young Marcel had come forward with his eyewitness identification of Ken Northbird. Carmody had buried the information on Eagle. He never turned it over to the defense, then disappeared somewhere in Cass Lake. Marcel wondered if his disappearance was a result of this case. Northbird's prosecution was then handed over to another attorney. Anderson in the public defender's office had suspected something stunk but was now out of commission. This was all stuff Marcy had told him at the US Attorney's office. There was more.

"It seems as though Carmody was involved in some extracurriculars in the Fossum case." Marcel talked low enough so that the other customers seated around him wouldn't hear. The restaurant was filling up with college kids ready to spend their financial aid checks on happy hour margaritas.

"There was an odd note about Carmody in another file I saw," Shannon added.

"Yeah what was that?" Marcel had ordered a garden salad which had arrived.

"His name was written on the corner of a note with an arrow drawn to the name Banks," she said.

"Clifford Banks?" Marcel took a bite of the salad.

"Don't know, but it seems like anything that happens on Leech Lake Banks has his fingers in it," she responded, and took a bite of her seafood burrito.

"So Banks lied." He had figured the snake son of a gun had been lying and now he wondered if Shannon had the same suspicion.

"I guess so."

"I think we should follow up on this. I am not saying we take the case, but it has my interest. This whole thing stinks. There is more going on that meets the eye and I feel like I was a pawn in everything that happened." Marcel's tone was very introspective. *Shit I am convincing myself here*, he thought.

"What about Vegas?"

Marcel had been considering that same question all morning. Since the fight he had felt invincible. *Superman could do both*, he assured himself.

"I got this."

"There is something else."

Now what? It seemed like the hits just kept playing in this thing.

"What?" He couldn't mask his trepidation. There was still a lot that had not been resolved between he and Shannon, and he didn't want to open any emotional doors just yet. It was becoming harder and harder.

"There was a guy who approached me after I left the PD's office. He claimed to be Anderson's son, but he was full of shit." Was that fear he heard in her voice? He had never once witnessed anything close to fear in Shannon.

"What did he want?" The idea that there was something nefarious going on was quickly becoming cemented in his mind.

"Wondered what I was doing in Anderson's office, warned me to leave the dead lawyer alone." It was definitely fear.

"Was he a PD?"

"No, I took off for the library and called the PD who helped me out. The public defender had no idea who he was, but I tell you what, he scared the shit out of me."

"Shannon, I think Banks is all over this thing; we gotta get Joanne up to speed," Marcel said in between bites. It was the reason he held his cards close when he met with Banks the night before. Banks was a hustler and Marcel knew right off the bat not to trust him. Marcel was also concerned about what type of involvement Tess played in the whole thing. She seemed to be the Chairman's new main squeeze and he didn't think he could trust her either. It made him thankful to have a friend like Shannon.

45

Joanne sat back on her sofa, completely exhausted. She hadn't slept in days, as she had run all over the Twin Cities lining up a major drug deal that she needed to deliver to Florence. Coming up with the cash was the first problem. She kept ten thousand in a safe deposit box in a bank near her home. A hundred thousand dollars, on the other hand, was a horse of a different color. The second problem was weight. One hundred thousand dollars worth of pills was also a lot of weight to physically move around. The final task was closing the deal with Marcel.

Coming up with the cash had been easier than she thought. The running all over town had frayed her nerves a little. Though it wasn't illegal to drive around with that much cash, any number of things could have happened that would have spelled disaster for her. If she were stopped by cops, they would be suspicious about the money. That could get her on their radar. Worse than being on the cops radar was getting robbed. If that happened, coming up with a second hundred thousand would be impossible. These people she had gotten the cash from were not the types to take their contract disputes to court. No sir, she would be in a shallow grave somewhere in the woods if that happened. Unacceptable.

The deal went down without any SNAFU's. The cash was delivered quickly, then moved out of the dealership to a location better suited for dealing in cash. Behind the scenes the money was all accounted for of course, though she was sure there was a heavy skim at all stops on the train.

Now all she had to do was wait. Her car would be delivered to her home address, the keys would be left in the ignition, and the drugs would be in the trunk. She was given a picture of the car, so she would be able to identify it if need be. Title itself would never switch hands. In two weeks she was to leave the car in a parking lot at the mall of America where it would be "stolen."

Joanne gated off her front drive and left her garage open. Her hope was that the driver would park the car in the garage. Her driveway was sheltered as it was. The house sat on three heavily wooded acres of land with two hundred fifty feet of lakeshore. The house was not visible from any of the neighboring houses, but all the same she didn't want any of her business out in the open.

Joanne had been so caught up in the drug deal that she had almost completely forgotten about the other aspect of what she was supposed to do for Northbird, which was get him out of prison. She had entirely forgotten about Marcel, Shannon, and Tavian for that matter. When the phone rang she had not been expecting a call from Shannon McCarthy. The call was a pleasant surprise. In fact it was a welcome distraction from the stress of committing the deeds that would either keep her in a position of status or send her away for a long time. She felt that this was what soldiers in their last day of a tour at the front felt like. It was a feeling of intense foreboding.

"Joanne, it's Shannon McCarthy from Wrongful onvictions class."

"Shannon, what can I do for you?"

"I spent the day with Marcel Wright. We took a look at some things relating to his brother's murder and came up with some information we would like you to take a look at." Shannon had a confidence about her that Joanne liked.

"So he is willing to work on the case?" Joanne hoped to high hell that she would like Shannon's answer.

"Yeah, he wants to investigate this further.C"

Joanne could hardly contain her jubilation. Everything was coming up aces right now. Maybe she could make it through this thing. Then she paused for a moment. *Why wasn't Marcel the one calling her?*

She didn't dwell too heavily on who actually called her, now was not the time to get bogged down with minutiae. Joanne didn't really need Shannon for this. It was fine that she was coming along for the ride, but she absolutely needed Marcel.

"Would you mind if I brought some of the stuff by tonight?" Shannon asked.

Shit! Joanne wasn't exactly sure how to proceed. She considered it for a long second. She was planning on receiving a major shipment of drugs within the next twenty-four hours, but she wasn't exactly expecting it to be dropped off in her living room. It was also entirely possible that the more normalcy she had in her life, the less nervous and therefore conspicuous she would be.

In the end, Joanne's curiosity won out. She wondered exactly what these two kids had gotten into. She assumed they learned about that greasy fuck Carmody, the original prosecutor in the case. Northbird had told her he was a corrupt son of a bitch who got taken off the case, and Joanne knew him by reputation.

"Yeah come on over, can you be here by six?" Joanne looked at her watch. It was four-thirty now. She wondered what time her package would arrive and then her mind came back to the present.

"Yeah I think so." Shannon didn't hesitate.

"Okay, you like Chinese? I will order up dinner."

"Yeah, love it," Shannon responded.

"Anything in particular?" Joanne continued.

"I don't like the really spicy stuff," Shannon responded.

"Sounds good, see you in a bit." Joanne hung up the phone having no idea that Shannon had more than one motive for coming over that night. Her mind had already wandered back to the drugs, like that was a surprise. It was where her mind was most of the time. An idea had formed somewhere deep inside her brain on her way out of the prison. The idea that Marcel would make the delivery had been the plan all along. But maybe, just maybe, it would be Shannon that would deliver the package to Marcel. That would give her an added layer of insulation. She admitted to herself that the plan was a little diabolical, but she wasn't interested in prison herself. She thought about Marcel; she thought he was the type of guy who could get this shit done for her. Joanne had always viewed Marcel as a bit of an oddity at St. Stevens. She had gotten to know his reputation during his first year. She had been on the admissions committee. She had read his essay, and she had been the one who brought him up to the board. He had lived a unique life, although he didn't mention having been the witness to his brother's murder. She was sure that outside herself and the principals involved in the trial, no one knew that fact about this young man. She believed that even Shannon hadn't known about that facet of his life until now. Marcel was a kid who had lived a hard life and thrived even in the most difficult circumstances. She knew that he could succeed amongst the sharks here at St. Stevens, and at bare minimum, provide a different perspective than the rich twits that filled her classes on a usual basis.

Joanne hadn't paid a lot of attention to the relationship Marcel had with Shannon. She often didn't pay attention to such things. Shannon had talked highly of Marcel last year, and Joanne had wondered if it was because she was banging him. After recent events, she didn't think that was true. Shannon certainly talked highly of Marcel because he was a talented thinker, not because of any sexual relationship. Joanne doubted very much if a sexual relationship existed. Joanne saw Shannon as being much too cold to have a relationship with a classmate.

In fact Joanne was pretty certain Shannon was a dyke. Definitely a lipstick lesbian, but a lesbian all the same.

Joanne had considered taking Marcel on as her own pet project even before Ken made his participation a requirement. She kept tabs on his progress from afar. She listened to Shannon's updates and she checked grade point averages. Joanne knew that he was near the top of his class after first year; good enough to grade onto the law review all though she also knew that he hated the idea of writing for it. Joanne could tell that Marcel danced to the beat of his own drum. He wasn't in law school to earn accolades and score a high paying job when he got out of school. He was doing it just to prove to someone somewhere that he could do it. She knew that was powerful motivation. She believed that if he ever looked deep into his soul, he would realize he was trying to quash his own self doubt not the doubts of anyone else. Joanne had known that no matter what Marcel had put his mind to, he would find success. She saw that in his work on the first assignment, and she knew that he was the right person to be working for the American Innocence Institute. She just hoped that things would go well for him in this en-deavor and he could continue on with his life uninterrupted. She was happy that he was in her class this semester. No one could accuse Joanne of being an altruist, however. Although she was glad that this was happening for Marcel, her bottom line was that he was a tool for her success. She wasn't about to fail; she had a retirement to start planning for.

46

C hairman Banks sat in his office contemplating his next move. Antonio was on
his way back from Duluth with a report
on what he saw. Banks figured he would be in his
office within a couple minutes.

There was always a danger of getting into
bed with an addict like Joanne but the deal was
exactly what he needed. Though he knew everything about the vending business he had gotten
into bed with, he was sure that they, Joanne in
particular, had no idea who he was. The money
from the prison racket was exactly the invest-

ment capital he needed to expand his operation and take the pharmacy legit. They had been producing prescription drugs for a few years now and selling them illegally, all the while working for FDA approval. Once the Leech Lake people were in the pharmaceutical business, the sky was the limit to what their economic infrastructure could become. His plan to give stock options to every enrolled member was a chance for them to obtain some financial autonomy. Having a company like that owned and operated by the tribe would give the people another source of pride that the state mouthpieces down in St. Paul would have a hard time deriding like they did the casinos. The beauty of white people was that they had very little shame when it came to the jealousy and contempt they had for the natives. There was a small group who couldn't stand for the Mdewakanton Sioux to be getting wealthy off of their casino and them not to be able to get their piece of the pie. It made him sick. But he did admit that casino's certainly had morally objectionable drawbacks. Pharmaceutical companies on the other hand developed drugs that saved lives. Hell what if the Leech Lake people's company was the one to develop a cure for cancer? Well that would be a feather in his cap.

Deals with people like Joanne were short term solutions to allow him to realize long term goals for his people. The one thing he held firm on was that none of the drugs produced in his lab would be sold to anyone on the streets, especially on the reservations. His drugs were designed for the sole purpose of easing the pain of those incarcerated in prison, or killing the white devils in the suburbs. The vending business had the perfect distribution setup. It was a major cluster fuck when that jackass Milton had put himself in a coma. Banks was now scrambling. Joanne's current moves were making him very nervous.

A knock on his office door yanked his thoughts from his scheme to the present time. It was Antonio.

"It's open."

The fireplug of a man who had scared the hell out of Shannon in Duluth walked through the door.

"It's not good, boss."

The report irritated Banks.

"What do you mean?" He asked, pushing the man for the details.

"Wright and the woman are working on Northbird's case. The woman was at the public defender's office. Carmody's name certainly came up." That was the last thing Banks wanted to hear.

"Any idea where they came from?" Banks asked

"Secretary at the US attorney's office said the Innocence Institute, they gotta be working for

Joanne," he responded.

"Good." It wasn't good news per se, but Banks never tipped his cards. If they were in fact working for Joanne, he might be able to have some influence over her. Especially since she was expecting a delivery of a hundred thousand dollars worth of pills that had not yet arrived.

Having Marcel Wright involved in this shit storm meant he had to be extra careful. Marcel knew things, that was a problem. If Joanne and the Innocence Institute got going on Northbird's case, there was sure to be press. A story like this was sure to go viral. That would in turn bring scrutiny to the reservation he absolutely didn't want right now, and quite frankly, Carmody was not a name he wanted to ever hear again. Marcel Wright had also struck him as a bit of a loose cannon after the fight. People like Joanne were simple to deal with. People like Marcel on the other hand, were much more difficult. Maybe it was time Tess got more involved.

Banks had learned that Wright was back in town only weeks ago from Tessa Whitebird, a woman whom he had had an affair with some years ago. He still saw her from time to time but after she had discovered his wife, the sex had stopped. He liked Tess and as such provided for her however he could. In return she would make some deliveries for him here and there. He was certain she didn't know what she was delivering; she thought she was shuttling used cars to their new owners. The car dealership was owned by a holding company he had set up out of the Uintah reservation in Utah. The Uintah provided the necessary protection for owners of the corporations so their identity could be kept secret. Even if someone had dug deeper into the corporation they would find that the controlling interest was held by the Leech Lake tribe. The car dealership was a legit business that masked something a little bit more sinister and it was untraceable.

"What do you want done about Wright and the woman?" Antonio asked.

"Keep an eye on them, we first have to figure out what their game is. If it looks like they are going to be a hindrance...well, then you get to do what you do best."

"You want me down in the Twin Cities?"

The thing that Banks liked about Antonio was his unquestioning devotion, it was why he had Carmody help out Antonio when he got into a jam. Antonio was about his business. He got done what needed to get done with a yeoman's work ethic. He was robotic in that once he was set on a task he wouldn't finish until it was over and he never questioned a directive.

"No, I am going to send our little honeypot in to handle this. If Wright's thinking with his dick we might be able to kill two birds with one stone, grab him as an asset and get rid of the woman all at the same time."

47

After everything that had happened over the last week, Marcel needed to unwind. The only place where he was free to do so was the gym, and that was exactly where he was headed. He hadn't worked out since the fight and there was a voice in his head begging for a grueling workout. There was something about an intense workout that cleared his mind; he supposed it had to do with the pain. The burning muscles, the heaving lungs, and the desire to go a little bit harder prevented him from living anywhere other than the moment.

Marcel wrapped his hands and went right into warm ups, not really looking around to see who else was at the gym. His warm up usually started with three rounds of jumping rope, at three minutes per round. During the one minute rest period he would drop in ten pushups. After the rope jumping, he went through an intense dynamic stretch. High knees, sprints, butt kicks, sprints, lunges, sprints, Frankenstein's, sprints, then more sprints. By the end of the sprints he had a good sweat going and he was catching his second wind. He grabbed a quick drink from the fountain and began getting his gloves on. As he was gloving up, an enormous black man walked through the front door. He had a gregarious smile and his eyes caught Marcel instantly.

"What up, Champ?" The man extended two gargantuan fingers in a victory formation.

"Hey, fam." Marcel nodded back.

Big Will was the guy at the gym whom Marcel was most fond of, though he hadn't seen much of him this summer.

"Congrats on the belt, man, that was a great fight." Will wrapped two arms around Marcel and bear hugged him off the ground.

Big Will got his name because of his stature; it was not an ironic name by any means. Big Will was a big guy. At six foot three and close to two hundred fifty pounds, he moved with a grace antithetical to his size. Will fought in the amateur division as a super heavyweight. He wasn't as skilled or as conditioned as Marcel but when Big Will hit you, you knew you had been hit. Marcel had sparred a few rounds with Will in the past to get him used to big punchers. Their first time in the ring had left Marcel with a black eye when he failed to slip a huge right paw. Marcel had overestimated his own quickness in comparison with the hulk of a man. Normally he was able to move enough to at the very least deflect the brunt of the punch. He had learned a hard lesson about humility that night. And defense. Since then the two had become close friends. Will had always hosted viewing parties for the big fights, and Marcel had been to his house a couple of times.

"Thanks bro. You were there?" It was more a rhetorical question. If there were fights, Marcel knew Big Will would be there.

"Come on, man, you know I was there." Big Will stepped back and looked at him "Damn man, it's been a while."

"Yeah, man where you been?" Will loved the gym, so not seeing him came as a surprise.

"Shit, man, I was working out of town this summer." Will beamed.

"Where?" Marcel questions

"North Dakota on the rigs. Tough work, but shit, here I am." He held his hands up in a whatever motion. "So I hear you know my lil cousin Tess?" The question surprised Marcel a little. He never knew that Tess and Big Will were related.

"Tess is your cousin?"

"Yeah, her dad and my momma was brothers and sisters." Will smile widened.

"Wow. I grew up with Tess, and her dad was never around. I guess that's why we never met?" Marcel wondered how much Will knew about him.

"Yeah, guy's a deadbeat man, I don't have any love for him. Shoot, I didn't even meet Tess until this summer. We kick it from time to time now, though," Will explained.

"See her lately?" Marcel asked.

"Yeah, we was just talking about you the other night. We went to the fight together, her and her scumbag boyfriend."

"Yeah, I saw her there." Marcel was delighted that Big Will thought the chairman was a scumbag.

"Hey fam, I am having some people over for the fight tomorrow if you want to come. She'll be there, I think she would like to see you. We gonna barbeque some shit up." Will smiled again. Outside of boxing, barbequing was Will's passion.

"Yeah, that sounds cool. What time you thinking?" Marcel asked.

Marcel found it was interesting that Big Will thought his cousin would like to see him. He wondered what their conversation had been. Marcel had wanted to catch up with her more but things really hadn't worked out. Now after his trip with Shannon, his involvement with Northbird's case, and his discovery in Duluth he really did have a lot to talk with her about. He wondered what she would have to say about all of it.

"Well shit, bro, I gotta get back to my work out, but I'll see you tomorrow night. Want me to bring anything?" Marcel thumbed the heavy bag.

"Hell no, we will have burgers, chicken, potato salad, and all the beer you can drink." He smiled that big smile again. He held out a fist for Marcel and Marcel hit him with a pound and then headed off to the heavy bags.

48

Tess got a call from the dealership telling her to drive a car over to Minnetonka. After she dropped the car off, her cousin Will would pick her up and she would go over to his house. Marcel was going to be there. Banks had asked her to get in touch with Marcel and get an idea of what the heck he was doing back in Minnesota. She had told Banks they were old friends, but she didn't think he knew exactly how close they were.

Will gave her a ride up to the Dealership in Blaine. The car she was delivering was a 2009

Buick Lesabre. She thought it was a pretty big car, a family car for sure. She had been delivering cars for the dealership for a couple of years. It was odd to her though, because the dealership wasn't like any other she had ever seen. It didn't really have any inventory. People didn't come in off the street and test drive a car, buy it, and then drive it home. Rather they would come in, meet with an agent, and give a description of the car they wanted. The price was agreed upon, and the car was delivered to them within a couple of weeks. The concept made little sense to Tess.

The car she was delivering was a four door model that was a hideous shade of gold. Whatever happened to the days of red, blue and green? Why would anyone buy this? The new family cars all had these ugly metallic tones, colors she didn't know the names of, nor could she describe very well. There was a GPS in the car with the delivery address already programmed in. These were a gift to the purchaser and they were always left in the car afterwards. The drive from Blaine to Minnetonka was exceptionally brutal this time of night. Tess absolutely hated the suburbs, especially the ones on the west side. There was always construction over here; the roads were always jam packed, and she didn't really know her way around. She was thankful for the GPS but it still took her the better part of an hour to get out to the house.

The GPS directed her to take Highway 7 out

through Minnetonka then turn onto Excelsior Boulevard. There were a lot of trees out here and it reminded her of home. The smell of the air did as well. It was a specific smell only people who lived near lakes could recognize. The air smelled fresher. There was an aroma of lily pads and leaves, fresh cut grass and the smell of the water that combined to contrast with the industrial smell of a city.

"I am definitely near a lake," she said to the rearview mirror. Farther in the distance of the reflection, Will was still behind her. Will drove a 1988 Firebird like the one in that old movie with Burt Reynolds. She thought it was a little lame but Will loved it. He kept it immaculate and parked it in the winter, which was when he took out his massive Dodge Ram pickup truck.

She took a left off Excelsior and followed the directions on the GPS. It lead her to a driveway that split into two directions. The first lead to a turnaround at the front of the house; it was gated off. The second branch meandered off behind the house and down a hill. Tess wheeled down the second until it was swallowed by the garage. She saw the garage door was open, only on closer inspection she wasn't sure it was a garage. It looked more like an underground parking lot.

"Must be nice," she sighed.

The door was open so she drove in. There was one other car inside the lot, a black Lexus.

"Now that's a sexy car."

Why would someone in this house want this car? It didn't fit this house at all. A budget sedan in a mansion of a house that clearly had an indoor pool. It also had three levels and this monstrous garage, not to mention a beautiful view of lake Minnetonka that couldn't be cheap. Tess didn't know that this was just one of the bays, not really the whole lake.

She pulled the car in, put it in park, turned the key off, left them in the ignition as ordered and got out of the car. Will had turned around at the top of the hill and was waiting for her. She walked up the hill and got in his car.

"Strange a house like this buying a car like that," she said to Will as she got in.

"Maybe it's for the guy's kid." Will's answer made sense and she let the issue go.

Another car was coming up the drive. This one was a BMW. Tess peered at the driver and saw a younger woman who bore a strong resemblance to the girl who was with Marcel after the fight. She wondered if it really was her and wanted to go back to get another look but thought better of it. She didn't want to get in trouble with work, but she thought she might mention it to Marcel when she saw him at Will's.

Will lived on the North side not to far off of Wirth Parkway, which wasn't a real long way from Minnetonka. He took 7 back to 169 North and then to 55 back towards the city. It took about twenty minutes to get back to his place, and there was a lot of work to do to prep for the barbeque.

"What time is everyone getting here tonight?" she asked Will when they were still about ten minutes away.

"Shoot, people could be there right now." Will wasn't kidding about that. At any given time there were usually between five and ten random people at his house. He had one of those big old houses with a lot of rooms and Will's personality was such that he attracted everyone. On a fight night there were upwards of thirty people in his place.

"Jayna will be there for sure, she getting the grill going. Probably Bunz, D, Ricky, Travon and his old lady, what's her name?" He paused. The characters Will knew had nicknames and aliases. No one went by their real name.

Bunz was Benjamin Bundy. He had played quarterback on Will's junior college team, and now worked for some insurance agency downtown. D was Drashaun Thomas, a guy that lived in the neighborhood. Ricky was Lee Steamboat, one of Bunz's coworkers. They called him Ricky after some wrestler from the 80's. Travon, who was actually Travis, was a stuffed shirt of a white boy who Will worked with. They called him Travon so he could at least be a little black. Travon's old lady was a really nice chick named Sarah or something like that. They were all good people, and Tess liked hanging out with them. Jayna was Will's girlfriend, or fiance. They had been engaged going on four years now and Tess wasn't sure she could call the woman a fiancé after all this time.

"What time is Marcel coming over?" she asked, more curious than anything.

"Could be here now, he didn't say. I am sure he will want to watch the fight." Tess thought that somewhere inside him, Will hoped that she would hook up with Marcel. She could tell that he really liked Marcel, not that it was a surprise, but Marcel was someone that Will looked up to, and with his personality and stature he didn't look up to many people.

"Cool." They pulled in to his driveway and she saw Marcel's motorcycle parked there, right next to Bunz' bucket, some sort of Chevy that was about twenty years old. She was excited and a little nervous too.

49

Shannon had just pulled into Joanne's driveway as the old Firebird with the enormous black man driving pulled out. The front drive was gated, and the other driveway to the back lead straight into a garage that reminded Shannon of a downtown parking ramp. Shannon almost thought she was in the wrong place until she saw Joanne come out of the house into the garage, and wave her in.

It felt a little awkward pulling her car into someone else's garage but it was so big that it didn't seem like a run of the mill garage. She pulled in next to the ugly copper Buick that was parked hastily next to a Lexus. Joanne thought it was an odd pair of cars.

"Did you have visitors?" Shannon thumbed the driveway behind her. She risked offending the woman whom she didn't know very well at all but needed some answers.

"Oh, they were just here to look at the LeSabre I am selling." Shannon could hear it was an obvious lie and wondered why she was being lied to.

"You're selling your car?" Shannon followed up.

"Its, uh, not actually mine, it belonged to my aunt who just passed away, we are liquidating her estate, this was hers. I am the executor." Another lie.

The conversation with Joanne was giving Shannon a real feeling of apprehension as well as suspicion. What Shannon knew about Joanne was that there was more to this woman than it seemed. What exactly did Joanne know? Shannon decided it was time to change the subject for now, but she would really be interested in taking a further look at this car. She took a quick peek at the license plate, hoping she could remember some of it later. The dealer plate confirmed Joanne's lies.

"I have our notes from what we found in the Northbird case. Ready to take a look?" She held up a manila folder.

"Come in, let's eat, we can discuss it over dinner." Shannon followed the woman out of the garage and up a set of stairs. The doorway entered into a giant kitchen with a granite center island that housed a stovetop and grill. The cabinetry in the kitchen was beautiful and the tile floor complimented exceptionally. How many millions did this cost? More importantly, how did a law professor afford it?

The floor plan of the house was open. The kitchen turned into the dining room separated only by the center island. There was a small oak circular dining table in the dining room with seating for four, though it seemed a little too small for the room. Beyond the dining room was a sitting room. The focal point of the room was a fireplace at the far wall that didn't look as if it had been lit in twenty years. Around the fireplace there were three uncomfortable looking pieces of furniture and above the fireplace was a wall mounted television. Shannon scanned for exits. An old habit.

Each took a seat at the table. Joanne had provided three cartons of entrees and two of white rice. One entre Shannon recognized as beef broccoli, the other was a chicken dish she wasn't familiar with, and the third was fried rice. Shannon absolutely loved fried rice. She slid the file over to Joanne and took a scoop of the rice from the container and put it on her plate, watching Joanne closely. Joanne took a little from each container and topped it off with some white rice. She opened a soy sauce package and sprinkled it over the plate, then opened the envelope.

As she read she took the first few bites of her dinner.

Hell of a poker face. Shannon observed a marked difference in her overall demeanor. She had been caught in the middle of something. Outside Joanne had been sweating, spoke in a fractured tone and minced her words. Now she was as cool as a cucumber. She took note of Joanne's ability to change faces so easily.

"Tell me about Northbird."

The two women ate and talked. Shannon explained what they had found; the mystery of Carmody, and the exculpatory statements. She also disclosed the stack of files the PD were concerned about as well. She left out the part about the heavy set man. That was something she wanted to hold onto until she knew more.

Joanne had several questions for her, some of which she was able to answer and some she wasn't. They discussed the case for about an hour.

"Excuse me, I need to use the restroom." Shannon politely demanded.

"Through there and to the left." Joanne pointed to the main entry of house, a spectacular foyer with a staircase leading up on either side. Shannon got up and went into the foyer and made a left. She looked back towards the dining room to ensure she wasn't visible from the dining room. She went into the bathroom and quickly went through all the drawers and cupboards. She didn't find anything, as she suspected. She removed the toilet paper from the holder and put it into the tank on the toilet. She then slipped out of the bathroom and headed up the stairs with as much stealth as she could manage.

She could hear Joanne cleaning up in the kitchen and knew she didn't have a lot of time. She made her way to the master bedroom and quickly shuffled through the drawers in the room, being careful not to disrupt their contacts too much.

50

While Shannon was rifling through Joanne's drawers, Marcel was at Will's watching the fight. Will's crew was all there. Will always traveled with a minimum of five people, but tonight there were closer to twenty. The crowd filled up his living room, spilled into the dining room and those revelers who weren't into the fight congregating in the kitchen. Will's living room was large enough to fit two sofas, both were filled. There were a couple women sitting on the floor. One of them had a toddler who was fixated on a ball he was playing with. Those in the dining area had arranged the chairs in order to have a sightline of the television. Will's living and dining area were separated by large double pocket doors that were broken. One of the doors stuck out of the pocket enough to obstruct the view from that side. Because of this, those folks in the dining room were squished together more than they needed to be. Marcel thought of goldfish.

The first fight of the night featured a middleweight from Boston with an undefeated record taking on a Rafeal Lopez, the man whom Marcel would be fighting in Las Vegas in the spring. Lopez had been in two world title fights; He won the first then relinquished his title in the second. This fight was for the vacant WBA title. If Lopez won, Marcel would be fighting for a world championship. Marcel navigated through the dining area, stepped over bodies and legs and finally made her way to a folding chair in the living room that had been reserved for him. The chair was positioned so that he would have a good view of his opponent, it also meant that others on the sofa behind him had to careen their necks a little to see around him. It wasn't an issue for anyone.

"Hey, you guys need to shut the fuck up." Will stood up and faced everyone.

"This is who the champ is fighting next," he continued on, embarrassing Marcel slightly.

"You're fighting this guy?" Bunz asked with

the excitement of a teenager. Next to Will, Bunz was probably the most star struck by Marcel. Having been a former athlete who didn't make it as far as he wanted, he had a great admiration for those athletes that had the opportunity to live their dream.

"You gonna be on ESPN?" was the next question. Several more followed. Marcel didn't have a chance to answer any of them.

"I thought I said to shut up!" Will interrupted them all.

A buzz of excitement rippled through the room. Marcel caught Tess stealing a couple glances at him. He saw her differently tonight. Their first encounter was frantic; she was a familiar stranger. At the gym she was his brother's girl and he was fourteen years old all over again. Here at Will's, they were on the same plane. I don't see her different, he thought. I see myself as an adult now, not a kid brother. There was something else, though, something he wasn't willing to admit to himself just yet. That seed hiding in the recess of his mind was this: maybe the reason he saw her different was because she was a threat and not the family she had once been.

Marcel was having a hard time focusing on anything but Tess tonight. She was an attractive woman for the most part, though she was showing signs of her age and the effects of a lifetime of poor nutrition. Every time the fight went to a commercial break his eyes would return to her. Had she been overlooked by a lot of other guys? The type of guys from good addresses with good jobs and direction. Though baggy and lined with the beginning of crow's at the edges, Tess still had magnificent eyes. Couldn't they see that? Why was it only the corrupted eyes of men like his brother and the chairman could see the beauty in those eyes? They were so deeply brown they were almost black, and there was a spark in them that Marcel could only describe as alive.

Tess wasn't overweight, but she wasn't fit like Shannon was either. Shit, what an asshole I am for comparing the two women, he thought. Marcel knew now that he had a crush on Shannon; he was seeing her in places she really wasn't.

I need to be watching this fight his inner voice spoke.

The fight lasted for only three of the scheduled ten rounds. Lopez exposed the prospect as a bit of a fraud, knocking him down in the first before finally obliterating him in the third. The prospect didn't have the power or the jaw to contend with a fighter the caliber of Lopez.

The excitement of the fights ending came to a crescendo when the fight was stopped, and as quickly as it built it went silent, with everyone looking wide eyed at Marcel. He was going to fight a guy that had just demolished his opponent in three rounds on ESPN and was now the

WBA world middleweight champ.

"He ain't shit, he is slow and not very accurate. All I have to do is move and counter," Marcel jockeyed, a move to reassure himself more than anyone else.

"You too quick for him champ," Will spoke definitively and the rest of the people in the room got in step.

Marcel's phone rang. Marcel saw that it was Jarvis on the line and got up from his seat.

"Jarvis." He held up his phone to let everyone know the reason he was going outside. Marcel went out through the kitchen to the deck in the back of Will's house and took a seat in one of the patio chairs.

"You see it." Marcel said, switching the phone on.

Jarvis began talking as the back door to the house opened and Tess came out. She gave Marcel a wink and an approving smile that let him know she wasn't going to interrupt, that she would wait for him so they could be alone for a little while.

It was the middle of September and the sun had already gone down. It didn't seem like that long ago that the sun was out until almost ten; it was a sign to all Minnesotans that summer was now over and the cold of winter was almost here. If the sun wasn't enough, the cool fall air was. The rains that had washed through the day before had carried with them a cold front. The ninety degree weather that had tortured them all summer had given way to a brisk fifty, almost too cold for his bike. He sat there on the deck talking with Jarvis, glad he had a sweatshirt. The street lights were starting to come on. They gave an enchanted quality to the evening.

"I agree," Marcel finished his conversation with Jarvis and hung up.

"So can you beat him?" Tess asked once Marcel was off the phone.

"Yeah, he is a guy that can be beat, he knows what it is like to lose. I don't. You can't put a price on that." Marcel was feeling more confident after talking with Jarvis.

"Yeah, I think you could kick his ass." Marcel could see her smile in the dimly lit Minneapolis night.

"Jarvis will have a good game plan." This was the fact that solidified Marcel's confidence after the beating he saw on ESPN.

"And what about you, what's your game plan?" Tess asked him.

"For the fight?" Marcel didn't think she was talking about the fight.

"No, for life, what are you going to do next?" The question was an honest one, but one he didn't expect from Tess. As kids, none of them really had dreams; they had never talked about the future. That thought made Marcel sad. The truth was none of them had believed they had a future, Marcel included. His brother's thinking had been correct. Henry hadn't had a future. The others didn't either. But now Tess did, and maybe he did too.

"Are you going to keep fighting, be the world champ?" she continued.

Marcel contemplated this question for a while. When he heard it like that, it seemed silly to believe that he, sitting here in North Minneapolis watching a fight on TV at the age of twenty- four, had any hope of ever being an undisputed world champion. Realistically he probably only had a couple years left before his skills started to decline. How many fights could he get in by the time he hit thirty? He would be twenty-five before he fought Lopez.

"I don't know. Maybe it's only a pipe dream at this point. I mean I am twenty-four years old and don't have any key fights under my belt." For the first time in his life he spoke with a raw honesty that he didn't even use in his inner voice.

"I think you can accomplish anything you put your mind to. Even as a little boy you were a pitbull. You got something in your head and you wouldn't stop until it was completed." Marcel could see affection in her eyes.

Marcel didn't really know what to say, but he didn't have to.

"And what about this lawyer stuff?"

"I don't know about being a lawyer. I don't know if I can sit in an office every day for the rest of my life, looking at computer screens and reading court cases." The thought of being a lawyer terrified him. It felt like prison. There was something about the rigidness of it all that scared him most. The unchanging scenery, and the inability to control his day that made him question whether or not he could ever practice.

"What? So no Law and Order for you? I hear you got your act together when it comes to all that courtroom stuff." He wasn't sure who that had come from but it was flattering nonetheless.

"I have my moments. It depends on what I am working on, I guess." He wasn't lying. There were facets of law that he excelled at without a doubt.

"You got any exciting cases now?" Tess asked.

Marcel's heart stopped for a moment.

Well, I guess I may as well tell her.

"Yeah, actually I am. I don't think you are going to believe me when I tell you who it is." Marcel wasn't completely sure how she would take it.

"Who?"

"Ken Northbird." The name cut the cool night air, saying it out loud sent a chill down his spine.

Tess didn't say anything. Marcel waited, ten seconds, twenty seconds. He became uncomfortable and thought about speaking again, then she responded.

"Ken Northbird! Are you flipping dense?" He could hear a building rage in her voice.

"He filed a petition with the Innocence Institute, he says he is innocent." Marcel tried to explain.

"Marcel, you saw him shoot Henry in cold blood right in front of you! How can you even think for one second he's innocent?" Her rage was turning to exasperation and he felt like she was probably on the verge of tears.

"You know Tess, after all these years maybe I made a mistake. There is evidence to suggest that it maybe wasn't him." If he couldn't convince her how could he ever convince a jury?

"Well if it wasn't Northbird, who was it?" she said through tears.

"You remember Antonio Eagle?" Marcel thought he saw her recoil when he said that name.

"Yeah."

"Did you know he was the first suspect the police had in mind?"

Tess stopped crying. Her face went from sadness and confusion to...*anger?* Marcel couldn't be sure. Something he had said had triggered something within her.

51

T ess' confusion turned back to rage. This rage was not directed at Marcel. This rage was directed at Clifford Banks. Antonio Eagle was Clifford's number one goon, and though she never considered herself a brilliant mind, she knew when she was being used. Clifford was using her as a pawn in a game she wanted no part of, especially if it came at the expense of Marcel.

Tess loved Marcel. She had loved him as a little boy back on the rez; he was family. She took care of him. Watched after him when his mom was too high to know she had a kid. After Marcel's dad went bat shit and ended up in prison, she had taken sole responsibility for him. Sure, Henry was his legal guardian, but she was the one who made sure there was food in the house and got him to school. Henry certainly never gave a shit about school. It was funny, she was only a few years older than Marcel and barely made it through school herself, but she knew that he deserved so much better than he got.

Tess now loved Marcel as an artifact from her past and a hope for a future whose prospect was quickly starting to fade as she approached her forties. Marcel had grown into a good looking man, strong and fit. He was making something out of his life; earning money as a professional athlete, but also investing in his future outside of the sport with law school. He was the type of guy who quietly gave back to his community by working with children and had a good heart. He was confident and people flocked to him. In Marcel she saw hope, and she desperately needed hope now more than ever.

For Tess, life had been a gradual downhill ride since the time Henry was murdered. When she was with Henry, she was on top of the world. He was powerful and he provided for her and her mom. They lived in a decent house and the bills were always paid. When he died they were no longer able to afford such a nice house. Though her mom worked for Chairman Bank's,

Micheal Poncelet

she wasn't making the kind of money Henry was hustling. In short order Tess had lost her entire family: first Henry, then Marcel moved to Colorado, and within a couple years her mom got sick. Tess spent two years caring for her before she finally passed away from cancer, leaving Tess all alone. The Chairman had taken care of her, and for a split second she thought that he could be her salvation. But that was fool's gold, like so much else in her life. Bank's had been married, and she had been nothing more than something on the side. He had no interest in taking care of her long term, so she had broken it off. The only reason she kept contact with him at all was because he was willing to pay for his indiscretion.

Tess moved down to the Twin Cities to live with her aunt and nephew. Tess' own sister was strung out, and she was unable to take care of the child. Drugs were an unpleasant fact of life, like mosquitos and sub zero temps. It made Tess sick that people had to accept that, but what choice did they have. Anyway, the boy lived with Tess' aunt, and now that her aunt was getting up in years, more and more of the care and support the boy needed came from Tess. Tess was struggling. It was a scramble to make ends meet. Tess had started nursing school, but had to drop out because she no longer had the time to take care of her aunt and her nephew and still pay the bills. Instead of making the good money that registered nurses made, she was a nursing assistant that made only enough to scrape by. Her aunt's social security check paid the rent in their shitty apartment in a Somali neighborhood that she thought amounted to a war zone, with shootings regularly and a stench that she couldn't escape.

Tess thought a life like this was no life at all. At thirty three years old, options were starting to run out for her. She couldn't see herself living in that same shitty apartment, subsisting on social security when she was sixty. She couldn't see herself living there at forty. The thought of suicide had been sneaking into her thoughts more and more every day. The payments she received from Banks kept her going. She stashed every one of them away in an account, hoping to heaven she would one day use it to finish school, or buy a house if she was too old to go back to school. That little stash was her suicide antidote for now.

Of course, that was all before she saw Marcel for the first time at the gym. The sight of him brought back all the old memories and created new possibilities all at the same time. Clifford had always had an interest in Marcel. Tess had thought it was because Clifford was a reformer and had a high opinion of the young boy who had broke the code and helped break the gangs on the reservation. That thought was reaffirmed after the fight when Banks invited him to return like a conquering hero. The information that she was hearing coming from Marcel right now painted a completely different picture, a picture that made all too much sense, given what she knew about Clifford's character.

Marcel said that Antonio Eagle was a possible suspect. If Eagle was in fact Henry's killer, then Banks' interest in Marcel would be more to protect his own asset than to welcome Marcel home. If Eagle had been the one who killed Henry, then Banks' certainly knew about it because Eagle didn't take a dump unless he had permission from Banks. It was entirely probable that Banks had ordered the killing. Tess knew that Banks wasn't above getting his hands dirty in the name of reform. Her mother had told her stories. Killing Henry and then sleeping with her was a whole new low, even for a guy like Clifford. She knew Eagle was capable. If it really was Eagle, she was in a dangerous spot.

Tess considered telling Marcel everything she knew about Banks, but wasn't prepared to do that just yet. She needed more information.

52

Shannon didn't find anything in Joanne's bedroom, so she slipped out and went down the hall, peaking in each of the doors. There were three more bedrooms on the floor. None of them had anything in them. At the end of the hall was another bathroom. She went in and locked the door behind her. First she pulled on the mirror to get to the cupboard behind it. Inside were several vials and containers, none of which was anything of any particular interest. Next she went through the linen closet. Inside was a wicker basket. Shannon opened the wicker basket and found a large ziplock bag that contained several pills. She opened the baggy and took out a couple of the pills and put them in her pocket.

Her expedition was interrupted by a knock at the door.

"Shannon?" It was Joanne.

Shit!

Shannon had been gone for a considerable amount of time and was also not where she was supposed to be. Her heart rate cranked up.

"Umm yeah, I went to the downstairs bathroom but the toilet paper was out." Shannon stood frozen in the linen closet. She doubted Joanne would come busting in, but if she did she was in deep shit. Little did Shannon know Joanne had just filled the toilet paper that morning.

"Oh, umm okay, sorry." She could hear Joanne walk back towards the stairs.

Shannon quickly stuffed the baggie back into the wicker basket and did her best to place it in the linen closet as she found it. She flushed the toilet for the sake of the ruse and washed her hands. She unlocked the bathroom door and made her way back down to the dining room. The table was all cleaned off, and the dishes had been put in the dishwasher.

"What do you want Marcel and I to do next?" Shannon spoke as if nothing happened.

"We will need to meet with Northbird, as a

group," Joanne spoke, Shannon felt like Joanne was doing her best to cover up her suspicions.

I wore out my welcome, I need an exit strategy.

"You know Joanne, I hate to eat and run but it is getting late and I have a pretty healthy drive home from here…" she just sort of trailed off.

"No worries, we will get to it tomorrow, get in touch with Marcel and let's set something up." It seemed Joanne wanted her out as much as she wanted to be out of that house.

"I'll show you out."

Joanne followed her to the stairwell down to the kitchen, and then down the stairs. Shannon knew better than to even glance in the direction of the Buick after her excursion through Joanne's house.

Joanne stood in the doorway of the garage and watched Shannon get into her car and back out of the garage. The sight of Joanne in the doorway staring out at her with the garage door closing between them made her feel a great sense of unease. She was getting a better picture of what Joanne was into and knew that everything was falling into place.

53

Tavian had watched the two cars pull into Joanne's driveway, but only the Firebird had left. The driver of the Buick was in the passenger seat. This was an odd development, so he decided to follow the car back to North Minneapolis.

He knew that Joanne was into something insidious. He had the basic outline now and he just needed a few key details to put the screws to her. Her handling of the Northbird case was completely out of character for her. First she had reviewed a case without the proper paperwork filled out. This had never happened before. Next she agreed to meet Northbird without any background research. Not only was this also unprecedented it was expressly forbidden as a matter of procedure by the A-I-I. Someone had gotten to her, but how and for what purpose? As of right now, he couldn't connect any of the dots to Milton or the pills. The most recent development, bringing in Wright, was also a highly unusual move. Outside the obvious ethical implications, there were also some purely moral issues that concerned him. Joanne's approach to Wright was cold and impersonal, not the act of someone working for the greater good, but rather someone who had a job to get done. That was typical Joanne.

There was a lot at stake and Tavian knew it. He hoped that the man and the woman inside this house would provide him clues. He had an assumption that this could be Joanne's drug connection. He wasn't exactly sure what role the car played in the whole thing. He doubted it was the delivery vessel for a small amount of drugs for Joanne's personal use, but it was certainly feasible that it was used to deliver enough for distribution. It was highly likely this was the major shipment that they had been waiting on for so long. If he could make a move on the two in the Firebird, maybe he could squeeze them just enough to get a warrant for Joanne's home and that car. He made a call to the field office and filled them in on Joanne.

Tavian followed them all the way, waiting for the smallest traffic infraction with nothing serious enough to warrant a stop and search. He ran the plates and everything came up aces on the owner William Curtis. He thought about getting a peak in the house but ultimately came to the conclusion that it was too risky. So he sat and watched, drifting in and out of his own thoughts until about eight-thirty when a man emerged from the house talking on a phone. To his surprise, the man was Joanne's student from the Northbird case.

How the hell was he involved in all of this?

If he had some sort of side connection to Joanne, that would explain her lack of concern for the moral and ethical implications. However, his reaction in her office seemed legit. If the man he thought was named Marcel had been acting, it was an award winning performance, and he needed to consider heading to Hollywood or Broadway. He was a future Oscar winner.

Could Marcel be pulling the strings somehow? Maybe he was supplying the drugs to Joanne? Marcel had connections to the man in Colorado. He certainly could be the one brokering the deal. Maybe Marcel was the kingpin. It didn't make sense. Marcel was new to the scene. Maybe he was simply a new employee. Whatever the situation, everything led back to the reservation. The reservation was the key to this investigation.

Well, well, well.

Shortly after Marcel exited the house, the driver of the Buick came out and took a seat next to him. Tavian wished he had ears on the conversation. There were answers abound in what the two of them were discussing. He watched them talk for about a half an hour before they got up and went back inside. The conversation was what Tavian had come to see. There were more pieces that he could use to fill in the puzzle. Now he had a decision to make: go back and keep an eye on Joanne or make an attempt to bring in the mystery Buick driver. Either way the end game was to get a look at that Buick. He hadn't slept in a considerable amount of time and didn't feel like he completely had his wits about him.

Think this through.

At this point he didn't really have any probable cause on the driver of the Buick. If he hung around his current location, he risked the Buick being disposed of. If he went back to Joanne's, he risked missing an opportunity to bring in a potential suspect he felt he had a good chance of flipping.

Call in the locals.

He picked up his phone and made a call to his agent in charge. They could keep an eye on the woman for the next twenty-four hours. He was heading back to Joanne's.

54

SAC Josef hung up the phone and reviewed all of the notes together. There were two new developments to digest. First the Northbird situation. There would be more to come on that case, but it wasn't a run of the mill operation. The second pertained to a Buick Lesabre delivered to Benson under some odd circumstances. It was enough to get a sneak and peek warrant. The warrant would allow an incursion into Joanne's garage to ascertain whether the car was in fact used in the traffic of illegal narcotics. There was enough probable cause for that. Josef wanted to act quickly, but he didn't want to tip Joanne off that she was being investigated just yet. He punched in the number for Kerwin Marshall, a Federal Magistrate for the District of Minnesota. He and Marshall had went to law school together and he knew Marshall would be a little more forgiving on the details of their probable cause than some of the others. Once the warrant was obtained, Tavian who had the car under his watch, would have the green light whenever the situation presented itself to enter.

His next course of action would be to find out where in the hell that car came from. He made a call to Paula Moreno in the fourth precinct to put surveillance on William Curtis and Tess Whitebird. The local police would be waiting to secure arrest warrants for them if Tavian turned up anything in the Buick.

Finally there was Marcel Wright. This kid just might be the key to finally bringing this ring down. He was smart and he certainly had a lot to lose. Interestingly enough, he seemed to have connections to every facet of the case. Maybe it was time to squeeze him a little and see which way he would go on this thing. Josef picked up the phone again.

"This is Josef. Let's put the screws to Wright."

He got the response he expected.

"No, I know, but we need to make him uncomfortable. If he gets nervous he will slip up.

If he is involved we will know about it right away. If not we pull him in, he definitely knows the players and we can put him to work. He isn't going to risk that title fight."

He listened to the response. He anticipated it. The time for patience had passed now it was the time to make a bold move. His guy in the field was not one for bold moves. He could make the slow play with the best of them but every once in a while needed a kick in the shorts.

"Look, we have been at this for two years, it's time to make our move. Go see Wright. Let's make this bust, and then you get to move on with your career. The promotion will be waiting."

55

The next day started off relatively quiet compared to the events of the last forty-eight hours. Marcel hadn't yet spoken with Shannon about her meeting with Joanne. He also hadn't spoken any more with Tess about Northbird and his brother. He had gotten up early for his morning run. When he stepped out the door of his apartment, he was greeted by a blast of brisk fall air. The cold front that had passed through had altered the weather of the city drastically. There was a heavy frost on the ground, and the temperature now that the sun was up a little was barely in the fourties.

Today is a day for Harriet Island.

It was earlier than St. Paul got going in the morning and the streets were still pretty quiet. He headed out past the Cathedral and down Kellogg into downtown. As he made his way past Crowne Plaza toward Harriet Island, he started to get the feeling he wasn't alone. He picked up the pace a little and took a quick peek behind him. His feeling was right; he wasn't alone. There was another man out for a run about a half block behind him. Likely a patron from the hotel. Nothing really to concern himself about. Marcel continued to Wabasha turned right and headed across the river. The man behind him followed.

Marcel crossed the bridge and turned right onto one of the paved trails that snaked out to the island. The man behind him continue to follow. Marcel periodically checked behind him; he had not yet approached nervousness, but now he was aware. Marcel devised a quick plan to weave around to see if the man was actually following him. When he took a right on the next path, and another consecutive right going back the direction he started, the man followed. This was confirmation the man behind him was much more of an issue than he originally thought. He picked his pace up again and headed toward the pavilion.

Marcel arrived at the pavilion ahead of his stalker and ducked into a cubby completely out of sight from the path. From his vantage point he got a good view of the man. He was certain that since he had the drop on the man he could handle whatever the man had planned for him. He just didn't want to give the man the initiative if he had a weapon of some sort.

As the man came into view, Marcel was hit with a feeling of recognition. It was Tavian Springs, Joanne's associate. The two had met the other day in her office. Springs hadn't said much. He just sat behind Joanne looking like a lackey or possibly a hired thug. Springs was a pretty studious looking fellow, and Marcel was certain he hadn't been viewed as a thug too often, outside of a few white people who always saw black men as thugs.

Marcel came out from his post and confronted Tavian.

"Can I help you with something, Springs?"

"What are you and Joanne cooking up?" Springs wasted no time.

"What are you talking about?" Marcel was starting to really dislike this guy.

"I know about the car," Springs shot back.

Marcel could now see that Springs' conditioning was nowhere near his own and if need be he could escape pretty quickly.

"Look bro, I don't have the first damn clue what you are talking about." Marcel was starting to show his frustration.

"Your girl, the dark skinned one in North

Minneapolis, dropped a car off at Joanne's house yesterday. A late model Buick, something Joanne would never drive," Springs explained.

"What are you talking about, bro? I don't know anything about a Buick, I don't have any dark skinned..."

Oh shit! Tess.

"Wait, are we talking about Tess, Native American girl?" Marcel asked.

"Could have been native, she dropped the car off and was picked up by a big black man driving an old Firebird." Tavian had finally caught his breath.

"Big Will? So you saw these two at Joanne's house? When?"

"Last night, I have been watching Joanne. I saw the two of them pull into her driveway. The girl driving the Buick. She drove around to the back of the house and then only the Firebird left, with her in the passenger seat. I followed them to see where they were going," Tavian explained.

"And you saw me talking with Tess on the deck." Marcel had connected the pieces a little earlier. He spoke now because he could tell Tavian felt uncomfortable telling him he was spying on them.

"Yes."

"Why were you spying on Joanne?" Marcel was starting to get the feeling that Tavian was a cop. He clearly had Joanne under surveillance.

Shit, am I under surveillance?

"Joanne is into some bad shit. She is a junkie, man, and if we aren't careful all our careers go in the toilet." Tavian had learned long ago that the best cover stories were ninety percent true.

"We have a case pending in Texas where we are days from freeing an innocent man who had been condemned to death. I can't allow anything she does to get in the way of that happening. Whatever Joanne is into could create serious problems," Tavian continued.

"What does any of this have to do with me?" Marcel questioned.

"I gotta know what you guys are into. What connections does your friend have with Joanne?" Tavian had a desperation in his voice that Marcel found a little disconcerting.

"Joanne's my teacher. As for Tess, I don't know anything about that. The first I have heard about any sort of connection between her and Joanne is right now from you." Though Marcel wasn't sure he would tell this guy even if he did know more. He certainly wasn't going to tip his hand to the guy about his suspicion that the guy was a cop.

"Look, if you hear anything, or see anything out of the ordinary, let me know. It is in both of our best interests." Tavian gave him a look that said everything else he needed to say. He turned and started his run back to the hotel.

Marcel wasn't exactly sure how to take the conversation but he thought it was time to bring

Shannon in on the whole situation. She was now as much a part of his brother's murder case as he was, and he wasn't going to be able to handle this situation alone. He walked over to a bench that looked over the river. River traffic was quiet this morning and there weren't any other people in the park. Across the river in the downtown area the traffic was picking up. The day was starting to get going.

Marcel took out his phone and scrolled through his address book for Shannon's number and banged out a message.

MEET ME AT HARRIET ISLAND ASAP

He hit send and waited for a response.

K B THERE IN 15

Shannon made it in less time. He had texted her an exact location where to find him.

"Marcel, how are you?" Shannon sounded tired but pleasant.

"Good, and you?"

"Good, you started the day early," Shannon said

Marcel looked down at his watch. He hadn't even thought about the time when he called. But now that she mentioned it, he realized it was only six fourty-five AM.

"Sorry, I didn't realize how early it was." Suddenly Marcel felt bad. His conversation with Tavian had spun him out a little and he wasn't completely in tune with what was going on around him.

"Oh no, don't worry about it. My guess is you have something pretty important." She was genuinely forgiving and Marcel was thankful. The conversation with Tavian was something he had to discuss.

"Yeah, I had an interesting run in with Tavian Springs. You know, Joanne's sidekick," Marcel replied "I think he is a cop."

"What? What are you talking about? When did that happen?" Shannon asked.

"Just now, he caught up with me here on the island." When he said this he realized that Tavian had to have had surveillance on him to know where he was. It wasn't as though he had been a creature of habit and ran through downtown every morning at five AM.

"What did Springs want?"

"He thinks Joanne is into something." Marcel didn't really know another way to describe it.

"Into something? What does that mean?" She sounded a little confused.

"Drugs, he has been watching her and saw something strange last night. He thinks she is going to screw these cases all up."

"How so?" She asked.

"He didn't specify, but he brought up something really strange to me." Marcel wasn't sure how much he was going to share. "He said he saw a car being delivered to her house last night, something really out of place."

"Interesting. Did he say anything more?"

343

"No, that was it," Marcel answered.

"What do you know about the car?" Shannon asked.

"Nothing, this was the first I had heard about it," Marcel responded

"Why did he think you knew anything about it?" Shannon continued the line of questioning.

"My friend Tess was the one driving the car that was brought to Joanne's house." Marcel considered leaving this part out, but decided honesty was his best policy in regard to Shannon.

"Interesting," Shannon said quietly.

Marcel desperately wished he knew what was going through her mind, but whatever it was he had to deal with it. He knew that Shannon was supposed to talk to Joanne about the Northbird case.

"You talk to Joanne?" Marcel changed gears.

"Yeah, she is ready to get going. She wants us to meet with Northbird, and to start getting a team put together." Shannon's voice changed again.

"She wants us to go to Colorado?" Marcel didn't like the idea.

"Yeah, she does." Shannon's response was compassionate.

"What do you think about Springs?" Marcel didn't want to get into his feelings about meeting with Northbird.

"I don't know. I haven't talked to him much," Shannon answered after giving it some thought.

"He's worried that Joanne is going to screw her Texas case all up. Why do you think he is worried about that?" Marcel questioned.

Marcel couldn't quite grasp how the drugs played into all of this. He didn't really know Tess that well anymore so anything was possible, but he seriously doubted that Will would be involved in any sort of drug trafficking. The appearance of the car was odd. What possible reason could Tess have for delivering a car other than drugs?

"I don't know, there has got to be more to Joanne than meets the eye." Shannon said.

Neither of them was aware of what was about to happen. Within a few hours, a chain of events would be set in motion that would alter both of their lives forever.

56

Tess was sitting in her Auntie's living room watching a Law and Order rerun when agents from the Drug Enforcement Agency and Officers from the Minneapolis police knocked on her door, announced their presence, and then broke through the door.

She had been up for a while, unable to sleep. Her mind kept swirling around Marcel. Seeing Marcel had brought her back to a happier time. Back when they were kids and they had everything in front of them. Being with Marcel had felt good. When she sat with him on the deck at

Big Will's house she hadn't wanted the night to end, but like everything else in her life it did.

Now here she was early in the morning with another conclusion in store. This finale was the end of her freedom. She had no idea why they were there but was sure she would find out shortly.

The agents were dressed like commandos. One of them was the biggest man she had ever seen in her life. He made Big Will look small. He carried a shotgun and had a mask on his face. He was the first through the door. While other agents continued through the house, he made his way to Tess who was sitting on the love seat in the den.

"Ms. Tess Whitebird, this is a warrant authorizing agents of the Federal Drug Enforcement agency to search the premises for illegal controlled substances." He handed her a piece of paper.

"It also authorizes us to detain you for a period of forty-eight hours. We are asking you to come with us. You have the right to remain silent, anything you say can and will be used against you in a court of law." The man's voice was deep and booming.

Tess realized that she was being arrested, though she didn't have any idea what for. She had never been involved in drugs in anyway. She had grown up in a cesspool of drugs and knew that the quickest way to end up in life's toilet was to get involved with dope. She had seen it time and again. She started to cry.

The DEA agents lead her Auntie and Deshawn down into the den as well. When she saw her aunt being led in by the men all of whom were armed and quite scary looking, her head started to swim. Things became blurry, and it felt like she was running out of oxygen. She collapsed into a puddle on the den floor.

57

Marcel and Will pulled up to a house in the 2700 block of Upton Ave. The house was fairly nice and the street was thick with old growth hardwood trees. Finding parking wasn't difficult, as most people either didn't park in the street or were at work this time of day. The North side was a working class neighborhood that had been plagued for some time with gang problems. This summer had been relatively quiet but it was still possible to hear gunshots in the neighborhood at night.

Marcel sensed something wasn't quite right

about the house but wasn't sure exactly what it was.

There were four steps that lead from the sidewalk to the top of a small but steep hill. The house was set back from the street about a hundred feet. Marcel and Will made the walk in silence, Will taking the lead. When the pair got within ten feet of the house, Will turned as if sensing Marcel's growing feeling of unease or possibly to signify his own level of discomfort with the house.

It sat completely quiet. There were no lights on at all inside. Normally this wouldn't be unusual during the day, but the sky was covered in dense wet clouds and rain seemed imminent. It was very dark for the time of day. Even with no lights, at the very least Marcel thought he would see a glow from the television.

"Tess' Auntie always has the TV on, and doesn't go anywhere, something ain't right," Will finally spoke as they got to the door.

He pushed the doorbell and waited. There was no response. He pushed it again.

Nothing.

Will took a firm hold of the knocker on the door and gave it several hard raps. There was still no answer. One of the neighbors had made her way over to the steps down at the sidewalk. She was an elderly black woman wearing a housecoat.

"Cops came and took them out of there." Her

voice was barely audible to the men. She was shouting but her vocal chords had grown week over her eighty years.

Marcel walked down the path toward the steps so he could hear her better.

"Excuse me?" Marcel asked the elderly woman.

"I said, the cops came and took Marlene away, her niece and grandson too," she repeated, a little perturbed at having to do so. Not so much at Marcel, as it was at her own frustration with her failing body.

"When?" Marcel followed up.

"This morning, I had got up to let the dog out, and saw them busting through the door." She repeated what she had seen a few hours earlier.

"Minneapolis police?" Marcel asked.

"Don't think so, they were all wearing DEA jackets." The old woman stood looking at the two men. Will had now come up behind Marcel to better hear the conversation.

"DEA?" Will finally spoke.

"You boys didn't have anything to do with this did you? Marlene is a good woman, takes care of her grandson you know, she don't need this kind of trouble." The old woman shot Marcel an accusing eye.

"No ma'am, I am a lawyer working with Marlene's niece," Marcel lied a little feeling guilty.

"And I am his associate." Will, ever the comedian, added to the lie.

"Well I guess they need one now, don't they?" The old woman shot them a suspecting glance, first one then to the other.

"I guess we should try and track them down." Marcel spoke to Will for the old woman's benefit.

The two men excused themselves and bounced back down to Will's car. Marcel opened the passenger door and got in. His hands were shaking a little. He flashed back to his conversation with Tavian the day before, and he knew that Tavian was behind this. Marcel was scared that he was going to get caught up in something he wanted no part in.

Will got in the driver side and put the key in the ignition.

"What's going on Will?" Marcel turned and looked at Will.

"I don't know, man, this shit is crazy," Will answered.

"No, I am saying what are you guys into?" Marcel made sure he was crystal clear this time.

"What? What the hell are you talking about?" The accusation had pissed off Will but Marcel didn't care.

"Look, some guy, I think he was a cop, tracked me down at Harriet Island the other day when I was out running. Said he watched you and Tess drop a car off at Joanne Hart-Benson's house in Minnetonka." Marcel laid the evidence out on the table.

"First I don't know any Joanne Benson. Second, Tess has been delivering cars for Blaine Auto for a couple years now. All she does is drive used cars to the people that buy them. It's all on the up and up." Will spoke with the pain of his friend's accusation readily apparent.

What neither man knew was at that moment the DEA was out looking for Will as well. They were raiding his house not far from here and had he been home he would be sitting in a federal detention cell himself.

"Think Tess knows what's in the cars?" Marcel dialed back his accusatory tone. There was something going on at North Metro Auto that wasn't quite square, and he needed to get to the bottom of it.

"What's in the cars?" Will answered, however Marcel thought the question was more internally directed.

"Have you ever heard of a car dealership that delivers used cars to people? It's a front. My guess is there is a treasure trove in the trunk, most likely drugs." Marcel vocalized what Will was coming to in his mind.

"Ah shit." Marcel could tell that Will was now contemplating Tess' involvement. Will started the car and pulled from the curb. The two men headed back to the east towards I 94.

58

Marcel and Will pulled into the parking lot across from Blaine Auto, the used car dealership that Tess had been delivering cars for. She had worked for them for at least two years that Will knew of, and now it turned out she was possibly delivering drugs.

The dealership was unlike any that Marcel or Will had ever seen before. It was an office in an office suite building. There were no cars parked outside, nothing to suggest it was a car dealership.

The two men sat and watched as agents carried out boxes from the office. They had arrived too late to find out any information on their own. Tess' situation was now firmly out of their control. Marcel wondered to himself if his own apartment was being poured over by federal agents at this very moment. After his conversation with Tavian, he wouldn't be surprised if they were there right now. Marcel decided they should go take a look and instructed Will to head over to St. Paul.

It took slightly over a half hour for the men to make the drive from Blaine to St. Paul. Will drove by the apartment building twice before stopping, just to ensure the feds weren't there before they went in.

The apartment looked deserted so the men parked on the street about a half a block west and walked back towards the building. Marcel led, Will not far behind. They entered through the front and eased up the stairs. They looked and listened for anything that would suggest a search warrant was being executed on his apartment. Nothing. They continued up the steps to Marcel's door. They stood outside for a moment, listening. There wasn't any sounds from the inside. Marcel took out his key and opened the front door.

Inside the apartment looked nothing like as he left it. It was trashed. Books and papers were strewn about the room, drawers were emptied. Marcel's first thought was that the feds had already been there. The more he saw of the destruction in the apartment, the more he began to believe he was the victim of a break in. His suspicion was confirmed when he saw the broken glass laying on the floor by the door to the fire escape. Whoever had been in his apartment had broken in the window and let themselves in. But why? He didn't own any expensive electronics, jewelry, or really anything worth breaking in to steal.

He went into his bedroom and saw the destruction was consistent with the rest of the apartment. The papers from his work desk were scattered everywhere, and he considered whether there was anything on his desk that could have been targeted.

Marcel quickly began gathering his papers, looking specifically for his file on Ken Northbird. It was gone. His notes and all the information that he had gathered in Duluth, all of it was gone. Who would take something like that? Who would have an interest in the case? Outside of Joanne, Shannon, and Tess, who would even know he was involved? Except Tavian Springs, and he was pretty sure a federal agent wouldn't break into a private residence and steal a confidential legal file. Unless, of course, Springs really wasn't a federal agent, but he would have access to the files anyway. All he had to do was have Joanne ask for them. Then something in his mind triggered Shannon's encounter in Duluth with the strange man who had followed her to the library. Could it have possibly been this same guy? Marcel thought it was time he get a hold of Shannon.

"Will, man, this is going sideways fast. If the Fed's have Tess they are going to be on to you too. You should probably get out of Dodge." Marcel turned to his friend.

"You think the Fed's did this?" Will asked.

"No, this wasn't the Fed's. This is about me, Will, you're a good dude and you need to get as far away from me as possible." Marcel demanded.

"That's not how I roll."

"Will, I am serious. I got this. For Tess' sake you need to lay low, find out all you can about what is going on with her and the second you can, get her out of here. Please!"

Will considered him for a moment. Then nodded in acceptance. He hugged Marcel then said, "You need anything, call." Then left out the fire escape.

59

Antonio Eagle had gotten the information his boss had asked him for. Clifford Banks was more than a boss, he was a mentor and a father figure. Antonio hadn't ever known his father, who was a member of the White Earth band. His father was home only on long weekends; he worked on the pipeline, which kept him away for long periods of time. Life had been pretty good as a small child or at least to the best of Antonio's memory. They had a nice place to live, there always food on the table, and his mother had seemed happy for the most part. That was until his father had been killed in a car wreck on his way back from North Dakota. Antonio was only five years old at the time. His mother quickly disappeared into an alcoholic haze, and he was soon fending for himself. That was when Clifford Banks came along. Clifford found him sleeping in the park. Antonio's mother had gotten drunk, locked the door to the house, and passed out all before he got home from school. Antonio had been seven. He didn't know what to do so he walked to the park and played on the jungle gym until he had gotten tired and he had laid down to rest his eyes a little and had fallen fast asleep. When he woke up, he was in Clifford's house.

Clifford had given him a ride home the next day. Clifford went in and had a stern talking to with his mother, and he instructed Antonio that if he ever needed a place to sleep or needed something to eat to come see him. A few years later Antonio moved with his Auntie to Red Lake. He had lived there with her and his younger cousin Jamie. He saw Clifford once in a while. But when he had snapped at school and plunged a knife into a classmate's neck and needed to get the fuck out of dodge, Clifford had been there to help.

Antonio didn't consider himself to have a temper. However, when a course of action needed to be taken, he didn't have any problems following through to the end. His classmate had

359

been an asshole who had stolen some things from his locker: a couple of cassette tapes and some pens and pencils, nothing of any real value. The value wasn't the point, the point was fucking with him in any form or fashion was not allowed. The way of life Antonio had grown up in was that once you have been fucked with you continue to be fucked with. A knife to the neck insured that the asshole would not fuck with him anymore, nor would anyone else in school be inclined to fuck with him. He was, however, in a heap of trouble but lucky for him he had Clifford.

Clifford brought Antonio down to Cass Lake and smoothed over the incident. His classmate had lived and Clifford made right with the family. He didn't really know what all smoothing over the situation entailed and frankly he didn't give a shit. He wasn't scared to go to prison. Even as a kid, his life was shitty enough that he couldn't see prison being worse. In prison he wouldn't have to worry about finding a place to sleep or something to eat, and he felt confident he could handle himself if anyone tried to fuck with him. And if he couldn't, he would be dead and it wouldn't matter anymore.

In return for saving his life he had to do some work for Clifford. Most of the time the work involved roughing up some drunk who didn't take care of business, or teaching some deadbeat a lesson about stealing from the casino. One such asshole had a problem getting drunk and sitting at a bus stop near the school and harassing kids as they left. After multiple warnings by tribal police and a stern warning by Clifford failed to have any effect, Clifford called in Antonio who smashed the guy's nose to oblivion along with breaking bones in his hands, arms, and ribs. He was a bloody pulp who learned quick to listen to Clifford's warnings and to stay at home and get drunk. Word got out about that incident and Clifford's warnings started carrying a lot more weight everywhere on the rez.

Antonio wasn't much on school. He didn't really give a shit about math or science, but he could bust a skull with the best of them. He had always fancied himself some sort of mob enforcer, like Joe Pesci in Casino, though he knew the jobs Clifford sent him on were small time. Small time until he was sent to deal with Henry Wright, at least. Wright was a piece of shit snitch who was going to bring down Clifford's entire empire. Antonio had walked up to the snitch in broad daylight and shot him right square in the head. The feeling of shooting the man in the head wasn't what he anticipated. He always got a rush of adrenaline from busting a skull and he thought killing someone would likely make him cum it would be so damn exciting, but it wasn't. Not to be misunderstood; he wasn't a blubbering pussy, bawling his eyes out about an innocent life lost. No sir that was not the case. He didn't feel an ounce of remorse, but it just wasn't the rush he was hoping for. It felt like brushing his teeth.

Antonio believed that Clifford continued to fix things for him because Antonio needed him. Clifford was ruthless, but he didn't care much for getting his hands dirty. Antonio had fixed it for him then went back to Red Lake. He was in Red Lake when he caught that big shot lawyer from Duluth screwing his little cousin.

Antonio had been working as a custodian on the night shift at the high school. He had come home early from his shift around ten o'clock to find the sorry son of a bitch, higher than a kite face first in his cousin's crotch. His fourteen year old cousin's crotch that is. Antonio knew that there was right and wrong in this world. Most of the time he couldn't tell the difference, but when he saw this, he knew that it was wrong. His cousin had been a witness in one of the son of a bitches cases and he had taken a fancy to the little Indian girl. Antonio had known about the expensive gifts he had given her but when confronted, she insisted she was still a virgin and nothing was going on. She had apparently been lying, and Antonio was as sure as shit not going to let the pencil necked son of a bitch get away with molesting a child in his damn house. He had snatched the son of a bitch by the collar and hammered him across the head with a beer bottle that had been sitting on the table. It had knocked the son of a bitch silly but not out. Antonio then dragged the bastard kicking and screaming out back by the woodpile, gave him a solid boot to the balls that had dropped him to his knees. Next Antonio pulled out his .40 Ruger P95, put it to the man's forehead, and pulled the trigger splattering blood and brains to hell and back. He then took the ax leaning against the woodpile and turned the son of a bitch into about ten different pieces. The toughest part was to get his torso into small enough pieces to be manageable. After the ax work, Antonio took the son of a bitch parts over to Skip Clouds and fed them to his dogs. Skip Cloud had about ten malnourished Shepherds and Rottweilers over at his place and they made quick work. Antonio laughed at the thought of the dogs shitting son of a bitch for the next two weeks.

After taking care of the son of a bitch, he had to take care of his car. Antonio drove his car down to Cass Lake and ditched it in the woods out by Bena. After ditching the car, he hitched his way back to Bemidji where he stopped into slims to get a beer and figure out what to do next. Six beers in and he still wasn't sure really what to do, so he called Clifford. As it turned out, Clifford had been overjoyed. Clifford had wanted the son of a bitch dead himself. Apparently the son of a bitch had been involved in the investigation into the Wright murder and had been the one who kept Antonio's ass out of jail. Clifford explained that the son of a bitch was a loose end they didn't need. Clifford was always talking about loose ends. Antonio didn't give two shits about any loose end, but he'd be damned if some fifty year old man, some fifty year old white man, was going to fuck his little cousin in his house. It didn't really matter that it really wasn't his house, it was his aunt's house, but as long as he was living there it was his.

Over the years Antonio had done a lot of work for Clifford. A little bit of everything, not just breaking bones. He had gotten good at killing. He guessed that came with practice, but killing wasn't all he did. Sometimes it was scaring people and sometimes, like today, it was search and recovery. That's what Antonio called it, anyway. It sounded like something Navy Seals would do. He had always thought the Navy Seals were real bad asses and now looking back at his life he had sort of wished he had become a Navy Seal. There isn't much more he would enjoy than stomping the life out of one of those towel headed terrorists over in the Middle East. Had he known a little more about it at the time, he certainly would have joined up. It was the only real legitimate career for a killer.

The most recent job was an especially important one for Clifford. These two assholes had been digging up dirt on shit that needed to stay buried. If this wasn't enough to let them know to leave well enough alone, then he guessed the next step would be to put one of them in the ground. This morning he had gone to the young guy's apartment, broken in, and taken the file on Northbird that Clifford was interested in. He had also trashed the place in the process, just to send a message to the shithead that he needed to come correct in a big hurry. He had considered bashing the little shithead's skull in right then and there. That hadn't been okayed by Clifford, so he knew he had to exercise some restraint.

60

Tess had been sitting in the interrogation room for the better part of nineteen hours. She was exhausted, hungry, and in dire need of a bathroom break. The bastard kept coming in and out of the room with different pieces of paper that meant absolutely nothing to her, asking her questions she didn't have answers to. She knew they were trying to break her and, to be honest, had she known anything at all she probably would have given it up much sooner.

The agent questioning her was a good looking black man named Tavian Springs. He had known a whole boatload about her, that was for sure. He knew about her connection to Marcel, that she had driven a car to Minnetonka the other night to some woman named Benson, and they knew about Blaine Auto.

Tess had told them she had no idea that the cars had drugs in them. She had told them that she had delivered between fifty and seventy-five cars in the last couple of years. She doubted they believed her story, but she was honest when she said she had no idea the dealership was a front for trafficking. Hearing it come out of her mouth she barely believed herself, though it was the truth. The thing they were trying to get out of her now was who was in charge. A question she could answer.

"Tess, we just have a few more questions for you, then you will be free to leave." The man spoke in a gentle voice

"How did you get the job at Blaine Auto?" he asked.

"I responded to an ad in the paper looking for drivers and got hired." The statement wasn't a lie but wasn't the complete truth either. There really had been an ad, and she really had responded. Her response was at the direction of Clifford Banks, who had been helping her land a job shortly after their affair.

"Who was your boss?" The man continued the interrogation.

"I don't know," Tess answered, though the absurdity of it all was still swirling around the room.

"Tess, after all this time, you are still going to bullshit me? I mean come on. You sit there and assume I am a complete idiot and that you can tell me you don't even know who your boss was and I am just going to sit back and say okay you're free to go, thanks for the cooperation?" This was not a rhetorical question the man sat waiting for an answer.

"I know it sounds silly..." she was interrupted by the interrogator.

"It sounds like a damned fairytale. I don't think there is anyone in America that doesn't know their boss. Who do you get up in the morning and hate if you don't know your boss?" The question made sense to her, but she didn't want to say.

"Look, I had a phone interview with some guy named Tappas. I can't remember his first name. A couple days later I got a call saying I got the job. I needed to pick up a car from the dealership and take it to the address programmed into the GPS. I was told to find my own ride home. I stopped in to the office where a teenage kid handed me the keys and I dropped off the car. A couple days later I got a check for fifty bucks and so it continued just like that." She was sure that the interrogator could hear the conviction in her voice.

"What was the teenage kids name?" The man continued the questions.

"I have no idea, he was a goofy kid that stared at my tits. I didn't sit down and have a conversation with him, just got the keys and left." She was starting to get anxious and wanted to escape.

"Sit tight, I will be back." And with that he got up and left.

61

There was a buzz on campus when Marcel walked into school on Monday. Marcel's life had been an out of control roller coaster for the last couple weeks, but he needed some normalcy. He didn't think he was going to get it here tonight, though that was what he had hoped for.

The news was all over. Joanne and her colleagues at the American Innocence Institute had gotten Esteban Diaz free. He walked out of the Polunsky death row unit this morning at seven AM a free man. Joanne had been the face of it all.

Marcel was a bit surprised she hadn't been arrested yet. This meant that Tess hadn't flipped.

Or didn't know anything?

Marcel hadn't seen Joanne since Tess had been arrested. He hadn't seen Tess either. He assumed she was remanded since he couldn't see any way she would be able to post bail. If she hadn't been released then she definitely hadn't cut a deal. Tavian was also nowhere to be seen. Marcel had thought that pretty telling. Tavian for all intents and purposes had disappeared.

There was other news as well, or at least what passed for news at St. Stevens Law School. In other parts of the country it was called rumor, but not here. He supposed that in this instance since the rumor was true that it was okay to call it news. The fact that no one had bothered to confirm the notion was an entirely different story all together.

He received no less than six congratulatory greetings, three from students he had never seen before. Word was going around about his big score on the last Wrongful Convictions assignment. They had also heard about the case he was about to be working on. He doubted his classmates knew the backstory and didn't really care. He was sure someone had been talking. Everyone seemed to know that he and Shannon would be working to set free convicted murderer Ken Northbird.

He made his way to the basement. Shannon

was waiting for him just outside the classroom. He hadn't seen her since they last spoke on Harriet Island the day his apartment was broken into. It was good seeing her again. He couldn't help but think back to the beginning of the year when they had shared that first kiss. That moment had disintegrated with their lives continuously moving forward and now they barely had time to speak.

She stood outside the doorway, her hair pulled back, dressed simply in a pair of blue jeans that fit perfectly and a St. Stevens University sweatshirt. He saw in her the raw beauty that he had noticed the first time they met during orientation. There was a determination about her that flowed from her appearance. She didn't need a lot of makeup, designer clothes or Coach bags to feel good about herself. Her self confidence was drawn from a deeper feeling of self-worth. He wished he had a better grasp of that self-worth in his own life.

"Hi, Shannon. What's going on?" He greeted her when he was close enough to still use a quiet voice that wouldn't interrupt anyone else around him that was now coming into the lower level of the school.

"Joanne needs to meet with us right away." Shannon's cool appearance gave way to a frantic tone.

She walked toward him, grabbed his hand and lead him out of the building to the parking lot.

"Get in." Shannon directed him into a Buick Lesabre.

Was this the car?

Marcel hesitated, instinctively he looked around to see if agents were waiting to pounce. It was quiet. There were some students walking around campus but no one with their eyes on them. He opened the car door and got into the back seat.

"Marcel, thanks for joining us." Joanne sat in the passenger seat.

Shannon hopped into the driver's seat of the car and started the engine.

"I don't know if you guys have heard, but Esteban Diaz was freed this morning." She paused, waiting for their acknowledgment. They both nodded and she went on.

"An important part of the A-I-I is public relations, similar to the US strategy in Vietnam. We want to win the battle of the hearts and minds of the people. We do that we gain influence over those running for elections; we can change the laws from the inside." She took a sip from her coffee mug and continued.

"Following up Diaz with another big win would do as much for the institute as any case we have had since its inception." Marcel was starting to see the showman in Joanne. It was a part of her he didn't like.

"Therefore, we have to get going on Northbird. We are all going out there tonight; I have a visitation set up for you tomorrow with North-bird." The words hit Marcel like a ton of bricks. He wasn't expecting to have to ever deal with Northbird face to face.

"What are we going to meet with him for?" Shannon asked, as if sensing Marcel's unease.

"You guys are the face of this case. You have to get in and get your hands dirty a little bit. Get to know the case from the other side."

"What about classes?" Marcel finally found words.

What about the DEA?

"I have spoken to your professors. They all agree that the Northbird case will be your number one priority. You can turn in related work product for credit in your other classes."

We are going to be traveling across country in a car packed with drugs. No way, I am not doing this. How can I get out of this?

Marcel couldn't come up with an answer.

"What are the specifics?" Shannon asked.

62

Three hours later Marcel, Shannon, and Joanne were on the road to Florence in Joanne's Buick. The plan was to check into a hotel in Denver when they got in. The three of them would make the trip to Florence in the morning. Ron Aristman would handle all the prison protocols. After the meeting, Joanne would fly back and Shannon and Marcel, along with Ron, would start assembling the team in Colorado. They could delegate authority as they see fit. Ron would sign off on anything Marcel needed. Joanne provided him with an A-I-I credit card to cover his expenses.

The trip itself took a little more than sixteen hours, most of which was a boring drive through Iowa, Nebraska and Eastern Colorado that Marcel sweated out nervously. It wasn't until just outside Denver that he could finally catch a glimpse of the Rocky Mountains he had left not all that long ago and he finally relaxed a little bit.

It was just before midnight when the trio finally got into town and checked into the hotel. The room reserved was at the DoubleTree downtown, and they all headed off to their separate rooms. He was surprised when there was a knock at the door.

It was Shannon.

"What are you doing here?" Marcel was pleasantly surprised. He slid the chain safety latch out and opened the door.

"I am not going to sleep. Wanna go see what kind of trouble we can get into?" She ignored his question.

Marcel regretted not showering, but there was little he could do about it at this juncture. He grabbed a polo shirt from the closet and put it on while she was standing there.

"One second." He excused himself to the bathroom where he took a quick shot of mouthwash and put on some deodorant. Shannon followed him in but walked past the bathroom to the window.

"What do you think of the mountain view?" She asked.

"Don't know, didn't look out," Marcel responded, spitting out the mouthwash.

"Pretty dark, I couldn't see anything." She turned and walked toward him as he came out of the bathroom area.

"Let's go," she said, and lead him out the door to the elevator.

The two of them hopped on and took it to the ground floor. Their rooms were only on the third floor and normally Marcel would take the stairs but tonight he wanted to get out of the building as quickly as he could. He wanted to get out on the street and smell the cool mountain air.

They walked for a few blocks and found a nice sports bar adjacent to the Pepsi Center. It was one of the few places around still open at midnight on a Monday night. The football game had just gotten over and there were still several people inside discussing the game over their beers and mixed drinks. A group of college aged kids were playing pool at the only table in the bar. Marcel and Shannon took a private booth and waited for a server to come around.

"This is a dangerous case isn't it?" Shannon asked.

"I think so. The mustached man in Duluth, my apartment being broken into, the possibility that Joanne is being surveilled by the cops," Marcel answered as frankly as he could.

"But you're still here?" Shannon asked him.

"Yeah, I guess I am." It was something he had thought long and hard about.

"Are you dangerous?" It was an honest question and Marcel knew that she was asking about more than just this case.

"No, I am not."

Maybe I am.

"Why did you agree to drive that car here?" Marcel asked.

"This is a big case, the stakes are too high," she answered.

"What if that car is full of drugs?" he pressed.

"I know you've done dangerous things before, Marcel. So what if it is?" Shannon looked carefully at him.

"That is a dangerous move." He shrugged.

"What about the tattoos, isn't that dangerous?" Shannon pointed to his left arm.

Marcel thought about their conversation in St. Cloud. About how he avoided these questions before. The time for avoidance had ended when he decided to pursue this case.

"We never got to talk about this before, but I think it is important for you to know. I know you know about the tattoos. I know you know about gangs." He had a hard time looking at her, but caught her eyes once and knew that he was getting a fair hearing.

"Like I said before when I was a kid, I was involved in some dumb kid things. I guess you could call it a gang. I mean, we got our ink, we did dirt. Yeah, my brother and our friends were a crew, maybe back then we were dangerous. But I moved on a long time ago." He had a hard time holding back the emotion.

"Gave up gang life to become a prize fighter?" It was an honest question.

"A lot of people think boxing is violence. Nothing could be further from the truth. Violence is an expression of rage, rage has no place in boxing. Boxing is about control, violence is the lack of control. Boxing requires discipline, violence destroys discipline. Boxing was the entity that removed my rage and prevented me from being a violent man," Marcel explained.

"So, you were violent before boxing?" she asked

"That's not me anymore. Understand, my brother was the gang, he was the shot caller. I loved my brother more than anything. You have to understand, we weren't terrorists, we were kids trying to survive and we did what we had to. Am I proud of that now? Absolutely not, but it made me who I am today. So...." he trailed off.

He hoped that Shannon heard his pain and the conviction in his voice. He was talking about something in which he truly believed for right or wrong. He hoped that she liked him all the more for it.

"Marcel, you know you can tell me about it, right?"

"Not tonight," Marcel answered.

63

Marcel was awakened by a knock at the door. He looked at the clock and it was a few minutes after eight. He went to the door and opened it without looking out through the peephole expecting to see Shannon but found an older man instead.

"I am Ron Aristman. I was instructed to drive you to a meeting." The older man was gruff but polite.

"I thought you were leaving at nine?" The truth was he thought he was going to be traveling with Joanne and Shannon. He had no idea who this guy was.

"Plans changed."

"What?" Marcel was confused.

"You and I are headed to the prison. Joanne is taking Shannon to meet with a potential witness."

Marcel didn't like this sudden change of plans one bit. He didn't know Ron Aristman from Adam. For all he knew this could be some kind of set up. Luckily Shannon was already up and joined them in the doorway of his room, which was held open by the older man.

"Good morning, Ron."

"Good morning, Shannon." He nodded back at her.

"You know Aristman?" Marcel directed to Shannon.

"Yeah, we met last summer." She smiled.

"Did you know about meeting with a witness?" He questioned.

"Yeah, sorry, I thought you knew. I am not going to the prison. You and Ron are going to meet with Ken." Shannon sounded distracted.

Marcel couldn't figure how there could be a witness to meet with here in Colorado.

64

Clifford Banks sat in his office reviewing the file on his desk that Antonio had prepared. He didn't like what he saw. Tess had been arrested for delivering the car. She hadn't mentioned him yet or the tribal cops would have already tipped him off. That was good news. He believed that she would hold out. There was another problem, however. Antonio's name had shown up in one of Carmody's files. If Wright and his cooz started checking into Antonio it would lead right back to him. Banks knew they were in Colorado right now. Antonio had just become a loose end.

Clifford knew Antonio well. He knew that there was no way that Antonio would ride along peacefully with the feds. Any encounter would be his last stand. With Blaine Auto having already been raided by the feds, the wheels would be in motion. It was time for Clifford to start anesthetizing everything. This was going to be the fire sale of all time. Everything had to go.

Banks thought long and hard. It would probably be good to isolate himself from everyone. Tess would have to be the patsy on this one. He loved Tess, more than any woman he had known before including his wife. But Tess had gotten high and mighty about his status as a married man and for political reasons, child support reasons, and alimony reasons he was not about to leave his wife. He wasn't about to stir a pot that didn't need stirring, so he had let her go. Really she had been the one who made his mind up for him. If she wouldn't have been so damn haughty he wouldn't have been able to kill her. It was hard enough as it stood, but she was a money pit who no longer gave it up so it was a move he could at the very least justify.

Tess wasn't the only one. He had to get rid of Joanne, too. Joanne had no idea who he was, but he certainly knew who she was and with Marcel's help the two of them were smart enough to connect the dots, especially if Northbird started flapping his gums to Marcel. He didn't have a plan for her yet, but he certainly had one for Marcel. He was going to be joining his brother in short order and Antonio would be able to handle it all.

He called Antonio into his office.

"I need you to go to the cities to bail a woman out of jail. When you get her out, call and I will give you further instructions." He looked at Antonio for a moment. There was a moment of sadness in his heart that quickly vanished. Antonio was a pure sociopath. He had no feelings, no remorse, and Banks was certain he really didn't have a soul. A man born of the devil. Clifford had taken care of the boy at an early age. His mother was a drunk who couldn't take care of herself much less this little boy, but the boy's father had been a good man. The two had been good friends, playing on a basketball team together at Cass Lake and making a run to the all rez finals. Antonio Eagle Sr. had been a hard worker and had supported Clifford's election as chairman. He had done a lot of work to help sway support amongst the Natives who were members of the unions. For that Clifford was grateful. Looking after the kid was the least he could do. Watching the kid grow from that scared little boy into the heartless killer he had become scared Clifford a little. He was still a young boy when he had nearly stabbed another kid to death for no apparent reason while the two were playing at school. Clifford had got him out of the shit and made things right with the family. He assumed at that point that his debt to Antonio's father had been repaid. Then after Whitefeather had been murdered, Antonio cleaned up some loose ends for him and Banks was now indebted to him once again. This begun a good working relationship where Antonio did the dirty work and Banks did what he could to cover it up. He particularly thought Carmody was a good piece of work. That had gotten several federal agencies involved, but by that time Eagle had perfected his craft and was nearly untouchable. However, he was quickly becoming a liability because of Wright and would make the perfect fall guy to take the heat for Blaine Auto.

The thought that the dealership was now offline had initially been a huge pain in the ass, but he was so close to FDA approval that he was fine with it. The illegal operation had run its course. It was time to shut down and go legit. As long as the feds believed that Eagle was the head of Blaine Auto, the secret would die with him. Most likely he would be killed during his apprehension by authorities, but if he wasn't, there wasn't anything the feds could do to get him to open his mouth. A fact Banks learned long ago was that if a man didn't have a soul there wasn't anything he could be tempted with. Antonio Eagle had no aspirations in life. There was nothing he wanted and very little he enjoyed outside of killing. The feds could try and squeeze him, they could offer incentives and plea bargains, and he wouldn't take them. He didn't give a damn about freedom or prison. Antonio believed that there were people that needed to be killed in prison just as bad as the people he had killed that weren't in prison.

Eagle would be more than happy to kill Tess, and Tess being murdered by Eagle would further bolster the belief that he was behind the Blaine Auto charade. He now needed to make a couple calls to his friends out in Utah to straighten out a little paperwork to put the icing on the cake for the feds.

If he played his cards right, Marcel could be dealt with at the same time. What Banks didn't know was that Marcel's business in Colorado was going to cause him huge problems. Had he known Benson a little better, he would have known that she was a junkie and wouldn't have been smart enough to avoid getting pinched.

65

Tess had sat in a federal holding cell in Elk River for a little more than four days. She had been arraigned and charged with trafficking illegal prescription drugs. The feds were still working on her to give up her supplier and her court appointed lawyer was putting pressure on her to do just that, but she wasn't about to mention Banks and she didn't have anyone else to give up.

She had gotten word from her lawyer that Clifford was sending someone to get her out. She no longer trusted him, but she was sick of sitting in this hole. She had gotten word from the guards that her bail had been posted and she was going to be released within the hour.

When she walked from the jail she expected to see Clifford waiting for her, but he wasn't there. Instead it was Antonio Eagle. Her heart stopped, and she got a sick feeling in her stomach. Antonio was not the type of guy who acted as a chauffeur. She though about what Marcel had told her about Antion possibly being the man who killed Henry and got seriously scared but didn't know what else to do.

"Where is Clifford?" she asked.

"Get in and I will explain." He directed in a cold voice that scared Tess even more. She didn't know what else to do so she acquiesced.

"You can call me Eagle," He instructed in the same heartless voice.

She got in the car and they pulled out of the parking lot onto highway ten.

"Clifford Banks instructed me to pick you up," He said not looking in her direction.

Neither of them noticed Springs follow them from the parking lot.

Eagle's phone rang and he fumbled in his pocket, causing him to swerve into the next lane nearly sideswiping a minivan.

"Boozhoo," Eagle answered. Tess was unable to hear the voice on the other end.

"Eyuh," Eagle continued to speak in Ojibwe.

"Ninishi?" A silence.

"Eyuh." He hung up.

Tess wished she would have learned her language better. She knew that he had answered in the affirmative twice but didn't know what nin-ishi meant.

"Where are we going?" Tess asked.

The man didn't answer for a long time. This was terrifying. It seemed to her he was thinking of an answer because he didn't want to tell her the truth.

"We are going to meet up with Clifford. He is going to tell you what the next move is." His voice never wavered and he still hadn't looked at her.

She knew that she wasn't the knockout she had been at eighteen, but guys like this still had a hard time keeping their eyes off her tits. The little bastard at the car dealership had only conversed with her tits in the time she knew him. She had a thirty-five-year-olds body, and maybe she hadn't lived the easiest life but she still had great tits and a dirty old scumbag like this was sure to take a look, that she was certain of, unless he had some other plan for her.

What could that be? Chopping me up in little pieces and leaving me in a ditch?

Her initial fears were on the verge of engulfing her when a calmer voice cut through the cacophony of terror inside her. Clifford would never hurt you, it said. Clifford loves you. Sure Clifford loves you, but you haven't given him any since you found out about his wife? The fear voice spoke up again.

What man is going to keep pissing away money on a lollipop that went dry? This is the end, missy, this is where Clifford finally cuts off the pipeline and shores up any possibility of a leak.

No, this is crazy. Clifford isn't going to have you killed. That would implicate him in this whole thing. He simply sent Mr. Personality so that he wouldn't have to worry about the guy charming her pants off and getting a little taste of the goods Clifford himself couldn't get. Likely the man next to her was a queer, and that's why he hadn't taken a peak at her tits. That certainly would explain the porn stache.

The fact that they were heading back to the Twin Cities gave her some solace. If Eagle was going to end her life in a blood bath, he would have turned off 10 onto one of the country roads outside Elk River. He would then drive her out in the woods or to some abandoned cabin. He wouldn't take her to a population center where witnesses were abound and could easily identify the wreck of a car he drove and give and them ample opportunity to see his face.

They continued to drive into the Twin Cities, exiting on Central Ave and turning south. They drove until they reached 694 and entered onto the eastbound freeway. They barely got to speed before they exited almost immediately on Silver Lake Road. At the stoplight on top of the hill her driver took a right and traveled down Silver Lake Road through several stop lights until they got to 39th AVE and the Silver Lake Village. The car waited for the light to give a green arrow and it made a left, traveled down a block to the second of two blue duplexes. The garage door opened on the two car garage and the driver pulled the car in and closed the door behind them.

"Come on inside, hungry?" Eagle asked.

"Famished, jail food sucks. Ever had it?" she responded, trying to get more out of him.

He said nothing.

The door opened into a split level house. She followed the man up the stairs to an open floor plan. The living room area was above the stairs. Directly in front of the stairs was the kitchen, and to the left of the kitchen was a dining room separated from the kitchen with a breakfast bar. To the right of the kitchen was a stairwell that lead up to two closed doors. She figured they were most likely bedrooms, and a bathroom. To the right of the stairs was a room that looked out over the living room. Tess surveyed the entire floor plan for possible escape routes. She couldn't be sure what was going to happen in the short term but she knew she needed to get out of there sooner rather than later.

"Have a seat." The man pointed her to a sofa in the living room.

The decoration in the house was Spartan to say the least. There was nothing on the walls of any room. The living room had a sofa, an uncomfortable looking chair and a television on a stand. It was an old style tube television, that seemed small in comparison to the standard fifty inch TV's most people had.

In the dining room, there was a table with two chairs. Nothing else. No clutter, no mail, no empty ice cream pails, nothing. The entire place gave her the creeps, just like Mr. Mustache.

He walked into the kitchen and opened the fridge.

66

Tavian pulled into the driveway across the street from the blue duplex. He certainly didn't like the look of the place. He made a call to check the title owner of the house; it was a rental owned by the man who lived on the other side of the duplex. He got a number and dialed it on his cell phone. There was no answer. Tavian felt the man in the car was a serious player in all of this. He made another call, this one to the local police department to run a check on the license plate of the vehicle that pulled into the garage of the duplex.

The registered owner's name was Antonio Eagle. Eagle did have a criminal record, but most of it was petty stuff, drunken assaults and some theft, nothing suggesting drug trafficking. It was also the same Antonio Eagle who was the registered agent for Blaine Auto in Minnesota according to the Unitah Tribe in Utah.

Tavian weighed his options. He had enough probable cause for a warrant but something bad could happen in the time that it would take to run it through the proper channels. On the other hand, he probably could justify breaking down the door based on the totality of the circumstance and his reasonable fear Tess' life might be in danger.

The duplex had a fence around the entire outside of the lawn. Behind the duplex was an apartment building that might provide him a better opportunity to see anything inside the house. That could shore up his suspicions. He didn't want to blow this one. They were so close.

He got out of his rental and double timed it up to the apartment buildings about three blocks from where he parked. He surveyed the apartments and selected one with the correct vantage point. He then found the building manager who said that the particular apartment was occupied. The two of them went to the apartment and knocked on the door. The apartment was occupied by a young Somali woman who spoke no English. The apartment manager said something to her in Somali and she let them in. She was in the midst of cooking in the kitchen and paid them very little mind. There was a unique smell to the food that Tavian couldn't place and instantly hated.

Tavian and the manager made their way to the balcony where he took out a pair of high powered binoculars and focused them on the duplex. The shades were drawn everywhere in the house with the exception of the sliding glass door that connected the deck to the interior of the building.

There was something disconcerting about what he saw. There was nothing in the house, no microwave, no dirty dishes in the sink, no clutter of any sort on the island. There was a table and two chairs in the dining room but other than that there was nothing. This house wasn't a residence. It was also unlikely that the house was a mere safe house. No this house was for more sinister purposes; this was a sterile house used to disappear problems. Tavian knew he needed to get over there quickly or Tess' life would be in serious peril.

He didn't bother thanking the apartment manager or the occupant. He bailed out the front door and high tailed it to the fence. He made the fence with a single bound, something that reminded him of the old Superman cartoons, and skipped up the stairs of the deck. He made a quick call for backup, then he drew his .40 caliber glock. In full stealth mode he peeked through the window. He was just in time to see Tess being lead up the steps, most likely toward the bathroom where she would be executed in a soundproofed bathtub. Tavian checked the door and by some wild stroke of luck it was open. He slid it quietly and let himself in.

The girl was crying and pleading with the man to not hurt her. Her pleas were falling on deaf ears. Tavian moved with catlike grace up the steps to the bathroom door. It was closed, so he kicked it in with his gun ready to fire.

Eagle was startled and unable to take a good aim. This didn't stop him from whirling to the door with his gun drawn. Tavian fired once, striking Eagle square in the chest and knocking him back to the wall in front of the toilet. Eagle's gun went off. Tavian saw the muzzle flash and heard the bullet whiz past him. The crack of it breaking the sound barrier shattered Tavian's eardrum as it buried itself into the wall.

"Drop the gun, DEA!" Tavian shouted, pure adrenaline pumping through his veins. There was no response from Eagle, who was lying unconscious on the floor and quite possibly dead. Tavian's bullet entered his chest very near his heart.

The woman in the tub had began screaming and was now completely hysterical. Tavian didn't pay her any mind, walking past to check on Eagle and secure his body. He first pulled the gun from Eagle's hand, then checked for a pulse. He couldn't find one; Eagle was dead. He then turned to the hysterical woman in the bathtub and reached out a hand to her. She scurried into a little ball in the corner of the tub, panicked.

"Tess, Agent Springs, DEA." He tried to calm her.

He reached for her again, this time with both hands. She was fighting him, her arms flailing wildly a blather of sobs and hysterical no's coming from her mouth. He finally got both arms around her, but not without taking a couple solid shots to the face however. He hoisted her from the corner of the tub and held her for several seconds, running his fingers through her hair and trying to calm her.

"You're okay, you're okay," he spoke, trying to reassure her.

It took several moments but the woman finally quit fighting him and just collapsed in his arms a sobbing puddle, thankful for his arrival.

67

Marcel sat across from Ken for the first time since they had faced each other in court more than a decade ago. Ken had aged considerably more than Marcel anticipated. Ken picked up the phone first.

"Marcel Wright, the man who put me behind bars." Ken's voice was cold.

"Ken." Marcel nodded.

"I never killed your brother, you know?" Ken voice quivered slightly.

"I know that. I know it wasn't you. I am sorry for what I did."

"Are you sorry about what you did to Harold Stone too?" Now the quiver in Ken's voice was gone and his words were a dagger to Marcel's soul.

"What? How could you possibly know about that?"

"You and your idiot brother had no idea did you?" Ken shook his head.

"No idea of what?" Marcel was in shock.

"That Harold's little brother saw everything. He saw your faces, he saw you pull the trigger."

Marcel's heart stopped and his stomach jumped up into his throat. He was speechless and didn't know exactly what to do.

"Why did you do it?"

"For Henry." The response was automatic and after he said it, he realized that he made a mistake.

"Because Harold knew that Henry was stealing pills from the factory and selling them, and Harold was going to tell Banks."

Marcel sat in silence.

"That's why Banks had Henry clipped," Ken continued.

"Antonio Eagle did it," Marcel said, making the connection after all these years.

"Tell me this, why me?"

Marcel said nothing.

"You owe me an answer, you owe me that much."

"Buckley. He must have known about that beating you gave me. I was a kid; I wanted to make you pay." Marcel dropped his head.

"Yeah, well, now I am going to make you pay." Ken stood up and Marcel's head snapped to follow. Ken turned to the guard and though he could no longer hear Ken he read his lips.

"I got it."

Shit, it was a setup. I gotta get outta here.

68

Shannon and Joanne sat in a parking lot of some abandoned factory in Commerce City. A black Ford excursion pulled up and parked next to them. A sturdy man with a crew cut hopped out and approached the window.

"You that scumbag Northbird's gal?" he asked Joanne with a gravely smoker's voice.

"Yeah, you the dirty C.O. he told us so much about?"

The man smiled, revealing a hot mess of crooked teeth and plaque.

"I can show your girlfriend there just how

dirty I am, if she thinks she could handle it." He leaned in the passenger window and winked at Shannon. His breath reeked of cheap whisky and gingivitis.

"How about you get your shit and just get out of here?" Joanne moved her hand toward his face to shove him out of the car.

"Take it easy, lady, I was just trying to be friendly."

Joanne popped the trunk. The man walked behind the car and started digging in the trunk. Shannon watched him through the rearview mirror.

"Buddy!" The C.O. motioned to his crony driving the Excursion. A man with a shaved head and swastika tattoo on his forearm got out. Joanne shot Shannon a look. Shannon shook her head.

They carried two heavy boxes each from the back of the car to the Excursion. When the boxes were loaded the skin head went back to the drivers seat but the greasy C.O. turned to Joanne.

"You ladies wanna come back to Buddy's place and party?" He raised his eyebrows in anticipation.

"Fuck off..." That was all the C.O. could hear her say.

An explosive whomp whomp whomp of a helicopter's rotors suddenly drowned out all the sound underneath it. Dust and trash started blowing and swirling all around them. The C.O.

Micheal Poncelet

looked at the two women in the car a befuddled look on his face. He had no idea what was happening.

When the connections in his booze soaked brain finally fired correctly, the confused look was replaced with anger. He turned to run but there was nowhere for him to go. A helicopter came up over the building and an armada of Denver police and unmarked federal law enforcement vehicles raced into the lot to encircle both of the vehicles. Shannon's phone rang.

"Hello," she answered barely able to hear over the sirens.

"Shannon, get out it's a setup." Marcel was barely audible over the noise.

"Too late."

404

69

orthbird had been a model inmate for his stay at Florence and was afforded more privileges than the general population. He had approached the FBI directly after his first conversation with Clifford Banks. He had written a letter to Banks about his plight and the chairman had responded. There was one caveat. Northbird had to do some work inside the pen for Banks. This was a risk that Ken was not going to take. He wanted out of this hell on earth and now had a potential bargaining chip, so he made a call to the FBI and was put in touch with Special Agent Buckley. That had been three years ago. Buckley had instructed Ken to go along with Banks to help him gather evidence. In the interim, Banks had played games with him and he got tangled up with that crooked son of a bitch Davis. Then, out of nowhere, Harold Stone's brother had shown up with a plan for how to get Marcel Wright and get out of prison. Buckley was dead and there was some new woman turning over old rocks on the reservation. All Ken needed to do was make the call. So he picked up the phone and called Special Agent Shannon McCarthy.

70

2007

Northbird was led in and took a seat across from Shannon. He looked at her for a considerable amount of time before picking up the phone. Shannon thought the look was of a man contemplating the entire existence of the world. There was an overwhelmed look in his eye, fear and gratitude, hatred and excitement all wrapped into the package that sat before her.

Northbird gave Shannon a nod of acknowledgment and began to speak.

"Thank you," Northbird spoke, relieved.

"I need you to answer a few questions for me," she spoke and set down her digital recorder.

"Anything."

"Henry Wright."

"Look, I swear, I didn't have anything to do with that murder. I wasn't anywhere around that night."

"Okay, so what proof can you offer?" Shannon responded.

"I know who the real killer is. I know the motive, you guys will have to put it together." Northbird looked at Shannon.

"Tell me the story," she said, also not breaking eye contact.

"Antonio Eagle killed Henry Wright, he was working for Clifford Banks." Shannon nodded.

"You know Banks?" Northbird asked Shannon.

"I am aware of Banks," she said.

"Banks is the Chairman of the Leech Lake Band of Ojibwe. He is a powerful man, he gets what he wants and he wanted Henry dead." Northbird spoke clearly and slowly.

"Why did the chairman want Henry Wright dead?" Shannon asked.

"Drugs. The Chairman was diversifying tribal business into prescription drugs. He had a factory that was manufacturing a synthetic opioid called Narcodone that was supposed to replace Oxycontin. It was a synthetic that was supposed to be way less addictive and cheaper. The problem was that FDA approval takes years and Banks didn't have the capital to sustain the factory throughout the trial phase."

"How do you know this?"

"Harold Stone had just started working as a shift manager at the factory. His brother told me about all of it. Henry Wright was also working for Banks, that's where everything went to hell."

"What do you mean?" Shannon prodded.

"Henry was skimming pills. Harold found out about it while he was in prison and used that info to leverage himself out of the pen and into a security job with Banks. Henry, his brother Marcel, and two other guys rolled up to a trailer house and killed Harold right in front of his brother. I am not sure if Banks knew about Henry skimming or if he was retaliating for killing one of his guys. My guess: it was the skimming because Bank's is a class A asshole.

"How do you know that Eagle was the trigger man?" Shannon continued.

"Travis Jackson was a witness. He was my cousin. He talked to that asshole Buckley about it and everything."

"Agent Buckley?"

"Yeah, Agent Buckley. He worked with that shithead Carmody and was the guy I went to when I learned about Banks...Fuck..."

"What is it?" Shannon was taken aback.

"Fuckin Buckley was on the take wasn't he?"

"So Travis Jackson saw the murder?" Shannon

ignored his question.

"Yeah, so did that little shit Marcel Wright, who lied his ass off in court about me." Northbird shook his head and looked up at the ceiling then back at Shannon.

"It was Buckley who turned Marcel, wasn't it."

Shannon affirmed.

"That son of a bitch."

"Mr. Northbird, this is a lot of hearsay. None of it useable in court. We are going to need more," Shannon said.

"I will get you whatever you need or a conviction. I just need two things," Northbird responded.

"What is it that you need?" Shannon asked.

"I want you to take down that bastard Marcel Wright. I want to see him locked away where he belongs,"

"And the other?"

"I need you to get me out of here."

"If what you say about being innocent is true, it is going to take at least a year and a half to make it through your appeal process, if you can get someone to take the case. After that, it is still a fifty-fifty proposition whether or not you are exonerated. On the other hand, if what you say about Banks and the whole conspiracy is true, then maybe we can work our way around the whole court process."

"Okay, I am listening."

Shannon walked out of the prison. Jefferson Buckley had been her partner out of Quantico. He had gotten cancer and died not long after her appointment with him. A letter had been delivered to her by his lawyer at his funeral service that confessed to a litany of major and minor corruption. The collusion with Marcel Wright to lock away an innocent man was probably the worst offense on the list. Ken Northbird corroborated everything that she had read from Buckley and added a whole lot more about Marcel Wright. She was determined to take them down. This was her first big break in the case. It was time for her to go undercover.

71

Marcel was in shock. He had heard the pops from the gun but he hadn't regis- tered that it was a gun. He saw the man running away. He was wearing a black hooded sweatshirt and grey sweatpants. He got about a hundred yards away and turned and looked back at the aftermath of the shooting. Marcel saw the man clearly. It was Antonio Eagle.

He looked at his brother again. Henry looked like he was having a seizure. There was a large pool of blood that was quickly expanding around Henry's head. Marcel bent down on one knee over his brother, and he saw that the top of his head from just above his right eye was completely gone. There was a disgusting looking gelatin like substance that was oozing from the wound. Marcel started to cry and he felt like he was going to throw up. He stood up and staggered back. He heard a scream from across the street and Tess came running screaming the whole way. Marcel had no idea what she was saying.

Tess was also crying.

"Call 911!" someone shouted.

Marcel looked for the shout and saw a man he didn't know nearby who was in the gathering crowd. Marcel sat down in the base of nearby oak tree and put his head in his hands. He didn't need 911 to know that his brother was dead and he was all alone.

Tess sat down next to him and put her arms around him and sobbed. They sat that way for some time. Crying together about the man they both loved more than anything in this world.

"I am so, so, sorry, Marcel." Tess kissed him on the cheek.

"Why?" Was all Marcel could say.

It wasn't long before tribal police and the FBI were on the scene asking him all sorts of questions. One of the cops, an older guy, who smelled like death was knocking on his door, spoke.

"Marcel, I am Special Agent Jefferson Buckley. Did you see Ken Northbird shoot your brother?"

Marcel nodded between sobs.

413

Kenny Northbird was a member of a rival gang. They had gotten into squabbles in the past, one a couple of weeks ago ending in a fist fight in which Ken had beaten the living shit out of Marcel. Henry had been there and watched the savage beating but stepped in before Ken went too far. That was all the encouragement Marcel needed from the old white man to say that it was Northbird's face he had seen when the shooter turned.

"Yeah. Ken Northbird shot my brother."

72

Marcel hopped into Aristman's Cadillac and ordered him back to Denver. He had no idea how in the hell he was going to get back to Minnesota. They had been set up, of this there was no doubt. All of them. He cursed himself. He should have seen this coming. He was sure the cops were all over Joanne and Shannon because of that damn car. He should have got out when he saw that car, but he had followed Shannon's lead.

His phone rang. It was Tess; she had to have been the one who set him up. But why? Marcel was certain agents had tapped his phone; he needed to be cautious on this call. Marcel knew Tess had been working for Banks all along. But was she setting him up for Banks to either use him or have him killed, or was she attempting to buy her way out of jail? He had to find out.

"Hello" Marcel spoke.

"Marcel, it's Tess, you have to listen to me. It is really important. Marcel you are in a lot of trouble. You have to meet me and I can fill you in. We have to get out of town in a hurry," Tess huffed.

"Tess I am in Colorado right now," Marcel answered.

"Are you with Shannon?" she asked.

"Yeah. Why?" Marcel wondered what she wanted with Shannon.

"Marcel, you can't trust her; she isn't who you think she is. I can't explain right now but if you meet up with me when you get back I will explain everything, gotta go." She hung up the phone.

Marcel figured from the phone call that it was Banks he needed to worry about. She was trying to lure him into a trap. She was also attempting to separate him from Shannon so that Banks could put him into a hole in the ground. If she was working with the cops she likely would have known that they already had Shannon.

"Take me down to the greyhound station," he directed Aristman.

He bought a Greyhound ticket to Minneapolis that was departing in just a few minutes. Once on the bus he brought up Shannon's number on his phone and clicked connect. Her voicemail picked up.

"Shannon, I am getting out of Denver. I hope you got out. I am going to run and hide. I got a nice payday from my last fight, should be enough to get me out of the country. Mexico, South America maybe. I want you to come with. I will meet you back in Minneapolis. If you are able to make it to the Greyhound station in twenty-four hours, I will meet you there."

73

Tess was sitting on the sofa wrapped in a blanket. She was still shaking from the ordeal. Springs was upstairs. She wasn't sure what he was doing, but she wanted to get out of the house. The fucking house that was deserted with the exception of a few generic items of furniture. She now noticed that the television wasn't even plugged in. She got up from the sofa and walked to the stairs. She looked up at the bedroom doors, one of which was now open. That's when she heard the report from a gun inside the bedroom.

She didn't hesitate. She didn't try and figure out what the hell was going on, she just ran; down the steps and out the front door. She turned at the street and sprinted as hard as she could for the civilization at the top of the hill on Silver Lake Road. She sprinted so fast that she was so far away that she never heard the second gunshot that killed Agent Tavian Springs.

Tess sprinted past the bank on one corner, across Silver Lake Road paying no mind to traffic or the lights. A Chevy Trailblazer had to lock its brakes to keep from splattering her all over the pavement. Tess made a beeline from the intersection to the gas station across the street.

Tess was desperately out of shape and tired quickly, but survival instinct had kicked in and pushed her further. She looked behind her to see if anyone was following, but they weren't. The street was filled with the bustle of the morning commute but none of them posed a threat to her. She slowed a little, feeling like she was about to puke, but continued running.

She entered the gas station, pouring sweat and panting so hard she could hardly speak. Her first call was to Marcel, to warn him. It was brief but she hoped she got the point across. Her second call was to Will.

"Will, I need your help, can you come pick me up?" She huffed.

"Where you at?" Will responded on the other end.

"Gas station on Silver Lake Road and…" She wasn't sure of the cross street.

"thirthy-ninth" the Clerk spoke to her, over-hearing the conversation.

"Thirty-ninth," she repeated into the phone.

"I will be there in about fifteen minutes. Don't go anywhere." She was certain Will could hear the panic in her voice. She was scared and couldn't hide it. Even the clerk saw it.

"Do you want me to call the cops, honey?" The elderly cashier spoke with concern.

"No, no cops. My friend will be here shortly."

She had no idea who had fired the last two shots. She hoped it was Tavian, but she didn't know why he would fire them. Her fear was that Eagle had somehow regained consciousness and been able to fire a couple more bullets at the agent who had saved her life.

Tess starting thinking about things and she began to cry. She had no idea how she had gotten herself into this mess. She had lived this life once before and had escaped. Now all of a sudden Marcel showed back up and the bullets started flying again. Tess knew that Marcel had to be involved. Agent McCarthy, who was pretending to be his friend, had told her as much. She had all kinds of questions for her about him. And damn if all this didn't happen because she dropped that car at his law professor's house. She desperately hoped that Marcel would get back here safely. She was in a lot of trouble but he was in more trouble.

Tess also thought about Banks. For Banks to kill her meant he had to be involved with the drugs. Banks was making deliveries through the car dealership. He delivered a shipment to Marcel's professor. Marcel's professor had him working on Ken Northbird's case. All of a sudden, a light went on in Tess' head. For the first time everything came clear to her and she knew exactly what was going on. It was Ken.

74

Clifford Banks was in one hell of a shitstorm now. He had gotten to the sterile
house an hour before Antonio had arrived
with Tess with the intention of being there first-
hand to clean up if things went south. Things
had, in fact, gone south, but in a manner that
he had never expected. Of course Antonio had
botched the operation. He was a killer, not a
thinker. He didn't get the girl finished off and had
gotten himself killed. That was fine. The agent,
however, had surprised Clifford. Clifford was
able to get a couple rounds into the agent and

take care of him, but the girl had disappeared. She had taken off out through the deck and had left the door open behind her. He followed out that way but couldn't see any sign of her. He had to be careful to not look too suspicious. He left quickly. He walked, passing a few houses before making his way to the street. The howl of sirens were fast approaching the house.

The cavalry is a bit late once again.

He laughed at the irony.

When he got to the street, he wasn't sure exactly which way to go. He decided it would be best to head to the sound of the traffic and ended up at Silver Lake Road. There were plenty of busy places for her to hide in plain sight and her trail went cold. Better to be in a business section than a residential section. If this was a white neighborhood, a brown man might make them nervous.

He had left his car in the Walmart parking lot so as not to draw attention, anyway. He shuffled inconspicuously to the Eldorado and unlocked the drivers door. He got in and started up the car. His gas light was on so he pulled into the service station next to Wal-mart to fill up. He almost slid his credit car into the gas pump, then decided it would be better to pay cash. No sense having a record of him being two blocks away from the house where his assistant and DEA agent were murdered only minutes earlier. He took the nozzle out of its holder and began to fill his tank. As he was filling the car up, an 80's era Firebird with a very large African American man pulled up, and Tess came out of the gas station and got in. He had to do a double take because he couldn't believe his own luck.

He hung up the pump and raced into the store to pay. Luckily there was no line and he was quickly back in his Cadillac. The Firebird was stopped at the intersection, giving him just enough time to catch up and follow it out of the gas station parking lot and back onto Silver Lake Road, headed south towards downtown.

Banks tried to give a couple car lengths between the two cars so as to not make it obvious that he was following them. The Firebird traveled through downtown until 94 and 35W merged, and then it headed west on 94. The morning traffic was dying down, so Banks had very little difficulty keeping them in sight. The Firebird headed west on 55 to Wirth Parkway. Banks followed.

Eventually the car pulled up to Will's house and the couple went inside. Banks parked a few blocks down and began walking up to the house. He pulled out the .357 Magnum revolver he had tucked into his waistline, opened the chamber, and replaced the two spent cartridges he had used to kill Springs.

75

Tess dialed Marcel's number, hoping to get ahold of him now that she was in a place where she could sit down and take a breath. There was no answer and his voice mail picked up immediately. She hung up the phone and looked out the window. What she saw terrified her. It was Banks, loading an enormous handgun.

"Will, do something! Banks is coming and he has a gun." Tess was getting frantic again.

"Calm down. Go upstairs and lock the door." Will was calm and determined.

Tess did as her cousin asked. He followed her up to his bedroom and took out a .50 caliber Desert Eagle pistol from his desk drawer. He then took a 12 gauge pump shotgun off the rack on his wall that contained various other hunting rifles. Will was an avid outdoorsmen and had a very ample supply of guns. He slid three shells into the breach and racked the slide.

"If he comes in, point and shoot." Will handed the shotgun to Tess. He then left the room, closing the door behind him. Tess rushed over and locked the door, then sat herself in the closet where she still had a vantage point of the front door. It didn't seem long before she heard glass breaking, and then she heard two of the loudest gun shots she had ever heard in her life. The shots came from inside the house, but she couldn't tell who fired them. She waited for an eternity; there was no sound. She listened for more shots but heard only silence.

The intensity was too much for her and she got up out of the closet and walked over to the door. She stood there with her ear to the door, listening. Her heart was pounding and beads of sweat were starting to form on her palms and her brow. The gun was getting slippery in her hand. She took her trigger finger off the shotgun and she wiped her palm on her jeans. She listened again and thought she heard footsteps. She unlocked the door and opened it just enough to peak down the steps. There was nothing. Then she heard the floorboards creak, and footsteps came closer. She raised the shotgun to her shoulder; it was almost too long for her small stature, but she managed. She held it up and felt for the trigger. The moment she saw Banks she was determined to squeeze.

The man coming up the steps said nothing, he hobbled a little when he got to the top and collapsed. Tess didn't fire. She didn't fire because the man who collapsed at the top of the steps was Will. He had been shot in the abdomen and was bleeding profusely, a trail of blood behind him up the steps.

"Will!" She screamed, dropping the shotgun. She burst through the door and went over to her cousin.

"Will!" she screamed even louder.

"He's gone," Will spoke, blood coming from his mouth.

"Will, you've been shot." Will looked down at his hands and stomach, all covered in blood.

"I guess I was."

Tess knew he was in shock. She sprinted for the ground floor of the house, forgetting she had her cell phone. Her mind was racing in circles. She got to the house phone and dialed 911.

The 911 operator tried to calm her down, Tess hadn't been the first person to call the emergency number about the shooting. A neighbor had called as soon as the first shots were fired. The police arrived on the scene while Tess was still on the phone. They came in guns drawn and quickly secured the room before starting to work on Will. Tess was cuffed and put on the sofa while the men worked. A few minutes later paramedics showed up and Will was taken to North Memorial.

Tess was taken to the police station for questioning once again.

76

Shannon tracked Marcel through his cell phone. They were tracking the Greyhound bus on I-70 eastbound out of Denver right now. On the way out she had gotten a call from SAC that all hell had broken loose in Minneapolis while she was gone. Agent Tavian Springs had been killed in a shootout in St. Anthony. The whole operation had almost devolved into a logistical clusterfuck when two government agencies were investigating separate aspects of the same conspiracy. Lucky for all of them that Marcel had blown Tavian's cover and had told Shannon about it. Shannon and Tavian had worked together to bust Joanne with all the dope in her car and they were able to put together a joint agency task force to clean up the mess. Shannon had operated under Tavian's lead. He was a good agent and hearing about his murder pissed her off.

It cheered her up learning that he had taken Antonio Eagle with him. She learned that Clifford Banks had taken a potshot at Tess and her cousin Will, and Will was in critical condition at North Memorial Hospital. Banks was now on the lam. The bullet removed from the wall at Will's house was the same caliber as the bullets taken from the scene in St. Anthony. It would take some time for forensics to confirm they were fired from the same gun but Banks was believed to be Tavians's killer. Tess was in custody and had started talking. As for Joanne, she had been detained in Denver after they busted Davis. Joanne had agreed to work with them the second Shannon and Tavian had her arrested.

An APB had been issued for Banks and it was only a matter of time before he would be apprehended. The only question left for him was whether the federal death penalty would be an option. The death penalty was an option through federal law even though Minnesota had not had an execution since the botched hanging of William Williams in 1906, over one hundred years ago. Minnesota was not a capital punishment state.

Joanne could anticipate spending her foreseeable future in prison. A search warrant had been executed at her place while she was in Colorado. The fruits of that search, combined with the drugs that she had been caught with in Colorado, were enough for the government to push forward a trafficking charge. Once the chemical tests were completed, they would finally have the connection to the prison ring and that would likely bring a RICO charge against her. Tess was in custody. Antonio was dead and that all but concluded her investigation. With the exception of Marcel.

Shannon could finally come out from the shadow she had been living in for almost two years now. But there was one more suspect to bring in. He would be the hardest arrest of all.

She would take great pride in seeing Ken Northbird walk free.

Finding Joanne's source and rooting out the corruption on the reservation had taken a lot more work than either agency had planned, but they had been successful. It was mentally draining. However, she never anticipated how it would feel to get so close to people that she was investigating. Undercover work was dangerous both physically and emotionally.

Shannon had pulled off an Oscar worthy performance; she had gotten a monster like Marcel Wright to believe they were friends. It wasn't difficult for her to separate herself from the part she played. Truthfully, it was more difficult kissing him. It scared her and made her feel filthy, which would make bringing him in all the more sweet. The FBI was her life. She believed in law and order. These were her strongest convictions and that trumped any emotion or feeling she could have for another person. Marcel Wright was killer, but he was also sincere and hard working. Maybe there was even something inside of him that could be redeemed. She didn't believe that he was the same guy now that he had been then, but she believed that he had a price to pay.

As the bus pulled to the side of I-90, Agent Shannon McCarthy pulled on her FBI windbreaker, unstrapped her service weapon, and stepped out of the Tahoe she was riding in. She approached the front of the bus with her gun drawn.

77

M arcel got a call from Jarvis informing him that Will was in critical condition, and that Tess was once again in custody. Jarvis warned Marcel that he needed to get out of town.

"I am in Colorado right now on a Greyhound outside of Denver."

"Get off at the next stop and get on a bus to El Paso," Jarvis directed.

"What about Will?" He wanted to see Will, and he wasn't going anywhere without Shannon.

"Kid, get off the bus and leave your cell phone

there. They can track you with it. Do it now and don't come back to Minnesota. I love you like you were my own son, and I never want to see you again." With that Jarvis hung up.

78

Shannon had missed Marcel by only a few miles. Only his cell phone remained on the seat where he had been sitting. The driver informed her that a passenger had suffered a panic attack a few miles back and had been let off the bus. She held up a picture of Marcel and the driver more or less identified him as the man who had been let off.

She immediately called her SAC to put out an APB on Marcel Wright. If she knew Marcel like she thought she did, he wasn't running. He was heading back to Minneapolis to say his final goodbyes.

"Get me to the airport," She directed the driver of the Tahoe.

"Where are you going?" he asked.

"To arrest Marcel Wright."

79

Banks wanted Marcel dead because of his obsession with loose ends. Banks was so spun that he hadn't ever considered that Tess had already given him up and the game was over. The FBI and DEA were both closing in but Banks was oblivious. He knew that the big boy had been taken to North Memorial. Banks figured that if the big man was there, Tess and Marcel would both be soon to follow. It was of no concern to him that it was likely there would be a police presence there as well.

80

Marcel changed his destination to St. Paul and found a mode of transportation way more low key than the Greyhound. He caught on with an over-the-road trucker who was happy to have the company and didn't ask any questions. It took him about fifteen minutes to walk from where he was let off by the trucker to get home and grab his motorcycle. There was an obvious police presence monitoring the front entrance but nothing on the shed where his bike was stored.

He quickly made his way to the Minneapolis

Greyhound station where there were more police waiting for him.

Damn it, I have to get word to Tess.

He had left his phone on the bus.

Library.

There was a public library not far from North Memorial. He used a public phone and left a message for her to meet him at North Memorial. He would say his goodbyes to Will and if Shannon had gotten his message they could leave from there. If not, he had made up his mind to hit the road either way. Jarvis had convinced him.

He walked into the hospital and approached the front desk.

"I am looking for Will Curtis?" Marcel asked the group of people behind the desk.

The man completely ignored him and a particularly unfriendly woman looked up at him. Marcel assumed it had been a hectic day in the ER.

"One moment," she responded without looking up.

She banged wildly at her keyboard and after a long minute looked up.

"I am sorry, sir, he is in surgery right now." She softened a bit "You likely won't get to see him tonight."

"How is he doing?"

"I am sorry, sir, who are you? That information is confidential."

"I just want to know how my friend is doing?"

Marcel was starting to show his exacerbation and frayed nerves.

"Sir, you are going to need to calm down or we will call security."

That was definitely not what he wanted to hear.

"Okay, thanks." Marcel turned, knowing that this was not a place for him to hang around. He started for the door. That was the precise moment Clifford Banks walked through. He had an unusual look in his eye somewhere between insanity and pure love. A man possessed by a demon he would never be free of. Marcel's brain didn't make a connection between Banks and danger right away, but realized quickly when the man pulled out a .357 revolver and pointed it at Marcel's face.

Marcel recognized the look on Clifford's face. He had seen it before a long time ago; it was the look of a man who was about to take a life. Marcel's mind went to Tess. She was still pulling the strings. She had called Jarvis knowing that he would tell Marcel about Will, and then she tipped off Banks. The whole thing had been one big damned conspiracy. Joanne, Banks, and Tess had all worked together to set him up, and now it was time to pay the piper.

Marcel turned and sprinted away from Banks. He heard an explosion behind him and glass shattering followed by a woman screaming. Marcel turned down a hall still sprinting and tripped over a wheelchair that sat empty around the corner. The collision sent him sprawling to the floor. He scrambled to get to his feet and he heard another explosion. This time the bullet whizzed past his head like a supersonic gnat. He ducked into a room to his left and locked the door behind him.

He found himself in some sort of office that luckily had a window to the outside. He grabbed a nearby medical book and threw it against the window until it smashed out. He bailed out the window and crashed to the ground. The ground was covered with rocks. The landing hurt, but he didn't feel it because of the adrenaline flowing through his veins. The situation he was in was very similar to a fight. He had tunnel vision. He focused only on getting away from Banks and getting the hell out of the hospital campus. He couldn't hear anything, including the approaching sirens.

He scrambled to a parking lot where he was hemmed in. He started to head for the exit where he was cut off by Banks. Banks raised the gun, and this time Marcel had nowhere to go. There were three quick explosions and Marcel was sure it was the end. Only it wasn't. The shots did not come from Bank's gun. Instead he watched Banks crumple to the ground in what felt like slow motion.

Shannon came around the corner with three members of the Minneapolis Police force as her back up. Her gun was drawn.

"Marcel Wright, get on the ground and put your hands behind your head," Shannon barked the order to him in a voice he couldn't recognize.

He turned around in disbelief to see Shannon, a woman whom he had considered his closest friend at St. Stevens, pointing a gun at him. He had no idea what to do.

"Marcel Wright, get on the ground now!" she barked again.

He made a quick move and another shot rang out. Marcel felt a burn in his leg and crumpled to the ground in a heap, blood spouting from his leg.

81

T he bell rang and Marcel moved forward to touch gloves with his opponent. The crowd for this title fight was the most raucous crowd he had ever fought in front of. The man across the ring from him was one of the most ferocious fighters he had ever fought against, though far from what Marcel would consider skilled. Marcel hated him. His opponent was aggressive, quick, and had tremendous power behind his punches, but no technique. Marcel knew that if he was sloppy that the man could be trouble. Marcel knew that If he wanted the title, he was going to have to have to dig in and be disciplined. His opponent continued his relentless attack throughout the first round. Marcel moved and countered but he still took several solid shots before the bell sounded, signifying the end of the first round.

He took a seat in his corner. He splashed some water around his mouth, took a couple deep breaths and closed his eyes while his cornerman applied more Vaseline to his brow. The second bell sounded. It signaled the end of the shortest minute of his life, and he came back out with a renewed vigor. He had a second wind that his opponent was not ready for. Marcel parried his opponents jab with his left and countered with a front right hook that landed square and buckled the man's legs. This time there would be no advice from Jarvis, so Marcel decided on his own that he would end the fight. He stepped in with a rear uppercut that picked up his opponents chin and followed with an overhand left that dislocated the man's jaw and sent him sprawling to the canvas with no hope of answering the referee's ten count.

After it was over, Marcel stood in the center of the ring with his hand raised. He was now the Federal Prison System Middleweight Champion. It was the highest title that he would ever have the opportunity to fight for. Marcel had plead guilty to second-degree murder under the Major Crimes Act. He was sentenced to thirty years to life in a federal prison. Parole was not an option under the federal sentencing guidelines but he avoided the death penalty from a first degree murder conviction.

After the fight, he returned to his cell in the Marion Federal Penitentiary. He thought about all the things that transpired for him to arrive at this place. Deep down he attributed it to the strength of his convictions. He loved his brother and believed that his actions, in accordance with his brother's value system, were the right ones. He had been loyal to a fault. After his brother was killed, his moral code was thrown into chaos. Jarvis had taught him about redemption, discipline, and work ethic. He had believed in those lessons. He believed that a zebra really could change his stripes. He had believed that leaving his old life behind was the right thing to do, and because of it he had chosen Shannon over Tess and Shannon had betrayed him. He had been wrong in so many of his convictions.

He was happy to hear that Tess had been freed. She cooperated with the police and they had been able to close their case on Clifford Banks. Will had survived and corroborated her entire story. The Feds had seized Banks' assets and turned them over to the tribe. For all the good he had accomplished for the people, his belief that the ends justified the means had been his downfall. He had become a man drunk on his own power, destroying lives in order to better the lives of his people and in the process pad his pockets. Clifford wasn't even really one of them. Jesus Ramirez had died of a result of the gunshot wounds he received in the shootout at the hospital. He was given a government funeral and buried in St. Paul. A fitting end for a man who caused so much destruction.

Marcel's life, along with his brother's, were destroyed by Ramirezs' ambitions. Antonio Eagle had lost his life blindly following the man he knew as Banks. And even though Eagle was a psychopath destined for a federal pen, the fact of the matter was: Ramirez had manipulated Eagle and thrown the man away when he was done with him. Marcel believed he deserved better even if he was the one who had actually killed Henry.

Ken was freed from prison. He had worked with Shannon on the case. Setting up Marcel was an added bonus. Freedom, as it turned out, meant a lot to Ken Northbird. He enrolled in college, got his degree and was contemplating a run for tribal government. Though Ken could have been a tragic victim of Bank's master plan, he didn't allow himself to be a victim. He lost ten years of his life to Banks and used it as motivation to give back to his people. Ken even traveled to visit Marcel and to forgive him for all the pain Marcel had caused him.

Joanne had plead not guilty. Her trial had been a media sensation, of course, and her team of lawyers dragged it out for almost six months.

With the trial winding down she had made a run for it and evaded authorities for a year and a half before she was eventually found in Rio. Authorities found her body in a low rent motel, dead from an overdose of heroin.

Joanne had believed that the world owed her something for what her husband did to her. She died alone and broke in a shitty motel feeling no more pain. Marcel had no doubt that her last thoughts were that she was the biggest victim of all of Bank's crimes.

Shannon's official report named Antonio Eagle as the perpetrator of the killings of Walter Carmody and Henry Wright. It was the last chapter in a sad life. Antonio had believed that Clifford was a father figure to him. Someone, possibly the only one on the planet. who actually cared about whether he lived or died. In the end, it was Clifford who sent him to his death as a way to cover up his own sins. Antonio wasn't innocent by any stretch of the imagination but Marcel couldn't help but think, what if Antonio had met Jarvis so long ago? What could Jarvis have done for him? Would his life have had a happier ending?

Tavian Springs, the man Marcel had known as Joanne's sidekick, had been awarded a Medal Of Valor for his part in bringing down one of the largest drug operations in the Midwest. All in all, the investigation shut down a five million dollar a year operation and the largest manufacturer of illegal prescription drugs in the country. Tavian had reached out to Marcel, had thrown him a lifeline, but Marcel had selfishly believed that the man was trying to destroy him. If only he had seen things a little more clear, he could have grabbed it.

Jarvis had tried to come visit Marcel but Marcel refused to see him. He had let Jarvis down and the one thing that Marcel wanted to give Jarvis was to allow the man to be true to his word. Marcel thought Jarvis really shouldn't ever see him again. Jarvis had a new protege, Deshawn Thunder. Deshawn had just won a spot in the Olympic games. It was another thing that Marcel hadn't given Jarvis that his trainer and mentor had deserved. There wasn't a lot that made Marcel happy anymore. Knowing that Jarvis was taking a fighter to the olympics was something that did. The man had sacrificed so much for him, for others and the only thing he ever asked for was that the people that worked under him be the best versions of themselves. It seemed like an easy request. Yet rarely was the man ever paid off. It was fifteen years in the making but maybe now Jarvis could reap the rewards of his sacrifice.

Tess Whitebird cooperated and all charges against her were dropped. She had returned to the reservation. She realized that her skills were best suited for helping her people the best she could. She was hired as an assistant by the new

Chairman of the tribe and worked diligently to set up counseling centers for young mothers and families to assist them in whatever way they could to raise the children. She participated in cultural events and put on Annishinabe cultural classes for the young people in Cass Lake. Tess had always believed that her worth had come by the acceptance of others, first from Henry, then from Banks. What she learned was that she had a value independent of anyone else. She had more to offer others than just sex. It was in giving that she became truly free of everything bad that had happened to her.

Shannon was given official recognition for her role in the investigation. She was promoted and was no longer in the field. She had written a letter to Marcel shortly after his conviction that he never opened. It had been five years since the judge had banged the gavel and sentenced him to life in prison. It had taken him some time but he had come to accept responsibility for his actions. He came to realize that the reason he sat here in this cell was because of his own beliefs, his own convictions. Convictions that were so strong, but at the same time wrong. He took the letter out from the special place in the mattress where he had kept it. He looked at the envelope for a longtime. He admired Shannon's perfect penmanship. Marcel considered what he had once believed about her, which was that he had loved her. Somewhere in that cold cell, locked away from society, he had finally made peace with everything that happened. He made peace with all the pain that was inflicted on him and he made peace with all the pain he had inflicted on others. He grasped the envelope in both hands and tore the letter into small pieces and threw it into the wastebasket in his cell.

About the author

Micheal Poncelet was born in Akeley, Minnesota on the bi-centennial of the United States. He attended high school at Walker-Hackensack-Akeley where he graduated in 1994. Extending his learning and life experience, Micheal went on to the University of Minnesota Duluth where he graduated with a degree in Political Science and Coaching. After graduation and unsure of what to do next, Micheal moved to Colorado where he worked for the Boulder Polo Club and got engaged to wife Shawna. Micheal and Shawna moved to the Twin Cities where Micheal was accepted to law school at Hamline University. Micheal worked as an attorney, prosecuting criminal cases in Sherburne County, and eventually opened a private practice. During this period, he found his two true passions: coaching basketball and writing. Micheal was a successful high school coach, being named mid-state conference coach of the year in 2016, before moving on to coach college basketball at Macalester College and he currently works on the Women's basketball staff at Bemidji State University. Micheal's first novel Wrongful Convictions was released on July 22nd 2019. Micheal and Shawna have two sons: Marquise and Vincent. Please follow Micheal on twitter @michealponcelet or like his facebook page https://www.facebook.com/MacCoachP. For information on upcoming releases visit https://michealponcelet.com/